The Name
Of
AnnaBella Cain

Kefira Zink

The Name
Of
AnnaBella Cain

The Chronicles of AnnaBella Cain
Book Three

The Name of AnnaBella Cain
Copyright ©2025 by Kefira Zink

Contact Info: kefirazinkauthor@gmail.com

ISBN: 979-8-9928400-4-9

Also By Kefira Zink

Table of Contents

Chapter One

AnnaBella Cain laughed as she stopped to dump more sand out of her shoes. She should have known from the last time she was in the Wastes that sneakers were not the best choice for walking over sand. But in her hurry, she didn't think to ask the Speaker for boots better designed to make such a trek. She asked for many things she really didn't need, like water and sunscreen, but not for something as important as proper footwear.

Admittedly, Bella never considered how much walking across hot, dry sand it would take to track down ten hidden mythical beings in ten also hidden oases within the Wastes of Taikarlu in an effort to save the Heka from Its entrapment and deadly fate. Because why would a seventeen-year-old girl ever think about such things, when six months ago they were just an average human going to high school and planning an easy senior year?

Bella had been introduced to the world of Taikarlu all at once and slowly at the same time. She wasn't given much time to really stop and think about the fact that her father was the Devil (but not really, humans get a lot of stuff wrong), she had mystical abilities that allowed her to join the ranks of the gods, and that those gods had a history that left her being the only one with the powers to save the ultimate god and lifeforce of literally everything in the universe before It died, taking everything else out with It.

So, for now, it was okay if Bella laughed with Ben as they made their way to the first oasis. The two gods, both teenagers in spirit if not in actuality, should enjoy their time travelling. Because what was coming next for them would shake them both to the core and change their lives forever....

And forever was about to become a really, really long time.

I wiped my hands down the front of my shirt, brushing crumbs from my sandwich off of them, then took a swig of water, put the bottle back in my backpack, and stood up. Ben also stood up, wiping crumbs from his mouth and sand from the seat of his shorts. Peanut butter and jelly sandwiches are good, but maybe not the best food choice for a hot desert.

Ben tilted his face towards the sky and shook his head while smoothing his long black hair back from his face. I had already given him the extra hairband I perpetually kept on my wrist so he could tie his hair up in a ponytail to keep it off his sweaty neck. In the ever bright sun of Taikarlu, his golden skin had seemed to tan to more of a brown color. Well, all of his skin except the spots splashed with burn marks from defending a village from a poisonous, bi-headed snake. As I stood on first one foot, then the other, to dump the sand that had collected in my sneakers out, I internally questioned how a god would be able to tan. Me, a human body, turning from a kind of pasty white to a more pinkish tone made sense, but a god? Shouldn't happen, right? Oh, well, another question for another time.

Either way, Ben's gray tank top, blue athletic shorts and hiking boots made more sense in this dry, sandy desert than my black t-shirt, blue denim jeans and off-brand sneakers. I should have asked the Speaker of the Commission of the Gods to give me some hiking boots. I was so hot and sweaty.

Ben slapped his hands together, exclaiming, "Whelp! I think it is time."

"Time for what?" I asked.

Ben laughed. "Time for you to choose a name."

I looked at him quizzically. "I have a name," I told him. "Actually, I have, like, three names."

Ben chuckled as he hoisted one of the backpacks containing all of our food and supplies onto his shoulders. "That's the point. Your mom calls you Anna, which is kinda your human name. Your dad calls you Bella, which makes that your coordinator name. But your full name, AnnaBella is kind of a mouthful. What is your god name gonna be?"

I pulled the other backpack onto my shoulders, and thought about what Ben was saying. He had a point; one I had heard before but not quite put that way. Gavya had told me when we were walking through the Wastes together to escape the Avenging Women that my dual name probably caused some identity issues, but I never really thought much more about that. Now Ben and I were walking through the Wastes, not to escape but on a rescue mission, and he was telling me the same thing.

At Dad's house I was always Bella, and at mom's I was always Anna. In Taikarlu, the realm of the gods and their helpers, known as coordinators, I was called Bella because that is what Dad called me and everyone else just copied him. In the earthly realm, I had become only Anna, because that is what Mom called me. After the human realm was given false memories that made us think Dad supposedly died, everyone there just copied her. But my full name was actually AnnaBella, and Ben was right. It is a mouthful to say all the time.

As I thought, I picked up sand in my right hand. I reached inside myself, to find where my power was, my Heka that felt like ice and warmth, and closed my eyes. "Take me to where Gavya and I hid," I told the sand, gently pushing it with my Heka. Since figuring out that the humans had decided to make me a god, I knew I had more than just the Heka power to force things to tell me the truth. I had more power than what I got just from being Dad's kid and a regular coordinator. Instead, I could use my Heka for anything within the rights of my godhood, and since what my exact godhood was, who my worshippers were and what their faith entailed was so far undecided, I kind of had free reign. Plus, since the Heka being supplied my Heka power, and we were on a mission to save the Heka being, I figured I could take a lot of liberties with what I could do. Not free reign totally, but pretty much do what was needed without considering how or if It worked that way.

In response to my urging, the sand started flowing out of my hands. Instead of falling to the ground, it streamed through the air to the north, creating a path for Ben and me to follow. We started walking, following the trail of sand. Ben had gotten into the habit of walking to my right, and slightly behind me. This way, he could pick up sand and add it to my right hand as the levels there ran low without disrupting my concentration or breaking up the path.

I had gotten good enough at using my Heka that I could concentrate on continuing to urge the sand on with one part of my mind and focus on having a conversation with Ben with another. I don't think I got this good because of practice or anything. I just had reached a point where I stopped questioning how things worked and assumed if I wanted to do it, then I could. I mean, wouldn't you after beating the Trials Arena better than Hercules, having your body and spirit split up then figuring out how to put them back together when the spirit was trapped in the gods' realm and your body was trapped in the human world, and then uncovering a thousand-of-years-old conspiracy to destroy the entire universe that started just because one man hated having arthritis?

With a part of my mind adequately fixed on the guiding sand, I turned the rest of my mind back to the question of my name. Anna. Bella. AnnaBella. Hmm. I didn't have a middle name, so I couldn't just drop the AnnaBella altogether and use that.

"I honestly don't know what name I should use." I finally told Ben. "All three of the names I am called each have their own importance to who I am. How did you end up named Ben?"

Out of the corner of my eye, I saw Ben shrug his shoulders. "Dunno. Why?"

"Maybe if I know how other gods got their names, I can figure out mine," I replied. "Do you honestly not remember how you got your name?"

Ben shrugged again. "I really don't. I have just always been Ben. Well, Benahahminen, but that is too much name for anyone, so I've always been called Ben. Just like I don't remember being created, I don't remember being named."

I nodded in understanding. The gods that humans believe in have always existed, since the first moment the Heka created the universe. It didn't matter if that god was only believed in back when humans first walked upright and never worshipped by anyone since, or if that god wouldn't have any followers for another million years. If they were, are or would be worshipped, all gods were created at the same moment the universe was. Well, all gods but ones like me. I was born human and then the humans decided that I should be a god, so I became one. I didn't know that they had decided that until later, but that is a different story. One I have already told, so I am not going to repeat it all here.

Suffice it to say, I am very unique in the world of gods because I was born rather than made, so I wasn't given a god name from the Heka at my creation, but a birth certificate by my parents who couldn't choose so just smooshed the names they both liked together. But, I guess, as far as Ben knew, normally a god's name just poofed into existence the same time they did.

"If you just knew your name the moment you knew you existed," I said thoughtfully, "that means the Heka created it when It created you. Maybe I have to wait for the Heka to give me my name."

Ben laughed. "So, what do I call you until we rescue the Heka and It can give you your name?"

At that moment, something appeared on the horizon. I felt the sand in my hand getting excited. "Call me whatever you want," I told Ben. I pointed to what I saw on the horizon with my left hand, showing him the oasis in the distance and grinned. "Just don't call me late to the party. You ready to find a mystical beast no one has seen in ages?"

I felt Ben grinning behind me and we both took off running towards the oasis. Laughing, we slipped and slid, tumbling as we tried to run across the shifting sand. After a few minutes, the ground became firmer, and the scrub brush that dotted the landscape started getting taller and thicker.

Soon, we were in the center of an oasis with a cave to our left and a refreshingly cool pond in front of us. Having been here before, I knew that the water in the pond was wonderfully soothing on the skin after the arid winds of the Wastes, and that it was the most refreshing drink I had ever tasted. Without stopping, I stripped off my backpack, kicked off my shoes and dived into the pond.

Ben stopped on the shore, watching me dip below the water and then bob up again, to float on the surface. He smiled. "You know your clothes are soaked now."

I swam back to the shore and climbed out of the pond. "I don't care. They will dry quickly in this heat." I nudged him. "C'mon. Jump in. You will feel so much better."

Ben looked around cautiously. I could tell he was sensing something watching us, just as I was. When Gavya and I were hiding out here before, we had both mentioned feeling something watching us from inside the tree lines of the oasis. Nothing ever came of it back then, so I ignored that sensation now, assuming it was probably the mystical beast we were there to find and if it was going to be violent or a hassle, I hoped it would be nice enough to wait until we had had a chance to relax some.

I nudged Ben again, then started pulling his backpack off. "Whatever is out there for us can wait a few minutes for you to take a dip in the pool. Cool off some, and we will be better able to think of how to get the first key to the Heka's cage from whatever beast we need to steal it from."

Ben nodded and sighed. "Fine," he groaned and then he slowly walked to the water's edge and sat down. He carefully untied his boots, took off each sock, placing it inside the corresponding book and set them to the side. Then he lowered his feet into the water. He stayed there with his legs dangling over so he only got wet up to his knees.

"Uh uh," I scolded, "all the way in. Or are you scared to wreck your perfectly coifed hair?"

Ben turned and looked at me, a playful smile creeping around the corners of his mouth. "My hair?" He wagged a finger at me, admonishingly. Slowly, he moved out of the water, back towards me, taking one step for each word he said. "It is not my hair you should be worried about, but my GRIP!" Yelling the final word, Ben's slow pace changed to a dash and before I knew it, he had scooped me up and jumped into the deep end of the pond, tossing me as he dived off the edge.

Even though I was already soaked, I yelped in surprise as I cannonballed into the water. Coming back up, I twisted to see where Ben was, and slapped my arms on the water to splash his face. He retaliated and we spent the next few minutes laughing, splashing each other, and enjoying the cool water.

My back was to the shoreline when Ben suddenly stopped laughing and his face went pale. I started to turn around to see what had make him go so still, but Ben shook his head once, telling me without words not to move. I went as still as he was, my chest heaving with the effort of going from roughhousing to silent in seconds.

"What is it, Ben?" I whispered as quietly as I could.

"A unicorn," he replied, breathlessly. "A pure white unicorn. I haven't seen one in a hundred thousand years."

"A unicorn?!" I gasped, trying to whisper. "A real live unicorn?" I knew that the point of coming to the oases in the Wastes was to find the mythical beasts that had been banished to these small parts of the desert when Taikarlu broke apart after the war, and been tasked by Malachi to hide the keys to the Heka's cage, but I never really stopped to consider what those 'mythical beasts' would be.

"Slowly, Anna." Ben told me. "Turn around really slowly. I don't want to spook him."

I did as Ben said, turning just a fraction of an inch at a time, desperately trying not to get too excited and make too much noise. A real freaking unicorn. Nobody would believe this, in Taikarlu or back home with Mom.

Finally, I could see the shore. Standing under a tree, nibbling at the grass around its roots, was an animal that looked just like all the horses from the movies little girls watch just before asking their parents for a pony for their birthday. The pure white hair along its body was almost blindingly bright, and its mane and tail were white with streaks of silver. The mane had three braids in it, tied at the ends with what looked like fine silver ribbons. The horse snorted and raised its head. Right in the middle of its forehead was a horn. The horn looked like twisted strands of crystals, each one shining a different color of the rainbow while also being see-through, like blown glass. It looked both fragile and dangerous at the same time.

The unicorn looked at me, and I looked at it. Its eyes were large and brown. Intelligence seemed to flow from its eyes and, without even knowing I was doing it, I started walking slowly through the water towards the beast.

Ben whispered urgently, "Anna, stop, don't."

I waved at him to stop talking. As I inched closer, my eyes stayed locked on the unicorn's. As soon as I placed my hands on the shore, to climb out of the pond, the unicorn snorted again and turned away, taking off at a run. As it ran away, I saw a small shape flanking its side.

"He is gone. You scared it away, AnnaBella." Ben said, breaking the trance I had been in.

"She." I retorted.

Ben waded over to me. "What?"

"Not 'he'," I told him. "The unicorn was a girl, and it had a foal with it."

Ben's face showed surprise. "A foal?" he repeated. "That means there's more than one. Maybe there is a whole herd of them. Anna, do you know what this means?"

I pulled myself out of the pond and sat on the edge. Looking at Ben, I shook my head. "No. What does it matter if there is one unicorn or a whole herd? It just means we have to figure out which one has the key instead of just knowing that the one we saw has it."

"It means they are not going extinct," Ben answered. "When Taikarlu was split up by the Wastes after the flood, we all assumed that the mythical beasts all had died and were now extinct. When Malachi revealed that mythical beasts were guarding the keys to the Heka's cage, I assumed that he had just somehow magicked one animal in each oasis to live forever to guard the key. But a unicorn with a foal means that there is at least three, a baby and a mating pair. Even if they are close to extinction, their species can be saved! Saved, and maybe reintroduced to the humans as real. Humans have not been nearly as creative since the mystical beasts disappeared."

Ben had climbed onto the shore by this point and was pacing in his excitement. "Bella, humans seeing mythical animals again, could you even imagine? They would believe in all the gods again. They would believe in Fury again! Oh, this could fix everything!"

"Ben," I said, much more subdued than him, "what are you talking about?"

Ben looked at me and his overly excited face drooped. "That's right. You were born, not made. You don't know what it was like to be a god when the whole world believed, before the war and the breaking of Taikarlu."

"I don't know what it's like to be a god at all, Ben." I reminded him. "I didn't even know I was a god for most of the time I was one. Before that I was just a normal human for seventeen years, then a coordinator for a hundred. A coordinator who was not allowed the knowledge of Taikarlu or the world that everyone else got automatically. I was kept in the dark of who I was for years, remember? It may have felt like a long time, but in reality, my spirit and body were only put back together yesterday. I only found out I am a god yesterday, and we spent today walking through the desert to get here. I don't know the stuff that even a god who was born instead of made would. Hell, I don't even know my name."

Frustrated, I stood up, wrapping my arms around my body, and walked away from Ben. Looking down at the oasis floor, I let my feet carry me where they would. Out of habit from my last time here, I found myself walking into the cave Gavya and I had shared as our makeshift home while we waited for Nummi to find a way to heal me. Looking around, I saw the remnants of a fire that looked like it was just put out yesterday and a pile of what looked like rotting berries that were definitely older.

I rolled my eyes at this. Of course. Time in Taikarlu was wonky. Wasn't that the first, or really only, thing Dad taught me about this place? Time is not the same in Taikarlu as it is on earth with the humans. A day here is a month there. Six months there is a hundred years here. The sun never sets in Taikarlu, so day has no meaning and night doesn't exist. I rolled my eyes again. I love Dad, but he sure left me a lot of blanks to fill in by myself.

To stop the tears that were threatening to spill out, I knelt down and messed with the extinguished fire. There was a lighter in my backpack, but I didn't want to do it the easy way. Instead, I stacked and restacked the wood, trying to get it into the perfect teepee setup that I had learned as a kid, camping with the Scouts. I focused so hard on making sure all the wood could get oxygen and a good burn, I didn't realize that I was using my Heka until the wood started to smolder.

By the time Ben followed me into the cave, carrying both backpacks and our shoes, I had a tidy little fire burning and had banished the majority of my frustration tears by rubbing my eyes with the back of my hand and pretending it was only the smoke.

"Hey." Ben said softly. "Sorry."

I looked up at him, hoping I didn't look like I had just been crying, and faked a smile. "It's all good. I was just being overly sensitive about there being stuff I don't know like most gods do. I just have some catching up to do."

Ben smiled weakly. I don't think I was very convincing at

pretending not to be hurt. "Well, didn't Mari say that was your strength? That you ask questions about stuff other people assume they already know?"

I chuckled lightly. "Yeah," I sighed. I took my shoes from him. Ben sat down the bags and put his boots back on. He had taken off his socks before swimming, so they were dry. I hadn't. I stripped off the wet socks, and laid them next to the fire to dry, setting my shoes close by.

"Well, here I am," Ben continued, patting himself on the chest, "a full-fledged god that was made rather than born, with all the answers. Fire away."

I looked at Ben. He sat on the cave floor, across the fire from me, and patiently waited. He sat down so gracefully that I couldn't help but keep watching him. Really watching him. As we both sat there, with the wood in the fire snapping and crackling the only noise in the cave, I noticed things about Ben I have never realized before.

Most people can sit peacefully, but will still fidget at least a little. Ben didn't. Even after watching him, and mimicking his stillness, for so long that my butt went numb, he still didn't shift or move. His face stayed calm and uncreased. I realized that the whole time I had known him, Ben had always looked just like any other teenager to me. But upon closer inspection, I realized his face wasn't just uncreased, but totally smooth. It was smooth the way a newborn baby's is.

There was something else about how still Ben was sitting that bothered me. At first, I couldn't figure out what it was, but then it dawned on me. All humans, no matter how still they can sit, move ever so slightly as they breathe. The shoulders go up and down slightly, and the chest rises and falls. Ben's didn't, because he wasn't breathing.

After another moment, I noticed my shoulders weren't moving either. Nor was my chest rising and falling. I wasn't breathing either.

"I am not breathing now, but earlier, playing in the water, I felt winded." I said to Ben.

"Yep." Ben replied simply.

"Why?" I asked. "Why am I not breathing now? Why did I need to catch my breath then if I don't need to breathe?"

"Because earlier you were thinking like a human, so you acted like one." Ben told me. "Now, you are thinking like a god, so you are acting like one. Gods are immortal. A little thing like forgetting to breathe, or just deciding not to, won't harm us. Heck, not breathing doesn't even get uncomfortable for gods. We don't need oxygen to live, just Heka."

"Oh." That made sense. Then I asked, "What else that humans do can gods just choose not to?"

Ben looked up, thinking, then back across the fire at me. "Do you want a full list or just the basics?"

"The basics, enough that I get it, I guess." I replied.

Ben tipped his head side to side, contemplating. "Eating, drinking, bathroom stuff, even female bathroom stuff, sleeping, getting pregnant, illness, get older. We can do that stuff if we want, but don't have to. Most gods don't ever bother with most of that, except the eating, drinking, getting pregnant and changing our age. Eating and drinking can be a way to connect with our worshippers sometimes. A lot of gods got pregnant or caused pregnancies a long time ago, but you know that from the myths. Some gods change their age, being older or younger, depending on the beliefs they want their worshippers to have about them. But for the most part, in Taikarlu, gods don't do any of that, and leave those things for when they are with the humans."

"What about injuries?" I asked. "You said illness, but not injuries."

Ben replied, "Obviously gods can be hurt." He gestured to his scars. "If something is powerful enough, and part of that god's legends and myths, that god can be hurt. But the god basically has to allow it." Ben stopped for a moment, thinking, then continued. "I guess if something was powerful enough, with enough authority, something could hurt a god against their will. I mean the Joint Commission can authorize the death of a god, in the form of spirit annihilation, if they have broken a rule in a severe enough way, so they must also be able to injure I would guess. But I have never heard of it being done."

"Do gods have love like humans do?" I asked.

"Yes and no." Ben hedged.

"What do you mean yes and no?" I pushed.

Ben sighed. "It's hard to explain. Gods can fall in love. Most gods choose to love someone on purpose. Some gods were made already in love with another god, and that became part of their myth story, so they can only ever love each other. But on the whole, gods don't fall in love the way humans do. We are immortal. We don't have hormones or a drive to procreate like humans. We don't fall in love; we choose to be in love. There are rare exceptions, of course, that usually have to do with myths that humans need or create, or with human-born gods. But by far and large, gods' love is more like high school love. Two gods will decide they like each other and spend a lot of time together for a while and then, for no apparent reason, decide to move on."

"Were Albert and Mari in love?" I asked out curiosity.

"Albert and Mari? My pretend sister and brother-in-law?" Ben asked. He laughed, loudly. "No. Their marriage was solely a ruse for the humans, for you. They are friends, I guess. But no, they were not in love or anything."

I sat back. These questions were interesting, but they weren't the point and I knew it. I needed to know how to be a god. Not just how they live, but how gods deal with things like worshippers, making myths and rules, what the world used to be like before and what we were here trying to save by saving the Heka. I needed to know how to know who I am now.

"Out by the pond, you said that I didn't know what it was like before. Before the Breaking of Taikarlu? What was it like? How is it different now?" I finally asked.

Ben answered my question with a question, which is always slightly infuriating. "What does it feel like to you when you use your Heka?"

"Like the pit of my stomach is frozen but hot at the same time." I told him. "Like I just ate a ton of ice cream and then drank a glass of warm milk. A warmth over ice feeling. Why?"

"How much Heka do you have?" he said, ignoring my question again.

I shrugged. "I dunno. I just use It when I need It. I never thought about running out or anything. Why? Is It limited? What happens if I run out of Heka?"

"Not limited like that." Ben started, then stopped and thought for a moment. He continued, "Don't think of it like a glass of water, where you can empty it and have to wait for the glass to refill. Think of it more like a dog. How much Heka do you have? Do you have a Chihuahua or a Mastiff? Is it on a leash and you are barely holding it back from running away or is it tame and in a cage?"

That analogy made me pause. I had never thought about the Heka like that. Every book I read as a kid that dealt with magic made it seem like magic was a form of energy. Use too much and you get tired and can't do magic anymore for a while. Or maybe use too much and you die. Not a single fantasy book I had ever read made magic seem like an animal inside you, a separate power. But I guess that's the difference between magic in stories and the reality of the power of gods. The Heka is Its own being, so why would It be limited by me?

I looked inside myself, using the meditative type inward looking type I learned in gym class when they taught us about yoga, and tried to see my Heka. I couldn't really see It, but sensed It. I used my senses to metaphorically poke It. How big are You? I asked it.

In my mind, my Heka felt huge. Huge, like Cerberus. But tired and weak, like if Cerberus was an old dog who only wanted to lay in the sun and not go on long walks anymore. Like, It could if you asked It to, and It missed the long walks, but Its tail couldn't wag quite so hard anymore. I told this to Ben.

"I remember when my Heka was Cerberus big. Cerberus big and Cerberus free. You wouldn't want to get in the way of Cerberus if He was chasing a rabbit, would you?" Ben explained.

I giggled at the image of Cerberus chasing a rabbit. I had met Cerberus in the Trials, and knew he liked sappy love songs and pop music, but rocked out too. The image of that Cerberus chasing a tennis ball or a rabbit in a field seemed silly, but at the same time I understood what Ben was saying.

Ben was still talking while I was imagining playing fetch with a massive three-headed dog. "My Heka used to be Cerberus off-leash and wild, untrained. Now," Ben sighed deeply, "now my Heka is a pet golden retriever. It does what I need, but is leash trained and won't go past the fence in the yard. I have to coax It to do anything I need.

"Before the Breaking, I could walk in Taikarlu or anywhere on the earth and know exactly where each and every one of my worshippers was and what they were doing. If they called for me, I could be there in a blink, or make it known to them that I was listening. They could actually see me if I wanted them to, or just feel my presence as tangibly as they could feel their own selves. They would be able to smell Fang's breath if I thought they needed to. I could perform miracles for them without a thought. You are injured and going to die, but have been faithful to me?" Ben snapped his finger. "Not any more. You have forgotten to give me the proper offering after the harvest?" Ben waved a hand. "There is no more nitrogen in your soil. Boom, famine. Apologize for that failing?" Ben held out his hand as if he was giving me something. "There, the corn is back.

"Imagine this type of god-worshipper relationship between every single god and every single human all happening at once. Then, add in the mythical beasts wandering around. Children of gods and humans being born left, right and center, with magical abilities and super-human strength or intelligence. The stories the humans told! There were alters on every street corner and in every home. Even the monotheist religions were everywhere all at once. There was so much Heka flowing through the human world because of the amount of gods, coordinators and hybrids running around all the time that no one doubted the existence of something bigger than themselves. No one could. Sure, atheism existed, but not like it is today. Atheists knew there was some sort of life force behind creation, and trusted that life force implicitly. They made having no god a type of god, if you know what I mean.

"We gods used to call atheists 'future worshippers,' because they wanted to learn about technology, science and math more than about the gods. And that was okay. No one cared, not us or the humans. Gods tried to sway believers to their faith, and humans tried to too, but that was to be expected. The world was full of Heka. Taikarlu was full of Heka. Each god was full of Heka. Even the Heka was full of Heka. It was wonderful and amazing and powerful."

"And now?" I asked.

"Now," Ben sighed, "I know I have worshippers. I know they are there and that they are worshipping me. I can receive their offerings and help them or harm them as warranted by their worship and my rules. But I can't be with them. They can't see me as a physical being. They can't feel me in the same way. I feel to them like a pleasant sensation that could actually just be gas. The humans used to tell the stories of the gods all the time, and know they were real. Now, the gods are history lessons, superhero movies, or just the way humans convinced themselves to have good morals.

"Part of the change is the Heka being locked up. We know that now, but for a long time after the Breaking, many people thought that the Heka had taken away the mythical animals on purpose. We thought It did it to limit humans' imagination, which in turn limits our abilities with them and our power. But since we know that the whole thing was Malachi, not the Heka, maybe it can all come back. We release the Heka, reintroduce the mythical beasts, and things get better. Maybe…" Ben's voice trailed off.

It always comes back to the Heka, I thought, and the fact that Malachi destroyed everything when he locked the Heka up. Malachi was angry with the world, angry with his god, Bob, and angry with me. He had been mad with Bob for making him a human that lived forever as a reward without considering the fact that Malachi was old, and suffering from an old man's body limitations, when Bob made him immortal. Bob never considered the fact that Malachi would still feel the pain from arthritis as an immortal in Taikarlu and, instead of talking to Bob about it, Malachi trapped the Heka and broke the world in revenge.

Then, when the humans decided I got to be a god, instead of choosing the options given to them by the Speaker at my trial, coordinator or human, Malachi became irate and separated my body and spirit to try to kill me. Thus, today's issues: the Heka slowly dying from Its imprisonment, and the keys to save It were hidden amongst mythical beasts that had been gone so long, we all forgot they were real once.

But Ben and I had found the first mythical beast. Unicorns are real, and there were at least two here in this oasis. Now the question was where were they hiding the first key to the Heka's prison and how to we get it from them?

"Tell me about unicorns," I said to Ben. "What are they like, or were they like?"

"Unicorns are the pretty well misunderstood by humans." Ben replied.

I laughed. "Yeah, isn't everything?"

Ben smiled at this and chuckled. "Yeah." Then he continued. "So, unicorns are thought by humans to be a lot of things, but mostly they focus on unicorns as a symbol of purity. Many traditions have unicorns being able to purify water, or humans, from illness and contamination at a touch of their horn. They are also seen as strong fighters, and are known in some myths to defeat elephants or other vicious animals. A lot of myths have them uncatchable, except by female virgins. Hence, the purity idea. Since there are many very real animals on earth that have one horn on their head, rhinoceroses and narwhals for example, most humans nowadays assume the old myths are really talking about those animals. That's basically what most human stories say about them."

"And the truth is?" I asked.

Ben sighed. "And the truth is, unicorns are very shy. It is hard for anyone, even other unicorns to form a relationship with them. But once a being does form a bond with a unicorn, that unicorn loves them fiercely. They are bonded tightly, no matter who they bond to, human, god, or other unicorns. It is forever. Nothing and no one external will ever break that bond.

"But unicorns are also very vengeful. If one party to a bond does something unforgivable, the other unicorn's absolute devotion will turn to absolute wrath. That unicorn will not stop until their errant bond mate is not only dead but thoroughly destroyed, body, mind, spirit, reputation, everything. They won't stop until the entirety of creation spits on the name of their former bond mate."

"Wow, so either complete devotion or complete animosity, no in between." I said.

Ben nodded, picking up a small stick that had been sitting next to our small fire and twiddling with it as he talked. "Pretty much. If you are in a bonded match with a unicorn, its complete devotion. If you ruined a bonding with a unicorn, its complete animosity. If you are neither bonded nor broken bonded, its complete indifference."

"What type of things would cause a unicorn to break a bond?" I asked.

"Killing another unicorn, unless it was to protect the bond mate." Ben explained. "Harming or killing of a child, any child of any species. Unicorns are fiercely protective of all children, of all kinds, anywhere. They have really sensitive smelling abilities and can smell emotions. Fear, happiness, distrust. Apparently, all things, humans, gods, other animals, produce a smell that matches their emotion.

"Unicorns can tell a lot by the smells on someone. So, if you were happy, they can smell it. If you were by someone else who was happy but you weren't, they could tell that too, even days later. So, they can smell that you have been near a frightened child, and were not moved to compassion or helpfulness by that child's fright, or even if you were excited or intrigued by that child's fear. They don't stand for that stuff at all and will a hundred percent turn on you for it."

"Wait," I stopped him. "So, what if, like, a child was hurt. They fell down and broke their arm and were scared and in pain, but the way they fell was comical so you laughed. You didn't hurt them, and didn't want them to be hurt, but laughed anyway? Or what if someone else near you wanted to hurt a child and you didn't?"

"From what I understand, which admittedly, I don't understand much having never had that type of relationship with a unicorn, each emotion and each person have a different scent." Ben explained. "So, the child's fear has one scent, their hurting has a different scent. If you laughed but actually cared for the hurt kid, you would have both the scents of kindness and compassion as well as humorous-type stuff. And if you were near someone who hurt a kid, they would know it was not you but someone else's foulness they smelled. I mean, at least that's what I understand. I know that unicorns are actually very fair-minded too, so they would loathe blaming someone for something someone else is actually at fault for."

"Makes sense, I guess." I replied. "What else breaks a pair-bond?"

Ben shrugged. "Like I said, they are fair-minded as a species. Anything they consider morally wrong will break a pair-bond, I guess. I didn't ever interact with unicorns very much, so I only knew cursory type stuff."

I thought about this for a moment, then said, "So, for Malachi to get a unicorn to hide a key for him, he probably would have to pair-bond with it first? How would we get that unicorn to give up the key then?"

Ben shrugged again. "I guess we hope that locking up the Heka, attempting to kill you, and attempting to destroy the whole of existence is on the unicorn naughty list."

I leaned back against the cave wall and let everything Ben told me sift through my mind. After a few minutes, something clicked. "Ben?" I posed.

"Yup?" Ben had also leaned against a cave wall and closed his eyes. He seemed as if he was resting.

"Unicorns protect children, right?" I asked.

Ben opened his eyes slightly and turned to glance at me. "Yeah. Why?"

I pushed myself to sitting up straight and asked, "What is a child to them? I mean, how do they define who is and who is not a child?"

Ben sat up too and looked at me fully. "I don't know. Where are you going with this?"

"I haven't had my eighteenth birthday yet." I reminded Ben. "In the human world, or well at least in the human culture I was a part of, child means everyone under the age of eighteen. I know other human cultures have different ages of majority, and even in the United States, the age that defines someone as an adult is kind of subjective depending on the topic, but basically eighteen is the benchmark most people use. So, would the unicorns see me as a child, even though I am a god, and my spirit is over a hundred years old?"

"That," Ben smiled almost conspiratorially, as if maybe he was starting to see where I was going with this, "is a very good question. One only they would be able to answer. Why does it matter?"

"Because Malachi tried to kill me." I replied. "If a pair-bonded unicorn would break the bond over harming a child, and Malachi tried to harm me when I was a child, they may be able to smell that on me, or something. They would break their bond with Malachi."

Ben interrupted me, finishing my thought. "And they would do anything they could to now protect you! They would break their promise to Malachi to hide the key, and give you the key to protect you."

"Is that right?" I questioned him.

Ben shrugged for a third time. "It sounds like a logical thought, so maybe, but I don't know for sure."

I thought about this idea for a few more moments. I didn't like how often Ben shrugged while explaining all of this unicorn stuff, but he was the best source of information I had. I would just have to hope we were right about how it all worked, and the unicorn would give us the key.

While I thought, I leaned forward and felt my socks. They weren't perfectly dry, but were close enough that I could comfortably put them and my shoes back on.

I sighed, hating the ifs and maybes, and spoke while I laced up my shoes. "Well, we can't know if we just sit around in this cave wasting time. I say let's go find the unicorns and see what happens."

Ben shrugged again, and held his arm out towards the cave entrance as if he was inviting me, saying, "You are the leader here, lead on."

I got up and walked out of the cave. "You really have to stop shrugging, Ben. It's kind of annoying." I teased him.

Ben shook his head, smiling. Then he shrugged again, exaggerating the motion, over and over. "I dunno, man. I kinda like this gesture. And annoying you is fun."

I rolled my eyes and ignored him, walking on towards the pond. From there, I started walking the same direction I had seen the unicorn and its foal run. I knew from my time in the oasis with Gavya that this oasis wasn't very big, and that it was mostly scrubby, overgrown vegetation. While not an actual forest, it had a sort of foresty type feel to most of it, and was probably only about a mile wide in each direction. So, I was surprised when the oasis suddenly turned into a traditional forest, and even more surprise when it kept going further than the oasis actually went.

As surprised as I was at these changes, nothing compared to my shock when the forest oasis suddenly opened onto rolling hills of beautiful green pastures. There was no way that all of this had been here before. There were miles and miles of lush green grass, wandering hills and valleys so wide that they would be visible all the way back in Taikarlu. I stopped at the edge of the woods, staring at the landscape, my mouth hanging open in surprise.

Ben was staring as well, just as surprised as me.

"How?" I sputtered, holding my hand out to gesture at... all of it.

Ben looked like he was about to shrug, but stopped himself. "Anna, you have to remember where you are. Taikarlu is not like the human realm. Distance means nothing just like time means nothing."

I looked at him, my confusion evident on my face. "But we are not in Taikarlu anymore. We are in the Wastes, or well in an oasis in the Wastes."

Ben shook his head. "You misunderstand how it works, Anna. Taikarlu isn't just the city. The Wastes are part of Taikarlu. Well, to be exact, the Wastes are a scar on Taikarlu where there used to be beautiful forests and hills and valleys, plains just like you see here. This," Ben gestured to the forest and the pastures, "this is all what Taikarlu used to look like before the Breaking. There was the city and the areas you knew before, like Area One and Area Two. There were also all the hells and heavens and afterlives and whatnot that were the dominion of each god, the places their believers went after death. But in between each of those spaces, Taikarlu looked like this. Well, some of it did. Other parts were swampy and others like the desert it is now, only not so harsh. All of this was just part and parcel with the city, part of Taikarlu.

"The city you know is made up of the four seasons that exist in the human realm, mimicking places humans live. But all of the places in the human world had some representation in Taikarlu before the Breaking. The main city was just the only place that survived the Breaking. But before it, the world of Taikarlu was one human type area butting directly against another one. You would walk and one moment be in a swamp, the next in the forest, the next in a huge metropolis. That's just the way it was."

"But the Breaking happened, Ben." I said, still confused. "The Breaking destroyed all of that in between space. That's what Gavya told me. How is this here, now?"

"It was." Ben replied, nodding. "It was all destroyed, and became the Wastes. I have no idea how it is here now. But it is. Maybe it's the unicorns magic or something. I really, really don't know how, but it is here, as if the Breaking never happened."

As we had talked, both Ben and I stood on the edge of the forest, looking out at the rolling plains. As we stood there, watching, I saw movement at the top of one of the hills. It was too far away for me to determine what was moving exactly. I only knew something was moving, and it was coming closer. As we watched, I saw the figure dipping below the hills into a valley, disappearing from my sight. Then I saw the figure, or figures really, crest the next hill, move into the next valley then crest the hill closer to us, again and again, until finally, the figures reached the top of the hill directly in front of us. The figures stopped on the top of the hill, and seemed to wait there, with just a small area of gently upward sloping land between us and them.

They were close enough now I could make out what they were. It was unicorns, a whole herd of them. Ben stepped around me, gasping in surprise.

"There are so many of them." He whispered, the awe in his voice barely constrained.

I whispered back, "What do we do?"

Ben furrowed his eyebrows, thinking. "I don't know. It's just... I mean, look at them." The awe returned to his voice. "There are so many. So many colors and ages and... It's like they never disappeared."

Ben stepped further out of the edge of the forest cover. I put a hand on his shoulder to stop him and he looked startled, like he hadn't even realized he was moving. He glanced back at me, and then towards the unicorns, his face reflecting the torn feelings he was wrestling with.

"I feel," he said hoarsely. Ben cleared his throat and spoke again. "I feel drawn to them, like I should just go walk right up to them. I don't know why."

I turned my gaze from Ben and looked at the unicorns, really looked at them. Suddenly, I felt it too, this inexplicable feeling of desire to walk towards the unicorns, to touch them, to sit with them in the long grass and nuzzle the babies and stroke their beautiful manes. I could see from where I was that they really came in every color. Soft blue and striking emerald green coats, white manes with gold or silver streaking, black tails with deep purple or baby pink tips. Each unicorn was a different part of the rainbow.

The foals were all light grayish colors with varying amounts of coloring in the gray. I could tell that the newborns were all a boring gray and as they aged, their colors became more and more pronounced, with the elders of the herd bearing blindingly intense coats and manes of pure gold and silver. The foals had tiny little bud tips on their forehead, while the elders each bore a single horn, three or four feet long, that looked as if they were made of twisted gemstones. One horn was emerald and ruby and sapphire, another was topaz, amber and pearl. Each horn was its own unique combination, and beautiful.

The herd stood silently, some nibbling grass, other standing, stately watching us. The foals were prancing slightly, just like any bored child would when forced to wait but not understanding what they were waiting for. A few unicorns seemed to be tasked with watching the foals, and were nipping at the sides of this foal or that one when they got too far out of line.

The urge to go to them was overwhelming. I gave up fighting it and slowly walked around Ben, out of the forest and up the hill. I didn't look back but knew instinctively that Ben was following me.

Once I was close enough to communicate, I stopped.

"Hello." I said tentatively. "I am AnnaBella Cain, and this is Ben."

"We know who you are," a voice spoke. I wasn't sure which one was speaking, but somehow knew that the deep, melodic sound must have come from one of the herd's elders.

"Do you know why we are here?" I asked. For some reason, I felt I had to be very careful with what I said. I knew if I said the wrong thing, or was not respectful enough, the herd would leave. I don't know how I knew that, I just did, so I continued to speak softly and slowly.

"Yes," the elder replied. I waited, thinking he would say

something more, but he didn't.

I took a breath, and spoke again. "We are here to save the Heka, and save us all. Malachi was bonded with one of you, and gave them a key…"

The unicorn interrupted me. "No unicorn would bond with someone as profane as Malachi!" he stated harshly. I could feel the unicorn getting angry and knew I had said the wrong thing.

"I'm sorry." I replied quickly. "I truly am. I never meant to insult you. I assumed that because Malachi said…"

Again, the elder interrupted me, his voice still harsh. "You assumed, yes. Gods and humans love to assume."

Another voice chimed in, but this one was softer. "Mawu, she is but a child. Be careful how you speak to her."

Mawu huffed. "She is a child and a god, Roshan."

One of the unicorns began prancing in front of another one. I assumed that the prancing one was Roshan, who spoke in my defense, and the one she was prancing in front of was Mawu. I have no idea why I assumed this, since the voices seemed to just float on the air rather than come from one specific creature, and their mouths didn't move as they spoke. But it was the best assumption I could make.

I turned to Mawu, and replied. "Yes, I am technically a god, but a really, really new one. I was born, not made, so…"

Mawu interrupted again, but this time his voice was not as harsh as before. "We know. Unicorns know about a creature's whole life from one smell. I knew exactly who and what you are before you ever walked out of the trees. I knew what you wanted and what your goals were before you spoke. There is no reason to tell me the things I already know."

I bowed my head slightly. "Please excuse my ignorance, Mawu. I did not know this and did not mean to insult your abilities or intelligence with my ignorance." The unicorns spoke very formally to each other, so I mimicked their speech and was formal in return.

Roshan spoke before Mawu could. "We know, child," she said softly. "Excuse Mawu's inappropriate behavior towards a child." Roshan turned to Mawu and bared her teeth, making a slight snapping noise at him. "Which a child she is, Mawu, god or not, and should be treated as such. Your disrespect will need to be dealt with." At this statement, several other unicorns huffed and pranced a few steps away from Mawu.

Turning back to me, Roshan continued. "AnnaBella Cain, your goals are admirable but are misplaced. Malachi's sour spirit was known to us long before he attempted to harm you. No unicorn would have bonded with one such as him, and if one had, that bond would have been broken as soon as he decided to harm an innocent child, to harm you. We know you seek a key that Malachi claims he hid with us, but we cannot help. Our lands are very small now, and broken. If the key was here, it is lost now to the Barren Place."

"The Barren Place?" I asked.

Before the unicorns could answer, Ben put his hand on my shoulder. "Um, Anna? What... What are you doing?"

Without looking back at him, I answered. "I am talking to the unicorns. Shush."

Ben pulled my shoulder to turn me to face him. He looked very perplexed. "Anna, the unicorns can't talk. Or if they can, they haven't. At least, I haven't ever heard them speak. Are you ok? I mean..." Ben's voice trailed off, his face showing his confusion deepening.

"This god cannot hear us." A third unicorn voice stated matter-of-factly.

I turned away from Ben, towards the unicorns again. "Why not?"

Ben and the third unicorn spoke at the same time. Ben started to say, "What do you mean why not?" but I cut him off with a wave of my hand to listen to the unicorn.

"I'm sorry. I don't know your name." I interrupted the unicorn who had been speaking. "I apologize for interrupting you, but Ben was speaking and I couldn't understand what you said."

Ben opened his mouth to speak again, but I shook my hand at him again to be silent. The third unicorn repeated himself. "I am Silvesse and I accept your apology."

"Thank you, Silvesse. It is nice to meet you. Why can Ben not hear you but I can?" I replied.

Silvesse answered, patiently. "That is not the question you should be asking, AnnaBella Cain."

I saw one unicorn, a much younger one than Mawu and Roshan trotting a few steps forward out of the herd and turned to them, assuming they were Silvesse. "What is the question I should be asking, then?"

Silvesse dipped his head a few times, saying, "The question is why can you hear us when all the other gods and humans cannot?"

Oh, I thought. I can hear unicorns speak when no one else can? "Could it be because of the job I worked as a coordinator?" I asked. "During my time working in Taikarlu, I only ever helped humans. But maybe the position in helping find the proper afterlife for people is actually extended to animals too."

Silvesse and the other unicorns made a noise that I assumed was a small laugh. "No, AnnaBella Cain, that would not be why." Silvesse explained. "Unicorns only have one potential afterlife; thus, no decision is needed about where we go. This is true for all the so-called mythical beasts. We are not immortal, but because after our deaths, we essentially are just reincarnated back into the herd. Most humans believe we are immortal. Our souls are immortal, even though our bodies are not."

"Oh." I replied. "I did not know that. Thank you for sharing that with me, Silvesse."

Silvesse bobbed their head again. "As far as the question as to why you understand us when others cannot, we do not have the answer either. There has never been a non-mythical beast who could speak to any mythical beast before."

"What about gods or humans who have bonded with a unicorn?" I asked. "Could they speak to each other?"

Mawu answered this time. "We unicorns can understand humans and gods as well as all animals and other mythical beasts, but they cannot understand us. Bonds that happened between mythical beasts and non-mythical beasts were capable because of a devotion that transcended the need to communicate with words. The only being that could ever understand unicorns was the Heka, until you."

Woah, I thought. Another thing where I was the only one able to do it. The idea of me being the only one to be able to do 'something' was starting to get to be an unnervingly normal turn of events. At some point, I would have to sit down and really think about what that meant.

But not now. Now, I needed to figure out the key thing. "Earlier, before Ben interrupted, you said that your lands were too small and if Malachi's key was here, it was probably lost to the Barren Place." I said, changing the topic back to what we had been discussing. "What is the Barren Place?"

Roshan responded this time. "The Barren Place is where you came from. These hills and plains are encircled by a small band of forest. In the south, there is the small oasis you arrived at our lands through, but everywhere else, past the forest is a land of heat and sand. We call this place the Barren Place. No grass grows there, and it goes on forever. If we leave the forest, and go into the Barren Place by the west, we can run for what seems like forever and return to the forest in the east, seeing nothing but sand the whole time."

Mawu continued where Roshan left off. "This has been true since the Flood. It was not like this before. Before the Flood, we could go anywhere, the city, the gods' places, the human realm, but then the Flood came. We were trapped in the waters for a long time. When the waters receded, all that was left was the Barren Place and this land here."

Now Silvesse spoke. "We have not seen gods, nor humans, nor anyone else since the Flood. We did not know if they were alive or dead or just gone. We tried to find them, but whenever anyone went into the Barren Place, no matter which way they ran, they always ended up back here, having seen nothing but more sand and more sand."

"Just like the gods." I told them. I felt the questioning from the unicorns and answered before they even asked. "The gods called the sand place the Wastes. It was the same for them. They could leave the city in any direction, walk through the sands forever and would end up right back at the city. They could, through their power, access their own individual afterlife places for their worshippers. But even then, it was surrounded by the Wastes, and they would wander the Wastes only to return to the same place they left."

"Then how did you manage to escape the Barren Place, or the Wastes as you call it, twice, AnnaBella Cain?" Mawu asked. "And how did you bring others with you? Ben this time, and Gavya last time?"

I sighed deeply. "I honestly don't know." I told the unicorns. "I think it has something to do with my Heka, but I am not sure. There are apparently a lot of things I can do that no one else can. Not gods, not humans, not coordinators, and apparently now, not even mythical beasts."

During my conversation with the unicorns, Ben had been standing silently, listening to the half of the conversation he could hear. But now he spoke up. "Anna, I am only getting half of this, but I think you are talking about why you can move through the Wastes when no one else can and the unicorns don't know why you can when they can't either. Am I right?"

"Yes, Ben." I told him. "They can understand you, but you can't hear or understand them. No one but mythical beast can hear or understand mythical beasts, except the Heka. I should have been translating for you, I guess. Sorry."

"Don't worry about it. I figured that, too." Ben said impatiently, waving off my apology. "But that is the point I am trying to make. You can traverse the Wastes, and even enter lands the Wastes hide from everyone else, like the oases and the unicorn plains. You can speak to the unicorns. Only you can do all that."

"Yeah." I huff. "We established that already."

Ben continued. "But not only you can do that. Everyone you take with you can do that too."

"No, they can't, Ben." I replied. "You can't hear the unicorns."

Ben held up a finger. "I can't yet. But you took Gavya into the oasis and left her there. She was able to stay in the oasis without you. It existed for her after you showed it to her. Maybe, once you give the ability to see somewhere or do something to someone else, they are able to do it. I can see the plains even though I never could before. Maybe you can give me the ability to hear the unicorns."

"That's a pretty big leap, Ben." I told him, feeling a little disbelieving. If he was right, then it was just more things I could do that no one else could. More confusing things. "Gavya stayed where I left her, in the oasis. And when she left the oasis, she went to the city of Taikarlu, like anyone else who walks through the Waste would. How do we know she didn't just come back because that was the only place she could go without me?"

Mawu answered instead of Ben. "This should be tested, this theory of Ben's."

"How?" I asked. Ben touched my arm, and I looked at him. He raised his eyebrows at me and I understood. "Oh, Mawu said we should test your theory."

Ben nodded. "Yeah, how?" Ben was looking out at the whole herd. I slyly pointed out Mawu to him and he looked directly at the unicorn.

Mawu caught my motion, and politely stepped forward so Ben would know where to look to speak to him. "This god Ben should go back into the Barren Lands alone, without AnnaBella Cain. He should go far enough away that he can no longer see the oasis. Then he should try to return to the oasis on his own. If he can, then he has gained the ability to find it from AnnaBella Cain. If not, then his theory is wrong."

I relayed what Mawu said to Ben, who agreed. "He is right. If I go into the Wastes, I should automatically go back to Taikarlu. If I don't and can find my way back to you, then something in me changed. I would assume that change was because of you, Anna."

"How would I know if you went back to Taikarlu?" I asked.

"Nummi." Ben replied, excitedly. "Nummi knows how to send himself to the cave. You can wait there and if I go back to Taikarlu, I will have Nummi astral project himself there to tell you."

There was a lot of assumptions being made in what Ben was saying, but he seemed very sure. I looked at him and he was grinning very confidently. I couldn't be as confident as he seemed no matter how hard I tried. Everything kept swirling around in my brain.

All of the 'only one' statements people had said about me started crashing into one another in my head. I was the only one who could have a human body in Taikarlu without it dying. I was the only one who could find the oases, or at least this one oasis, in the Wastes. I was the only one who could hear and understand the unicorns. I was the only one who had spoken to the Heka since the Breaking. I was the only one who could invert time everywhere, on every plane of existence at the same time. I was the only one who asked the right questions. I was the only one, the only one, the only one, over and over and over.

Ben and the unicorns all were chattering. Ben couldn't hear the unicorns so he didn't know what they were saying or that they were even saying anything, but the unicorns could hear him. It didn't matter, though. It was as if the whole herd was speaking all at once, and between their voices and Ben's, the words, their excitement, their confusion, all crashed around me, becoming a clash of noise and chaos in my ears. The voices of everyone saying I was the only one in my head and the real voices of those around me became too much. I felt like I was going to explode.

I put my hands over my ears and screamed. "Shut up! Just shut up! You're wrong, it's not me. I can't! It's too much." I started crying. Hot tears rolling down my cheeks, I clenched my eyes shut and turned away from the unicorns and Ben, still screaming. "I can't do this. I can't be the only one!"

My throat felt like it was on fire, my stomach rolled and I couldn't catch my breath. It felt as if the world had suddenly changed its axis and left me feeling unmoored. I sat down, then laid on the grass and curled up into a ball, tucking my head down into my arms to hide.

Ben and the unicorns went silent, watching me, but I didn't notice. Inside my head, everyone was still talking loudly. I could hear Mari, Nummi, Ben, my father. Everyone one who had ever said that I was the only one. I could even hear the voices of the doctors who had treated me when I was just a human, the ones who thought that I was a normal human who had been injured in a car accident, but had been surprised I made such a miraculous recovery. Every doctor that had said "Anna is the only one I have ever seen to have these problems. Anna is the only one I have ever treated to recover like this." Their voices were there too, with all the rest, clanging inside my mind with the other gods, the other humans saying over and over, "the only one, the only one." I could hear them all.

But especially loud among them all in my head was my father. "You are special, Bella. You are my only child and always will be. You are the only one I want." I heard him say over and over above the noise of everyone else.

Slowly, the other voices faded away, until it was only my father's voice left. Then, his voice started to change. It wasn't my dad's voice anymore, but someone else. Something else.

It was the Heka. "You are the only one who can save me." It said.

I opened my eyes. I was in the nothing I went to when the Heka and I spoke. In that place, where it felt like the universe was just being born and just dying at the same time, everything else faded away. My cheeks still felt wet from my tears as I looked into the never-ending abyss.

"I can't." I told It. "I can't be the only one. I'm scared."

"So am I." It told me, softly.

I wiped my face and slowed my breathing. "You are?" I asked. I sat up, tucking my legs under me.

"Yes." The Heka replied.

"What are you scared of?" I asked It.

"Everything you are." It answered me. "Your fears are my fears. That we can't do this. That we will be alone always. That we will get it wrong and everyone will die because they trusted us."

"We?" I said.

The Heka sighed, not with frustration but a weary sigh of one who has had to be strong for too long. "Yes, we, AnnaBella Cain. We are connected, you and I. What you feel, I feel. What I feel, you do too. If you hurt, I hurt. If you cry, I cry. If you are happy, so am I. And if I am scared, you are scared. We feel everything for and with each other."

"Oh," I responded, the idea of this, of the maker of everything feeling scared with me actually making me less scared somehow. "Why?"

The Heka sighed again. I could tell It couldn't answer me. It wanted to, but couldn't. I guess we really could feel each other's feelings.

"Why can't you tell me?" I asked.

"Because you are not ready." It said.

"Ready for what?" I pushed.

I felt the massive pressure the Heka felt, like It was carrying a huge burden by Itself and really, really wanted to put the burden down, or at least ask for help with it, but couldn't. "You are not ready for the answer." It said.

"When will I be ready?" I whispered. "Will I ever be ready?"

The Heka was quiet for a long time. I would have thought It went away, but I could feel It hadn't. It was thinking. Finally, the Heka did walk away. As It left, It said, "When you know your name, you will be ready. What is your name, AnnaBella Cain?"

As quickly as I entered the nothingness, I was back on the plains with the unicorns and Ben. I felt the grass underneath me, and Ben's hands on my shoulders. Apparently, he was trying to comfort me and had no idea that I had left to talk to the Heka.

"Anna," Ben was saying softly, "it's ok. I'm here."

I sat up and turned my face towards Ben. Apparently, my body had continued crying while I was gone. Everything was still confusing and overwhelming, but somehow it felt better than before. I wasn't sure if it was seeing Ben look so concerned or what the Heka had said to me, but even though nothing had changed, I felt comforted.

Ben wrapped his arms around me, gathering me into his lap in a big hug. I let him, and melted into the comfort I felt there. I hoped that, if the Heka could feel when I felt lonely and scared, It could also feel when I felt comforted. Maybe It could feel Ben's hug.

When I was sufficiently calm, Ben asked me, "What happened?"

"Everything became really overwhelming." I told him. "Then, I went to the Heka. It told me our feelings are connected. I think we both just got really scared of messing up, and with both of us scared like that, it was too much."

Ben nodded, just accepting what I said as fact. He didn't even question me going to the Heka, or what that meant. "Makes sense. You both would feel really lonely, with so much riding on you."

I didn't respond and Ben didn't push me to. He just held me and we sat there for what felt like a really long time. Finally, I moved out of Ben's arms. He stood, then helped me stand. The unicorns had apparently gotten bored waiting. One of the older unicorns had taken the foals off into the distance and they were running and leaping around like foal horses do. The rest of the adults seemed to be clumped into groups, chatting quietly among themselves.

When I had brushed most of the grass off my pants, Roshan, Mawu and Silvesse left the group they had been talking with and turned back to me. "Are you feeling better?" Roshan asked me.

"Yes, thank you." I replied to her. "I am sorry about that."

Mawu snorted. "No need to apologize."

Silvesse took over speaking. "We could see that you went elsewhere. Your Heka grew immensely. Did the Heka tell you what you needed to hear?"

Surprised, I asked them. "You can see my Heka?"

"Not in the way you think," replied Mawu. "You became so very full of It that it would be apparent to anyone what had happened. We assumed there was a connection between you and the Heka. This just confirmed our beliefs."

"Yeah," I snorted, then muttered under my breath, "You have no idea how connected me and Heka are." I took a deep breath, let it out then responded to the unicorns properly. "Yes, the Heka and I are connected. I know that now."

Ben grunted questioningly, but I ignored him. "The Heka and I are emotionally connected. We feel what each other feels, apparently. Maybe that connection bleeds over from feelings to abilities. Maybe that's why I can do things like speak to you unicorns and find places in the Wastes and all that other stuff."

The unicorns snorted in agreement and Ben nodded, saying, "Makes sense to me."

"I think," I started, then stopped. What was I thinking? I knew something was brewing in my mind, but it seemed fuzzy. Then I realized it probably wasn't me thinking. It was the Heka thinking and I was just along for the ride. Whoo boy, this could get confusing if we could think each other's thoughts along with feeling each other's feelings.

I waited to see if the thought became clearer. It did, and I continued speaking. "I think we don't need to test if Ben can leave the oasis and return. I think we need to test if a unicorn can leave the oasis and find Taikarlu."

"What's the difference?" Ben asked.

"The difference is the key." Mawu replied, catching on to what I was thinking.

"Exactly." I said to Mawu, then turned Ben. "Mawu said the difference is the key, and he's right. We have been thinking the key is a physical key, but we were wrong. The key isn't a real key, like for a lock, but the key to unlocking Taikarlu, to undoing the Breaking."

Mawu agreed. As he talked, I told Ben what he said. "The Great Plains were separated from the city and the human realms by the Barren Place. Just as the city was locked away from the Great Plains. If AnnaBella Cain is correct, now that she has come here, it should not be anymore. She has unlocked it from its isolation and unicorns can now go to the city, and gods can come here."

Ben gasped, putting the pieces together in his mind. "So, every oasis in the Wastes would be the key to another land occupied by a different clan of mythical beasts that were isolated by the Wastes in the Breaking. Each one, as you find them, will become unlocked, un-isolated, and connect with all the other unlocked ones. Once you have unlocked them all, you can release the Heka from Its cage because Its cage isn't in the Wastes, but is the Wastes itself!"

"That's what I think," I told him, "and the Heka thinks so too. Or at least I feel like It does. That part is confusing. I am not sure what is my thoughts and what is Its thoughts. Never mind, anyway, yeah.

That's what we think." I turned to the unicorns. "And you all agree?"

All the adult unicorns in the herd snorted and bobbed their heads up and down, in agreement. At least this communication I didn't have to translate for Ben.

Mawu called out loudly for a volunteer to go into the Barren Place. A young unicorn pranced forward. Her emerald coat was still tinged with slightest bit of gray, while her mane and tail were struck through with the tiniest strands of gold. On her head was a horn made of onyx, sapphire and pearl.

"I will go, Grandfather." she said. I translated for Ben.

Mawu snorted. "This is my granddaughter, Dulcea. I would be proud for her to volunteer to be the first unicorn in the city of Taikarlu in millennia."

Ben answered before I did. "Dulcea, you do your kind proud. Thank you for your bravery. Go south out of the oasis. You should come into the winter lands of the city from that direction. Go to the warmest, summer part and find Nummi. I will give you a message to give him to let us know you made it."

As Ben had talked, I saw him begin to almost radiate godliness. He looked taller, statelier. His hair seemed to shine and his skin was a pure light brown, with his scars gleaming white in contrast. They were not scars but badges of courage and strength.

His form didn't actually change, I realized. I was seeing him through the Heka's eyes. I was seeing him in all the glory of a god, how the Heka had intended him to be. How his worshippers would have seen him before the Breaking. And he was beautiful.

He turned to me and a slow smile came over him. He was feeling the change I was seeing. He was becoming a god in the fullest sense again. Something had changed in him that made him become unlocked like the land had become unlocked, and he tapped into the Heka in that new, full way. He believed in the Heka fully again.

"Back to the cave to wait for Nummi?" he asked me, holding his hand out to me.

I took his hand and the three of us, Ben, Dulcea, and me, walked back to the oasis while the other unicorns snorted and pawed the ground, sending their hopes of safety and success with her. Ben held my hand all the way back to the cave, where he let go of my hand and scribbled a short message on paper from our packs for Nummi to explain everything. Then he gave it to Dulcea, who held it gently in her mouth and took off from the cave at a fast trot.

"What now?' Ben asked me, after Dulcea was gone.

I sat down against the cave wall, exhausted. "Now we wait to see if Dulcea makes it."

Ben sighed, and sat down next to me. As if he could read my mind, he pulled on my arm until I was lying down with my head in his lap. "Rest," he commanded me, "I will keep watch."

I did as Ben ordered, falling asleep almost instantly

Chapter Two

The gods did not know how to react when the bright emerald unicorn trotted into Hills of Taikarlu. They stopped where they were and stood in shock, mouths hanging open. Those on the furthest edges of the Hills had already been aware something had changed when they saw a forest grow along the edge of the city where only seconds before there had only been sand, and so were more prepared for the shock. But even they did not expect a unicorn.

The unicorn, oblivious to the reaction the gods were having to her presence, continued on her mission. She had long since expected the forest to end and turn into a sandy desert. When it didn't, giving way to the city instead, she knew that AnnaBella had been right. She kept moving, a growing trail of gods, coordinators and humans following in her wake, as she made her way to the Business District.

Once or twice, the unicorn stopped, sniffed around, then continued moving. Eventually she made her way to a small building with a brass plate next to the door that read "Annex." The unicorn huffed at the door of the building, unsure how to move through it. She pawed at the door until a young woman in a saree heard the noise and came to investigate. Opening the door, Gavya was shocked to see a unicorn, but stepped to the side letting it through into the library of the gods. The trail of beings that had followed the unicorn waited outside the Annex to see what would happen next.

The unicorn turned to Gavya for a moment, sniffed, then continued trotting through the halls. In the middle of the Annex sat a group of several gods conversing quietly. The unicorn walked up to what appeared to old man, stopped, lowered her head, and dropped a piece of paper in his lap. The man, Nummi, thanked the unicorn and read the note, hiding any shock he felt.

"Well done, Dulcea." Nummi told the unicorn. He patted the unicorn's neck. "Well done indeed. Off you trot, head home to your herd. I must contact Anna and let her know you have arrived." Dulcea snorted and head butted Nummi gently, then turned and walked back to the entrance of the building.

Nummi followed her to the door. Gavya held the door open for the unicorn, who ran through it and galloped back the way she came. Gavya, and a host of other beings, stared at Nummi.

"A unicorn!" Gavya exclaimed. "What does that mean?"

Nummi smiled. "It means AnnaBella has unlocked the first key and the Wastes are healing." Murmurs of excitement waved through the crowd, but Nummi ignored them. "She still has a long way to go, but it is a good start." Nummi turned away from the crowds and into the Annex again, to find a quiet place to settle down and free his spirit to tell Anna she had succeeded.

As he did so, AnnaBella woke up with a start. She felt something tighten deep within her, as if her skin had suddenly become just an inch smaller and her insides were being pinched with the too-little space. As she sat up and moved out of Ben's protective arms, she realized that it wasn't her skin that shrunk.

"The Heka," she said aloud, breathlessly, "Its prison just got smaller. Dulcea made it to Taikarlu."

"How do you know?" Ben almost asked her, then thought better of it. Instead, he asked, "What do we do now?"

"We wait for Nummi to tell us," she said, standing up and gathering her things, "then we run."

I cut Nummi's time of astral projecting short. As soon as he confirmed what I already knew, that Dulcea had made it to Taikarlu, I told him that we needed to go. And go fast. The Heka was running out of not only time, but space. My skin felt tight, like I had a bad sunburn and the skin would crack and peel if I tried to move too much. If that was how it felt for me, I couldn't imagine how it felt for It.

Once Nummi had departed, we had gathered our belongings and cleaned up camp, Ben and I headed out into the oasis.

"Which way, boss?" Ben asked me jokingly.

Rolling my eyes at his comment, I responded. "It doesn't matter which way we go. Any way except south. We already fixed south, so point a way and we go that way." I turned around in a circle and randomly chose a direction. "West. We go west."

"After you." Ben held out his hand in invitation and I started walking, with Ben right behind me. The oasis went on longer than it had before and we could see to the south that the oasis turned into lush forest instead of desert. The physical landscape of the Wastes had changed.

Eventually, the oasis ended and we entered the western Wastes. Ben stopped to pick up sand and put it in my hand, but I stopped him.

"I don't think I need that anymore." I tilted my head to the side, trying to analyze what I was feeling, what I was doing. I didn't think that I was using any Heka, but I knew something had changed. Or maybe I just was noticing things I hadn't before.

"What changed?" he asked.

I tried to think of a way to explain it. Finally, I said, "You know how the Wastes turned to forest when we unlocked it?"

"When you unlocked it," Ben corrected me, nodding that he understood.

I ignored his correction and continued. "Well, the forest felt, I dunno. I guess you could say clean. The Wastes don't. They feel dirty, almost. Like, the Wastes are wrong and the other is right. The oasis feels more right, more clean, than the Wastes, but still polluted some. And I want to go to the cleanest place, the rightest place. I feel a need for the clean place. Does that make any sense?"

Ben nodded again. "Yeah, it does. If the Wastes are the Heka's prison, the places that aren't the Wastes would be the Heka's freedom. If you feel what the Heka does, then you would feel Its desire to be in the freedom places. The oasis would be the door to a freedom place for It."

"Exactly." I said, glad he understood my weird connection with the Heka or at least just accepted it. I mean, I didn't understand it, so at least Ben wasn't asking me to make that make sense.

Ben and I set out walking again, trusting my intuition, or Heka connection, to guide us the right way. We walked in silence for a while, finding a pace that didn't feel too slow for the sense of urgency that was growing in me, but not so fast that we felt like we were running.

After a time, Ben spoke up again. "Hey, Anna. What did you mean when you said the Heka's prison got smaller?"

I thought about it while we walked. "I am not sure. I just felt it. If the Wastes are the Heka's cage as you said with the unicorns, then every time we claim a piece of the Wastes back, every time we connect the mythical beasts' lands back to the gods' lands, the Wastes will get smaller. The Wastes getting smaller means that the Heka's prison get smaller. And, I dunno, I might be wrong but it feels like it is getting really uncomfortable for an infinite being to be in a smaller and smaller finite space."

"You only fixed one, though." Ben countered, again changing my statement of we to a statement of me.

"I know," I told him, "and that's the scary part. If it hurt that much for just that one part of Its cage to go away, how much worse will it be when we undo the fifth area? Or the ninth?"

Ben didn't have any more of an answer than I did. We kept walking, the forest and fields of the Great Plains receding behind us and dunes of empty sand before us. For a long time, Ben and I walked in silence.

As usual in Taikarlu, telling how long we were walking was hard since the sun never moved from its zenith. But after what at least felt like hours, I suggested to Ben that we take a break. He agreed and the two of us dropped our packs on the hard sand and then sat down ourselves. Ben rummaged through his bag and produced two bags of potato chips and some water, giving one to me and keeping the other for himself.

As we munched on our snack, I asked Ben more questions. "Why did you, Nummi, Mari, and Albert decide to come look for me?"

"Like Nummi told you," he replied, "we escaped the war between the gods. Me, Albert and Mari escaped before the flood, and Nummi after, along with a bunch of other gods. When we thought the Heka had been defeated, because Its power waned, we stayed in the human realms because we didn't know how to return to Taikarlu or what awaited us there. We thought the gods fighting on the side of forcing the Heka to step down from being in control won. We know now that the Heka was trapped, which I guess is the same as defeated."

I nodded. "Yeah, It was a sort of defeat, but not how you guys thought."

"Exactly." Ben explained. "The goddess of the hunt had been our spy in the camp of the gods, but during and then after the Flood, we never heard from her. We thought maybe she had been found out, or whatever. Defeated like the Heka, and that maybe all the gods on the Heka's side were imprisoned or something. This was before we four came together. For a time, all the gods who fled to the human realms were just wandering around, lost, confused and alone after the Flood."

"Wow." I said sympathetically.

"Yeah, it was a bad time all around. Cut off from our worshippers, well, those of us who had them already, we just felt weak. Impotent. Even Albert said he felt drained, and he still doesn't have worshippers yet." Ben sighed, his face showing how hard it was for him to remember that time. "Eventually, gods started running into one another. At first, you'd get really panicky if you ran into another god.

But soon, we all realized that it didn't matter which side you had been on during the War, gods or Heka, if you were stuck in the human realm, we were all on the same side now."

"What side was that?" I asked.

Ben gave a sarcastic grin. "The side of how the hell do we get home now? I ran across Albert first, in Mesopotamia, and we decided to stick together. For Albert, I think he was scared to be alone in the world when he had no worshippers. As a god with no worshippers yet, and not even the archeological remnants left behind of worshippers long gone, he would have been the weakest of us all. So, for him, pairing up with a god with at least a few living worshippers left around would have been some protection."

"Protection from what?" I asked. "Other gods?"

"Yeah, maybe." Ben wavered, bouncing his head back and forth as if weighing that answer. "Other gods, other who knows what. Remember the world had just fallen apart. We didn't know which way was up anymore or what new things there might have been that we should be scared of. When the whole world is full of unknowns, it becomes really easy for your mind to invent horrors to fear."

Even gods were afraid of the monster in the closet or under the bed? That idea was surprising to me. Most faiths I knew of tried to portray their god or gods as omnipotent, never scared of anything, power house beings. To know Ben knew what it was like to be scared of what you don't know was comforting.

Ben continued talking. "I liked having Albert around because, even though I am a god, I am only a teenager. My personage as a god is a teenager, so I am very much just a teen in a lot of my thoughts and actions. It was helpful, especially in trying to navigate the human world, to have an 'adult' around. Or at least, have someone the humans perceived as an adult around to do the adult stuff.

"Anyway, in about the 1000's, Albert and I found Mari in Europe. We had run across other gods here, now and again, so we were polite and thought we would keep going our way and she would keep going hers. But then she told us that she had heard of a god that had come to the human realm after the Flood rather than before it. Albert and I agreed to help her look for this god, so we could hear his story about what happened in Taikarlu.

"We found him in the southern Americas and, after we heard his story, Mari, Albert and I just stuck with him. He said that he had heard from the goddess of the hunt that there were things happening in Taikarlu that didn't make sense. His communications with her came very infrequently, and usually really delayed. Humans catch on quick when an old man lives for a long time and when a young man never ages, so we had to move around a lot. That meant the goddess had a hard time finding us.

"After a while, though, we got a message that the coordinator Nick Cain had gone to the human realms. We had known that a system of traveling back and forth between Taikarlu and the human realms had been set up for a while now, but none of us gods who ran and had been in the human world when it was set up were logged into it. Besides, we really weren't sure if we should go back or not, if it was safe to. So, we stayed with the humans and waited for news from the goddess, something that would tell us what we should do.

"Nick Cain coming to the human realm was not something we expected to hear. Then, the goddess sent a message telling us all about you, your trial, and whatever. We were so shocked to hear Nick had a kid. He never even seemed to care about going to the human realms at all before everything went sideways, let alone having a child like every other person was. So, to find out he not only broke the rules and had a kid, but took that kid to the Trials, was shocking.

"But then the goddess told us something else. She said she had been watching that child, who had been ordered to stay in Taikarlu as a coordinator by the courts. It seemed like there was something wrong with her, meaning you. Then she said someone told her that the courts had ordered the TIMS to go to the earth and 'clean up the mess left by Nick Cain.' That order included making it seem as though Nick Cain died, but made no mention of making it seem like his child had died too."

I interrupted Ben's story. "Wait, why did it matter that they made it look like my dad died but said nothing about me?"

"Because," Ben explained, "if you were the child of a human and a coordinator or god, and the powers that be wanted to maintain a cover story for the humans, why would they only give Nick a convenient exit story and not you? They wouldn't. If Nick was 'dead' to the humans who knew him and you just 'vanished,' how would your mother have reacted?"

I thought about that for a second. When she thought Dad died, and I was injured, in the car crash, Mom was sad over me losing Dad but was a crazy mess of worry about me and my health. If Dad had died and I, who should have been with him, was just gone? Yeah, Mom would have burned down the whole world just to find me.

Ben saw what I was thinking on my face. "Yeah. Not a good loop hole to leave open, right?"

"No," I replied chuckling. "Mom is not someone you want to piss off, not even if you are a god."

"So, you see why the goddess thought that this supposed oversight hinted at a bigger problem." Ben continued. "Then, there was the whole issue of the TIMS building you a bathroom in your apartment in Taikarlu. Why did you need a bathroom if you were no longer human?"

"That is the same thing that tripped me and Gavya up and led us to figuring out I still had a human body." I told him.

Ben nodded. "I don't know how Malachi managed to slip all these mistakes right under everyone's noses. Maybe everyone was so focused on themselves and freaked out that a coordinator broke the rules so spectacularly. They were more worried about an association with you staining them that they missed the evidence of wrongdoing that was right in front of their faces.

"Either way, the goddess of the hunt, true to her name, sniffed out these issues and put us on the job of hunting down your human body, if it existed." Ben paused for a moment. He looked around, as if he suddenly felt weird talking about all of this out in the open and was worried someone might overhear. Suddenly, he stood up. "Let's start moving. I want to find that next oasis."

I caught Ben's paranoid feelings and did as he said. Standing up, I collected our trash and shoved it quickly in my bag. Then I gave myself a second to determine which way we should go. Everything felt darker than it had before we stopped, more polluted. There was a small spot to the west that seemed less bad, but there was a haze between us and it. I didn't know what that haze was, but something in me recoiled at the idea of walking through it.

I mentally shook myself and thought that I was letting Ben's sudden worry about being overheard get to me. I oriented us to the west and led us in a straight line towards the less-dark place, haze or no haze.

Ben and I continued to chatter as we walked now. We didn't speak of anything important, just focusing on random things like our favorite movie, or that teacher from our chemistry class and their penchant for wacky hairdos. The more we walked, the closer we got to that haze feeling. I hadn't told Ben about it, but he seemed to be getting more nervous the further we walked, just like I was.

I had assumed the haziness would creep over us slowly, getting thicker with each step. Instead, we slammed right into it like running into a brick wall. All at once, I was sweating and clammy. Fear skittered up and down my spine and I really, really didn't want to walk any further.

I looked over at Ben to see if he was feeling anything. He had gone pale and his right hand was trembling, but his face looked determined, as if he was pretending nothing was wrong.

I finally gave in. "Ben, stop."

Ben breathed a sigh of relief. "It's not just me, is it? You feel it too? Like someone is listening?" When I nodded that I did, he sighed again, "Oh good."

"Give me a minute," I told him. Then I closed my eyes. Could the Heka feel this too? Did It know why it felt like this? I waited to see if there would be some sort of response. All I got was the sense that something was angry. We had gone too far from the city, and whatever it was in the desert that kept gods from finding the oases was not happy we had almost made it to a second one.

I breathed in slowly and then blew my breath out, trying to steady my nerves. Could that angry thing actually harm us? Wasn't it Malachi who had done all this, creating the Wastes, and with him gone, wouldn't that thing separating the gods from the rest of the Wastes be gone too? All I got in response was a very unsettled feeling, as if the Heka didn't know either.

I told Ben. "I think something wants to keep us from finding the second oasis. It's mad at us, and I don't know if whatever it is can actually harm us or not."

"Do we keep going?" Ben asked me.

"Do we have a choice?" I retorted. "If we stop, the Heka will die and so will everything else, including whatever is guarding the Wastes."

Ben took in a deep breath and stood up straighter. "Right." He looked around and then loudly proclaimed, "Whatever or whoever you are, we are here to help. We want to save you too, so maybe take it down a notch? You got a job to do, I get that, but work with us a little here?"

We waited for a minute, glancing around the empty desert, to see if anything happened. When nothing did, Ben and I looked at each other and shrugged. Ben chortled, chiding himself. "I half expect a great crash of thunder or something." Then, he started walking again.

Right as I was about to say that I thought that too, Ben screamed. Not a warrior yell of power, but a high-pitched shriek of terror and pain. I ran to his side as he fell into the sand, curling up on himself, still screaming. By the time I reached him, the sand around him was turning a rusty red and was damp with his blood.

"What happened?" I said, panicking. "What did you hurt? Ben!" I pulled on his torso to roll him over. His hands were wrapped around his right leg, blood oozing between his fingers. I pulled his hands off his leg so I could see the wound.

There was a gash on his leg from below his knee down toward his ankle, spiraling around the leg from the front to the back. It looked as if he had been hit with the end of a whip. The cut itself was less than an inch wide, but was clear down to the bone and bleeding heavily. The edges of the skin around the cut were mottled a sickly, unnatural green color.

My mind raced with all the facts I had learned in first aid classes. I tried to remember how to make a tourniquet and where to use it for a cut like this. I threw down my pack and scrambled to dump everything out of it, in hopes of finding something like a stick. My mind haphazardly remembered the idea of using a belt and a stick to cut off blood flow to an open wound.

Finding nothing of use in the bag, because why would two gods need a first aid kit, I threw down the bag. Ben was still screaming and, while I knew he was in pain, it made hard to think. Eventually, I took off my shirt and wrapped it around the wound. The shirt was filthy with sweat and grime after a long time of walking through the hot, sandy dessert but it was the best I had. Plus, Ben was a freaking god, right? He didn't have to worry about silly things like bacteria and infection.

But then again, he shouldn't have to worry about injuries from angry, invisible whips either. I wrapped the shirt around his leg, tying the ends together as tightly as I could. I hoped that I could pull it tight enough to put pressure on the leg and stop the bleeding. I wanted to get the bleeding stopped so Ben and I could get the hell away from here before whatever wielded the invisible whip decided to come back for more.

On the edge of my vision, I could see what looked like the oasis. I really hoped that it was the oasis and not just a mirage. "Ben," I yelled. "Ben, you need to pull it together. We have to get to the oasis."

Ben stopped screaming, mostly, and looked at me. I felt bad, being so mean to him when he was hurting, but I had to be mean to help him. Ben panted, biting his lip and squinting his eyes as if it took all of his control not to scream again. "I can't walk." Ben told me, his voice ragged.

I grabbed Ben under his arms and tried to lift him up. "Yes, you can." I grunted, hauling his shoulders up in attempt to get him to stand. "C'mon. You gotta get up. I can't carry you." I pulled on him again, trying to pull him to his feet.

"I can't, Anna." Ben shrieked. "I can't."

"Yes. You. Can." I said through gritted teeth. Between each word,

I pulled up on Ben, trying to force him to stand. Finally, he got his left leg under him and helped me help him stand. I swung around so he could use me as a crutch. "Here, lean on me. Let's go."

I started walking, half dragging Ben. He looked back over his shoulder at the mess I left. "Our bags." He started to say.

"Leave 'em." I told him. Nothing in there was really necessary for two gods anyway. It's not like we could die from dehydration or hunger. Or at least I didn't think we could. I mean, yeah, we knew Ben didn't need it, but I was still in my human body as a god. Maybe I actually did need to eat and sleep and whatever, just like when my spirit and body were disconnected.

Oh well, different problem for another day. Right now, I had to get Ben to safety. I looked down at his leg as we trudged through the sand at a much slower pace than I liked, that feeling of wrong and worry still plaguing me. I didn't see much blood soaking through my shirt, which was good. But I did see the sickly green color slowly creeping up his knee. Damn, I knew I should have tried for the tourniquet.

It seemed to take ages to walk to the oasis. The whole way, I had to half carry Ben while fighting off the growing sense of doom filling my mind. I didn't know if the doom feeling was because of Ben's leg or from the haze or the Heka worrying, but it really didn't matter the source of the feeling. All that mattered was getting to the oasis as quickly as possible and that feeling was slowing me down.

Finally, the empty sand started to fill with scrubby plants that started getting taller and denser. Before long, Ben and I were on the shore of a pond. As I set Ben down, I glanced around.

"This is the same oasis we just left." Ben wheezed, as if he was reading my thoughts.

"Hold on." I told him and then dashed off towards where the cave was in the other oasis. The cave was right where I expected it and looked exactly the same. I went inside the cave and saw nothing. There was no debris from when Gavya and I camped there, and no burn marks from the firepit Ben and I had cleaned up before we left the other oasis.

I ran back to Ben, wheezing. "It's not the same." I told him, gratefully. "it just looks the same, has the same layout and everything but the cave is empty when there should be all that stuff in there."

Ben was lying down on his back. He raised his right arm above him and gave me a thumbs up. He was sweating profusely, deathly pale and shaking. Ben's breathing was shallow and strained. I took the bandage off his leg and regretted it almost immediately.

The green ragged edges of the torn skin were now black and flaking off. The wound was still bleeding but the blood now seemed to have an odd green tint that was definite not normal. The greenish color of his blood matched the green spreading on the skin of his leg, and I assumed it meant whatever infection or poison the invisible haze had used was in his blood now.

In an attempt to clean the wound, I scooped handfuls of clear water from the pond and dumped them directly into the wound. Apparently, this was entirely the wrong idea because, as soon as the water touched him, it began to bubble and Ben screamed even louder than before.

"Shoot, sorry. Sorry." I said, using my bloody shirt to try to mop up the water still in the wound. I was running out of ideas on how to help Ben. All I could think was that, if Ben was a human, doctors would probably amputate the leg. But I didn't have a way to amputate Ben's leg, and even if I did, how would he be able to walk afterwards? And would that even work, considering he is a god, the whip, or what I assumed was a whip, was an invisible one wielded by an invisible foe and apparently coated in or made of some form of poison?

"I need help." I whispered to no one in particular. I looked up, at the treetops of the oasis, and said it again louder. I sat down on the ground, next to Ben's head and screamed, "Help me, please. Someone or something, please."

Out of the corner of my eye, I saw movement in the treetops. I turned to my right to look for what moved, and saw a fluttering out of the corner of my left eye. I turned again, only to see nothing.

Then the singing started. The most beautiful birdcalls I have ever heard played among the treetops. Birds were singing back and forth to each other, the sound becoming the the saddest orchestra I ever heard. A few birds flew across the sky and then darted back into the tree's foliage to hide again. They had looked as if they were shining.

I asked for help again, this time much firmer, and calmer. "Please, whatever you are, can you help me? My friend is hurt. I think he is dying. Can you help?"

The birds kept singing, their song getting louder as if more birds were joining in. A few more birds flew from treetop to treetop. Eventually, there were scores of birds moving around in the treetops and singing a sweet, sad melody.

I asked one more time. "Can you help? I'm sorry, I don't know your name, or have anything I can give you in payment, but I would be eternally grateful if you could help my friend. His name is Ben and he is a god and he is really, really a nice person. If you can help, if you did,

I know he could help you in return, maybe. We would help you, any way we can, we would repay you your kindness."

One bird, with shining white feathers all over from its head to its tail, a very small bright orange beak, coal black eyes, and impossibly delicate feet flew down out of the treetops and landed near me. The bird hopped on the oasis floor a few times, cocking his head back and forth as if it was examining me. Then it hopped towards Ben's injured leg, cocking its head back and forth again.

I waited patiently, letting the bird finish its examination of the wound. When it hopped back, towards me, I asked it, "Can you help him?"

"Caladrius." I heard the bird say in the most musical voice I had ever heard.

"I'm sorry," I told the bird. "I don't understand what you are saying."

"My name," the bird replied. "I am called Caladrius. You said you did not know our name, so I told you."

"Caladrius," I repeated, "nice to meet you. I am Anna and this is Ben." I looked at Ben and saw that he was fighting to remain conscious. "He really needs help. Can you... Do you know of anything around that can help him?"

"We can." The bird answered.

"You can? You and your other bird friends, Caladrius?" I asked, hopeful.

"No." The bird replied.

This confused me. "No, you can't help? I thought..."

"No, my name is not Caladrius." The bird answered, clearing up nothing for me. "We are called Caladrius, me and all my, what did you call it? My bird friends? We are Caladrius and I believe we together can heal Ben."

I sighed in relief. That made more sense. "Thank you. Thank you so much. What is your own name if it is not Caladrius?"

The bird turned its head to the side, and repeated, "Caladrius is our name. I am Caladrius, we are Caladrius." A second bird fluttered down to stand next to the first. It looked exactly identical to the first, except its beak was black like its eyes. "She is Caladrius." The first bird finished.

"Oh, I think I get it now." I told the first Caladrius, trying to remain calm while internally panicking over how long the formalities of introduction were taking. "Well, it is a pleasure to meet all of you, in any case. I would really appreciate it if you could help Ben."

The first Caladrius chirped at the second one in a way I couldn't understand. The second one flew off to the treetops, signing a tune that sounded excited. Suddenly, the ground around Ben and me was covered with what looked like hundreds of Caladrius. They were all the same shining white color, their feathers in various states of pruning, and they all either had an orange beak or a black one. They all looked at me with impossibly large, jet-black eyes that spoke of ancient knowledge and wisdom.

The first Caladrius turned to the other group and sang loudly. Even though its song had no words, it seemed to speak of urgency and pain, fear and longing. The rest of the group picked up on the tune and sang with what I assumed was their leader.

After the whole group sang together, the birds all hopped closer together, in a tight group, wings touching wings. The first Caladrius hopped closer to Ben's leg. "This is poisoned. A poison even the gods cannot withstand. I do not know if even all of us together can take this sickness from Ben."

"Please try," I whispered to Caladrius. "I need him."

"And the Heka needs you," the Caladrius responded matter-of-factly. I didn't even question how the bird knew this. It continued, "We will try. If we can remove the illness, we will be able to look at your friend. If not, if we look away, he will die."

All the birds at once turned towards Ben's face. His eyes were closed, so I touched him gently. "Ben, open your eyes." I said gently. "Open your eyes and look at the Caladrius."

Ben weakly opened his eyes. He caught the gaze of the first Caladrius and they stared at each other. I heard a song start at the back of the group. It sounded like a mourning song.

"It is not working, AnnaBella Cain." The first Caladrius told me, not taking his eyes off Ben. "The poison is too strong. I want to look away. Already, those at the back, the furthest from Ben have fallen from trying to heal him."

"No." I said almost silently. "No, don't look away." I stopped looking at the Caladrius, and instead looked at Ben. I looked deep into his eyes and felt for my connection to the Heka. "I know you feel what I am feeling, Heka. I need Ben. I can't do this alone. I can't save you alone. Help me. Help me save him so he can help me save you."

The Caladrius song grew louder and more mournful. Ben groaned in agony and fought the desire to shut his eyes.

"Do not look away, Benahahminen." The Caladrius told him.

The song grew louder and louder. Ben groaned more and more, and I pleaded with the Heka. None of us looked away from each other. Then, all at once, the Caladrius' song changed. It took on a hopeful note. I wanted to look at Ben's leg to see if it was working but I didn't dare take my eyes off his. The Caladrius' song kept changing, becoming less mournful and more hopeful.

Suddenly, the entire flock of Caladrius let out a shrill note. At the same time, Ben closed his eyes and screamed out again. Panicking, I yelled at him. "Don't close your eyes, Ben! Don't close your eyes."

The first Caladrius brushed his wingtip across my hand in a comforting way. "It is done," it told me. "Ben is healed. My flock, with your help, took away the poison."

I looked down at Ben's leg finally and saw the torn and blackened edges of the wound pulling themselves back together. The green tinge to his leg was already gone. Ben stopped screaming and sat up, breathless. He had stopped sweating and his color was returning to normal.

"Thank you!" I told the Caladrius. "Thank you so, so much."

"We were not able to fix everything." The first Caladrius warned me. "He will still have a scar and it will ache from time to time. But he should be well enough to help you on your journey after a small rest."

The Caladrius hopped into my lap and pulled at the sports bra I was wearing with its beak. "And you, AnnaBella Cain, daughter of Nick, son of the Heka, you took some of the poison too, like we did. We can dispel it from us, but you? You cannot, not the way we can. I am not sure what will happen to you because you took on the god poison. It may stay with you and cause issues when you least expect. Be wary."

I nodded that I understood the Caladrius, but my eyes were following Ben. As the Caladrius spoke, Ben had sat up and slid himself closer to the pond. Using his hands as a cup, he had drunk some water and was now sitting peacefully on the edge of the pond, looking at his reflection in the water.

The Caladrius kept speaking to me. "We must go now. We have to take care of the fallen and dispel the poison we took from Ben over the land before it harms any more of us. We will return later, after Ben has rested."

This statement caught my attention and I turned to the Caladrius. "Wait," I told him. "What do you mean take care of the fallen? I thought the fallen were just Caladrius that had looked away from Ben."

The bird seemed to shake its head. "No, dear AnnaBella. By fallen, I meant that they had died."

Oh. That quickly, I went from elated that Ben was okay to sorrow that some of the Caladrius had given their lives to save him. "I'm sorry." I whispered to the bird on my lap. "I never meant for you to harm yourselves to help my friend."

"Do not be sorry, AnnaBella. This is what the Caladrius were made to do." The bird hopped off my lap. The rest of the flock parted in the middle, allowing the first Caladrius to hop along the ground in between them. As he hopped, I saw at the back of the flock, several birds were lying in the dirt. They were no longer a shiny white, but had now gone a dull gray color. I stood up and followed the first Caladrius to its fallen flock mates, carefully moving so as not to step near any of the birds, living or not.

As I neared one of the fallen birds, I bent down and stroked its feathers. They weren't soft like I anticipated. They felt like wood, hard with a grainy feel. "I am sorry," I told the dead bird. "Thank you for your sacrifice."

The flock of Caladrius called out in a short burst of mournful song. Then, all but the first two took to the skies. I called out to them, to thank them for their help again, and then looked down at the two remaining birds. "I will take care of the fallen for you, if you wish, as my tribute and thanks to them. Is there any special way you care for your fallen?"

"We bury them," replied the second Caladrius with the black beak. "We sing to them as we bury them. We sing of heartbreak and hope, love and loss. I think a human voice can sing that as well as a Caladrius." The first Caladrius made a movement of its head that looked like it was nodding in agreement. Then, the two flew off to join the rest of the flock.

I looked around at the ground and counted seven birds who had passed away. Carefully, I pick up each one and brought them over next to Ben by the pond. I did this one by one, handling each bird gently in my hands. The biggest one was as long as my hand, from fingertips to wrist, and the smallest was only as long as my pinky finger. I cried carrying the small one. For some reason, I thought it was a baby Caladrius, and it made me sad that it had tried to help the adults and failed so badly when it was so young.

Once the birds were all lined up, neatly, I sat next to Ben. "I need to dig them graves." I explained to him. "Are you okay here while I do it?"

"Yeah," he replied, his voice probably not as strong as he wished it was.

"Okay." I told him then stood up. "I am not a really good singer. Can you sing something for the birds while I bury them? Something sad and hopeful?"

Ben thought for a moment, then nodded his head yes. "I think I know the perfect thing." He began singing a song in a language I didn't know. The melody was perfect for what the Caladrius has said and even though I couldn't understand the words, I could feel their meaning in my heart.

I started to cry in earnest while I dug seven small holes in the dirt, right next to the lake. Then, I laid each bird in their own hole, and covered their bodies up. Finally, I found seven small stones and placed one on each Caladrius grave, to mark them. As I worked, I listened to Ben's song and the song coming from the Caladrius faraway.

Ben finished singing and I sat down next to him again. "That was beautiful. What was it?" I asked him.

Ben sighed. "It is the song my worshippers sing at funerals. It asks me as their god to take their loved one to be with me and to keep them safe until they meet again in the afterlife. I remember when I could hear that song as if I was standing right next to them, before the Breaking. It was always hard to see them hurting in a way I couldn't fix. But, at the same time, I knew that all of my worshippers went to an afterlife I had created, one of peace and happiness, where they really did meet their family again. So, I knew they wouldn't be sad for too long."

"How did you choose the afterlife you gave your worshippers?" I asked him.

Ben looked at me with a sense of grief but also something that felt like pride. He took his time choosing his words. "I just thought about what I would want if I was human and had to die. Then I made that for them."

I opened my mouth to ask another question, but Ben stopped me. "No, not all the gods used that same thought when designing their afterlife. My people live a very hard life, so I made sure their afterlife is very easy in return. I didn't give them a whole lot of rules to follow, so there was no reason to have a good and bad place, a punishment and reward type thing. They lived, so they should all be rewarded in my eyes. Sure, my people made up a lot of rituals to honor me, but I never asked them to. They thought of them on their own, and, to me, that makes them more special and appreciated. Other gods have other ideas, and they do things that match their ideas and rules.

"And before you ask, no. I don't think any of the other gods made up rules or afterlives in a wrong way and that mine is right. We all made things differently. There are billions of humans alive right now, and trillions and trillions who have lived before and will live in the future. What is right for one is not what is right for all the trillions and trillions. That is why there are so many gods, because humans are all unique and each one needs a different god, a different belief to follow, and that's okay."

I held my hands up hands, smiling. "Okay, okay. No need to get defensive. I'll stop not asking questions." I joked. Ben laughed at this, but then looked at the tiny graves of the Caladrius and stopped laughing.

"Hey," I said, all hint of joking gone, "I think if they sacrificed themselves for you to live, they would want to you actually live, you know? It's okay to laugh sometimes."

"I know." Ben replied, looking away from the graves. He turned his legs to let them dangle into the water of the pond and ran his hand down the now fully healed scar wrapping around his right calf. "It's just, I was thinking, why did it happen at all? I mean, what did happen? Why was I hurt? How was I hurt in the first place?"

"I don't know." I told him honestly. "I know it felt like the area just before the oasis was hazy, like it was dirtier than the rest of the Wastes or something. Like there was more 'bad' there. But how could that be?"

Ben shrugged. I moved over next to him and we sat there, silently, waiting for the Caladrius to return from purging themselves of the poison. As we sat, I carefully poked at the feeling of the Heka inside me. The Caladrius had said I might be tainted from the poison I took from Ben and, even though I was scared to, I wanted to make sure the Heka was okay.

It only took a small poke to know. I entered the nothingness that was the Heka's cage quicker than I ever had, and with even less warning. Instead of feeling as if I had moved toward the Heka, it felt as if the Heka had grabbed me by the shoulders and yanked me into Its cage and was holding me tightly, almost shaking me.

"What was that?" The Heka asked me, Its voice trembling with fear and anger.

"You felt that?" I asked It.

"Yes," It replied harshly. "I felt all of that. You were scared and angry and then you were burning. It hurt to touch you. Then all of the sudden all of that was gone and you were incredibly sad and I had no idea what happened. Why did you block me?"

I gaped in surprise. "I didn't block you. I wouldn't even know how to block you if I wanted to."

"But you did." The Heka said. "What happened?"

I told the Heka about Ben and me walking through the desert, the haze and his injury. Then I told It about carrying Ben to the oasis and the Caladrius healing and dying for Ben and me helping them. As the

Heka listened to my story, I could feel It pushing against the sides of Its cage in frustration.

"The haze," the Heka told me when I finished, "it must be a trick leftover from Malachi. A spot where I can't go, hidden in the Wastes."

I repeated Its words. "A spot where you can't go? How could there be a spot where you can't go in your own creation?"

The Heka had the emotional reaction akin to throwing Its hands in the air. "I don't know." It growled.

The Heka had never been this angry with me before, or at least had never shown me anger like this. I was scared. Instead of being scared for the Heka, I was scared of It, and It knew. I felt the Heka settle down, lowering Its anger level by sheer will. It couldn't tame back all of Its frustration, but It was better than before.

"I'm sorry." Thew Heka told me. "I shouldn't have grabbed you like that and forced you here, but I was scared something happened to you. If you were to be hurt, or die, I don't know that anyone could take your place."

"I know." I told the Heka comfortingly. "We're both scared. And when two being share emotions and both get scared, it probably is too much for either of them to really handle. This is going to be dangerous, apparently, this mission of going through the Wastes, opening up oasis after oasis. Your cage will get smaller with every land I open up, and I think pretty soon it is going to get even more uncomfortable than it already is."

The Heka nodded, or at least it felt like It nodded. "I felt that when the unicorns were released. Everything feels squeezed and pinched, which is strange when I also feel like I am floating in a vast empty universe."

I noticed that how the Heka talked to me had changed. Before, the few times the Heka had, for lack of a better word, snatched me out of reality, It sounded other-worldly. Like what you suppose the creator of all the gods and universes would sound like to human ears. But now, the Heka sounded more like me and Ben. Like, if anyone else heard Its voice, they might think the Heka was just another normal teenager. I wondered when this change had happened, and why.

Maybe It just sounded like this because of the fear of dying, the fear of me dying and leaving It alone. Maybe the Heka just needed to reassured, like anyone else when they got scared. So, that's what I did. "Hey, listen. We're gonna figure this out, Ben and me. He is all fixed up and we will release the Caladrius. Your cage is going to get a little smaller with each oasis opened, but that will just mean we are one step closer to finding you. We are one step closer to saving you. So, even if it is scary, remember it's a good thing.

"And you are going to have to trust me." I told the Heka. "You have to accept that sometimes I am going to have normal, human feelings about stuff, like get upset, or angry, or scared, because I am partly human still. Human feelings come part and parcel with a human body. But just because I feel these things, doesn't mean that you are in danger or need to react. And it definitely does not mean you should yoink me to you if I check in with you like I just did. You never know when I might be just looking for the Heka power in the heat of a battle instead of looking to talk to you directly. And since apparently something is fighting back against us making it through the Wastes, a battle may actually happen."

I took a deep breath in. If the Heka could get scared like I did, maybe the Heka needed someone to be the adult for It and know the right things to say. I tried to think of what Mom or Dad would tell me in a situation where I was scared and didn't know what was going on and had to trust that they did. I tried to pretend I was as adult as them, to make the Heka feel better, safer. "Trust that I am coming. Trust me even if something blocks you from seeing me. Trust that, when you need to know something that you may not be able to see from your cage, I will call to you and tell you. And trust me when I tell you Ben and I will save you. We have to, because if we don't, the world ends. So, there is no choice but for us to succeed." As I spoke, I felt the Heka relax more and more. It was convincing Itself to trust me.

"I can do that. I do trust you, AnnaBella. Of course, I do, because... Well, I do." The Heka sounded a little more like Its all-powerful self again, which made me feel better too. The Heka finally let go of me and I immediately slipped back to myself.

When I came back to, in my own body, Ben was looking at me with an odd smile on his face. "Heka get a little heated there?" He asked me.

"Just a little." I replied, rubbing my shoulders. The Heka was not a physical being, or at least had never presented Itself as having a physical body to me before, but somehow the spiritual yank It gave me made me physically hurt. "It doesn't know what that haze was or how it hurt you, either. But agrees that it probably is a left-over Malachi trick."

Ben pointed behind me, saying, "The Caladrius returned while you chatted with the Heka."

I turned and saw the entire flock of small white birds standing near the graves I had made for their friends. One of the Caladrius, I think the same one as before, hopped over to me.

"You have done our flock mates well, AnnaBella. Thank you." The first Caladrius bobbed its head in a sort of bow.

"Thank you for your help, Caladrius. Ben's leg is much better." I replied. I turned to Ben and asked him, "Can you understand the Caladrius when it is speaking?"

Ben shook his head, "Nope. I just hear bird chirping, but at least that is better than the unicorns, who made no sound at all."

I told Ben I would interpret for him again and then returned to talking to the Caladrius. "Tell me about your lands here. What were they like before the Floods and what are they like now?"

"Before the Floods, our lands were great. We had many places we could go." The first Caladrius told me, and I relayed to Ben. "We could go to any of the lands in Taikarlu or the human realm. We were with Roman and Greek kings, unicorns, bunyips, griffins, the gods and others. We could fly where we wanted and stopped only to help the sick. Sometimes gods would use us to help heal those humans who had found favor with them. We were free to go anywhere and come back here to our roosts at will."

The Caladrius stopped speaking. It flew towards the lake, darted down into the waters and then bobbed back to the surface, having gotten a small drink of water in the process. When it returned to land near me, it apologized. "I am sorry, I have not needed to speak this much in a tongue Heka power could understand since the Flood. During the Flood, while the rest of the animals and gods were trapped, the Caladrius flew constantly. There was nowhere to land. We flew and flew so long that we thought we would perish in the skies.

"But then the waters receded and land was visible once again. Happy, we Caladrius landed here in this oasis to rest. When we had rested enough, we took to the skies once more, excited to see what remained of the lands we were fond of before the Floods. But we soon discovered those lands were no more. If a Caladrius flew past the borders of the oasis, they would see only sand for miles and miles. Eventually, even though they had flown straight in one direction, the Caladrius would find themselves right back where they started in the Oasis.

"Many of us tried to find a way to the other lands. But they were no more, and, until you came AnnaBella, daughter of Nick, we believed all the other lands had been swallowed up by the Nothing. We were alone in the world, with the Nothing and its empty sands surrounding us. We waited here for the Heka to come free us, but instead came AnnaBella and her injured friend Benahahminen."

Ben and I listened to the Caladrius' story. It was just the same as the unicorns' and the gods'. I told the Caladrius this and then asked if they would be willing to try something for me.

"What would you like us to do, AnnaBella?" the Caladrius asked.

"Attempt to fly to the unicorns." I told them. Many of the Caladrius started hopping around, squeaking and shrilling in what I could only assume what frustration or disbelief.

"Please." I tried again. "The unicorns, after telling me about their lands, were able to go to the city of Taikarlu. Their home oasis was unlocked. We believe that the oases are like keys, hiding each mythical beast away from the rest of Taikarlu, and the Nothing, called the Barren Place by the unicorns and the Wastes by the gods, is where the Heka has been held hostage in a cage. Every time Ben and I go to an oasis and speak to its inhabitance, we unlock it, and we break one more piece of the Heka's cage. If we are right, you should be able to fly to the unicorns or even the city now."

The first Caladrius turned and whistled at the rest of the flock. Several birds, some with black beaks and some with orange, took off to the skies. It then turned to me. "We have sent several Caladrius to the land of the unicorns. They will fly at different speeds, each stopping within earshot of the next. If they reach the unicorns, they will send a song back to tell us."

"Thank you." I told the Caladrius.

"While we wait," Ben asked, "Can I ask what your wings are made of? They seem like they would be soft, but Anna says they are hard like wood."

The Caladrius with a black beak hopped over to Ben. "I cannot answer your question since, to me, my wings are made of feathers, and I do not think that is the answer you seek. Feel free to pick me up and examine me, if you would like. But be careful, my bones are hollow like most birds and my feet are very delicate."

Ben took the Caladrius up on its offer, very gently scooping it into his hands. While Ben examined the Caladrius, I picked my shirt up out of the dirt where we had left it and began attempting to wash the worst of the blood and muck out in the pond. I listened to Ben and the Caladruis while I did this so I could help Ben ask the Caladrius to do things, like lift one wing so he could touch the underside and lift a foot. The Caladrius patiently followed all of Ben's directions as Ben carefully turned the bird this way and that.

When he was finished, Ben set the Caladrius down gently. "Thank you. I am still not sure what your wings are made of, but you are most wonderfully made in any case."

The Caladrius fluffed it wings at the compliment. "Thank you for being gentle. It was strange, I have never been touched by a human before. Excuse me, a god." Just then the Caladrius showed us a new trick by blushing at its mistake. The birds face turned the slightest shade of pink, which intrigued Ben even more.

"Wow," he said, ignoring the mistake and the bird's obvious embarrassment, "you can blush. That takes an interesting blood system for a bird. Can I ask one more thing? Why do some of you have a black beak and some of you an orange? Does that signify anything?"

The first Caladrius answered Ben's question, giving the Caladrius he had picked up a chance to run away. "Those of us who have an orange beak are male. Those with black beaks are female. To mate, we lay eggs in nests high in the trees, and we mate for life. Before the Floods, humans would trap many of us as pets. They would have to take only young ones, or else a bonded Caladrius would pine for its lost mate and die in captivity. If kept away from other Caladrius, the captured young will bond with a human or god captor, if they are kind and compassionate to the Caladrius. But it would only take one moment of seeing another Caladrius for the captured one to break its bond with the captor and form a new one with its own kind."

"That is very interesting." Ben told the Caladrius, and I could tell he was making mental notes to write down at some point. My shirt was as clean as it was going to get, so I wrung it out and pulled it back on. There were still some stains on it, and it was still very wet, but I ignored that. The wet would dry and the I couldn't do anything about the stains.

Soon, a fluttering started running through the flock. I asked the Caladrius what was happening.

"They are returning the song." The first Caladrius told me. "The song says that they found the unicorns, and there were gods among them."

"It worked. There are gods in the unicorn lands, and now there are Caladrius." I told Ben. Immediately after saying this, I felt my skin tighten like it had after the unicorns were freed, but this time it pinched and burned so much, I passed out.

Chapter Three

Ben sat with Bella until she woke up. "The Heka's cage got smaller again, didn't it?" He asked her. Benahahminen was the perfect choice for a travelling companion for Bella. He caught on quickly to the things that would affect her and never questioned her ability to do the impossible.

Bella sat up, rubbing her neck and stretching. "Yeah, and this time it hurt. A lot."

"It's only going to get worse." Ben replied. "If you are already passing out from the pain of it, what will happen when It's in the smallest possible cage, when we unlock the tenth oasis?"

"I don't know." Bella sighed. She knew that she would have to find a way to shield herself from the Heka's thoughts and feelings at least a little. Otherwise, Its pain from a cramped prison could very well kill her human body.

Ben gave Bella some time to recover, as he also recovered, gathering water for her from the pond into a makeshift leaf he used as a cup. He spent her recovery time thinking. They needed to get to the third oasis, and all the other ones, fast, but still had to contend with whatever that thing that hurt him was and Bella's connection to the Heka that seemed to be slowly killing her.

Ben believed it was his job, as traveling companion, to find the ways to solve all their problems so that Bella could just focus on freeing the mythical beasts. But he had no idea how to solve these things. Bella's powers were different than anything he had ever encountered in his millions of years of existence.

And even though he was millions of years old, inside he still felt like a teenager. His worshippers had always envisioned him as one, and he had never forced them to change that idea. Ben didn't like forcing his worshippers to do anything, but right now, this desire to respect his worshippers was biting him in the butt. Since they always saw him as a teenager, and he never forced them to change that, his mind really was just like a teen's. Ask him to do basic algebra on a standardized test, he would sweat a little but would be fine. Ask him to solve the riddle of how to protect the strongest god in the history of existence from dangers he couldn't even see and his underdeveloped prefrontal cortex would short circuit and look for an adult to help.

"I am a god," he whispered to himself. "I can figure this out."

Ben had graciously given me time to rest after I fainted, probably also needing more time to get over his injury, but I knew we had to get moving. Maybe without our packs, we could move through the Wastes to the next oasis faster. As long as that haze was left behind, that is.

"You ready?" I asked Ben, standing up.

"Are you?" He retorted.

I nodded, and headed out of the oasis in a kind of southwesterly direction. Ben didn't even question my choice of direction this time, just fell in step next to me. The oasis itself felt clean, but I could feel on the fringes of it the dirty feeling. I headed towards that feeling and just let it take me where it willed.

Ben seemed to be deep in thought, so I left him alone as we walked. The oasis ended abruptly, a wonderfully cool forest changing into an oppressively hot, sandy desert. I kept us walking in the same south-western direction for what felt like hours.

Eventually, I felt the haze in the distance. I stopped and asked Ben if he felt it too.

"Do I feel what?" Ben gave me a puzzled look.

"The haze." I answered, gesturing towards it. "It's the same haziness that was in the Wastes before the Caladrius oasis."

Ben looked at me, his face blank, as if he had no idea what I was talking about.

I stamped my foot and groaned. "The haze." I repeated. "The thing that whipped you and cut your leg? Right before you stepped into it you said it felt like someone was listening to us and made that big announcement that whatever it was should chill because we were trying to save it too. Any of this ringing a bell?"

Ben still looked confused. "I remember the part about feeling like someone was listening to us and me being silly and overdramatic when you said you felt it too, but there was no haze that whipped me."

My mouth fell open. Was he pranking me? "You're shitting me, right? You honestly don't remember your leg getting ripped open to the bone and screaming and me having to half drag you to the oasis?"

"Oh, I remember my leg getting hurt, yeah." Ben said. "But there was no haze. I have no idea how or why my leg got hurt. One minute you and I were being silly about people listening to our conversations, because I always get paranoid when I talk about the goddess of the hunt being our spy, and the next I was in agonizing pain. There was no haze."

"Well, it was there. It was the haze that hurt you." I told him, shocked that I never realized he didn't know it existed. I looked from Ben to the haze and back again. "You honestly can't feel the haze in the distance?"

Ben shook his head, no.

"How far out do you think it is?" he asked me.

Closing my eyes, I let my Heka feel out the distance between us in the mildly wrong feeling Wastes and the presence of the haze. It felt like I could almost touch the soupy, stickiness.

"Not far," I replied, opening my eyes. "A mile maybe."

Ben looked down at his feet and kicked at the sand. He was scowling. He must be worried about getting hurt by the invisible haze again, I thought.

"You could go back." I told him. "You could go back to the city and wait with Nummi and Gavya and all of them."

Ben looked up sharply, his face surprised and hurt. "Do you want me to go back?" he asked, his voice betraying the hurt he felt more than his face did.

"No!" I said quickly. "I don't want you to go back. I just thought, maybe, you didn't want to stay and risk the haze again. You're not obligated to come with me, you know. I just wanted to give you the option, you know, to bail out."

Ben's face fell, the hurt replaced with guilt. He looked down at the sand again, kicking it into little piles. "I know I am a liability. You don't have to pretend, Anna."

"Benahahminen, look at me." I said sternly, using his full god's name for the first time ever. I tried to use the same tone my mom did when I said something bad about myself that was totally untrue. I must have done it well because Ben looked up at me with the same sheepish, guilty face I would have when Mom used my full name to reprimand me. "You are not a liability. No way. I don't know what I would do without you. I probably would not have made it this far."

"Yeah, you would have." Ben countered. "You could do all of this by yourself. You don't need me."

"Okay," I said, still trying to channel Mom's chiding tone. I copied her favorite line to use when I was depressed and not feeling great about myself. "This is not you. Tell me what has gotten into you, Ben. What is going on in that head of yours?"

Ben turned away from me and groaned. "Ugh! Leave it."

"Nuh uh," I pulled on his shoulder to make him face me. "What's up?"

For a moment, Ben looked anywhere but at me. I crossed my arms over my chest and tapped my foot impatiently. Finally, Ben groaned again and looked at me.

"I am a horrible companion," he groaned. "In all the hero myths, the companion helps the hero solve issues and protects them from danger and stuff. I can't figure out how to stop the haze. Heck, I didn't even know it existed until five seconds ago. I can't figure out how to protect you from the Heka's feelings. I can't do anything."

Much to Ben's disbelief, I laughed. I laughed so hard, I bent in two, clutching my stomach. "That's what you think?"

"It's not funny, Anna!" Ben exclaimed. "It's true."

I stopped laughing as quickly as I started, looked Ben straight in the face, and said, "Bullshit."

My sudden change in mood caught Ben off guard. "What?" he said, bewildered.

"Bullshit." I repeated, harshly. I spoke fast so he couldn't interrupt me. "Who has trusted me to know what to do at every turn, even when I didn't trust myself? Who encouraged me to just go with my gut, and never for one second doubted that the Heka and I have some weird connection that is helping me as much as it is hurting me? Who got injured by the haze and who do you think would have been injured if you weren't there? Who has made sure I eat and drink and rest because I still have a stupid human body in the middle of the land of the gods and have to do that stuff even when I don't feel like I want to? Who is educating me on what it even means to be a god?"

I stopped, panting slightly. I lowered my tone and spoke kindly to him. "You did, Ben. That was all you. And you did it all without complaining. Not once, ever. This whole mission has been complete shit for you, and not once have you given up or got sassy or stopped trusting me. I don't know what myths you have been reading, but in all the ones they gave us in the human realms, it's the hero's job to solve all the issues and the companion's job to keep the hero motivated. Now, I don't know why you are assuming I am the hero in this story, but if I am, then you are an awesome companion."

"Dude," Ben said, seeming slightly less dejected, "you are so the hero. I know my place. I am just the lowly companion. You got all the extra special magicky, connection to the greater being stuff, and that is one hundred percent the hero position."

I smiled. "Well, fortunately, this is not some myth in a storybook, but real life. The hero and companion roles are not as cut and dry in the real world."

Ben rolled his eyes at me, his self-doubt forgotten at least for the time being. "Where do you think all those myths and storybooks came from, Anna? You have been in Taikarlu for a long time. Don't you get it yet? They are all real. I mean, yeah, the humans got some parts a little wrong, but the myths about heroic journeys to save the world are real, and you are in one."

"If this is a heroic myth," I rejoined, "then some crazy, out-of-left-field, just in the nick of time, deus ex machina will appear to solve the haze problem, won't it? And if I am the hero, then some random thing will happen where I come just to the edge of death, but will miraculously survive the Heka's cage issue just in the nick of time."

Ben smiled. "Well," he said slyly. "If it is a Greek tragedy, you, the hero, will die but that will be what saves everyone. Or maybe you will die, but no one will foresee your resurrection."

I smiled back at him, glad to see his mood had improved. "And if it a romance, you and I will fall in love. Yeah, I get it."

As soon as the words left my mouth, I wished I hadn't said them. I tried to look at Ben without him seeing I was looking at him. Did he think I said that to flirt with him? Did he have feelings for me? I shook my head trying to rid my mind of these thoughts. It was just a joke. Why was I freaking out about it so much? Did I have feeling for Ben?

Oh, crap. Who is writing this myth and why did they think it was a good idea to pair up two teenagers on an epic quest to save the world? Jeez, this was every B-rated Hollywood teen movie ever.

Ben was not looking at me just as hard as I was not looking at him. One of us had to break the tension before it got weirdly out of hand. C'mon, that deus ex machina would be really good right about now, I thought. But, alas, we were not really in a Greek myth or Hollywood movie, so nothing happened.

"So," Ben finally said, breaking the awkward silence, "the haze?"

"Um, yeah," I replied, "it's about a mile ahead. Do you think we just keep walking and will figure out how to deal with it when we figure out how to deal with it?"

"Sounds like a plan to me." Ben said. He cleared his throat, still not looking at me. "Or, well, a non-plan."

We started walking again, not speaking and avoiding each other's gaze. Occasionally, I glanced at Ben when I thought he wasn't looking at me, trying to determine what he was thinking. But he was obviously trying to keep his face neutral. Once or twice, I thought I caught him glancing at me the same way I was glancing at him, but that may have just been my mind playing tricks on me. I watched way too many movies and read too many books, and doubted that those type of romantically charged, will they or won't they situations happened in real life.

I was just about to tell Ben that we had reached the haze when the ever-imposing bright sun seemed to disappear. It wasn't suddenly nighttime dark or anything, just more like we had stepped into the shade of a beach umbrella. But the sun in Taikarlu was always at its zenith and imposingly bright in the Wastes. So, this didn't make sense.

"What the…" Ben said, looking up at the sky.

"The haze is right there." I told him, gesturing out in front of us. "I know it is but suddenly it doesn't seem so strong anymore."

Ben nodded. "And the sun isn't as bright. Do you think they are related?"

I shrugged in response.

He continued, "Do you think it is a good thing or a bad thing?"

I shrugged again. "Deus ex machina?"

Ben rolled his eyes. "Do you really think 'the god from the machine' will happen in the land of the gods, Anna?"

"I dunno." I told him. "You were the one to say that we were living in a Greek myth. Why wouldn't some random thing come out of the woodwork to save us at the last possible moment?"

"Because," Ben snapped, "this is real life, not a myth that humans misinterpreted for centuries. Most of the deus ex machinas in the myths are humans misunderstanding how the gods work."

"And?" I argued back. "If the humans could misunderstand the gods, why couldn't the gods misunderstand the Heka?"

Ben opened his mouth, then closed it several times. "True," he finally replied. "So, what do we do now, oh hero of the Wastes?"

I playfully slapped Ben on his shoulder. "Shut up." I chided. "I don't know. Maybe we step into the haze and see what happens?"

"Last time we did that, an invisible whip almost took off my leg." He reminded me.

"I know." I told him, frustrated. "But this time, we know what can happen and can react. We aren't going in blind."

Ben didn't respond. Instead, he looked around like he would somehow be able to see the edges of a haze that I only felt as a dirtiness to the air and he apparently didn't feel at all. Very slowly, he lifted his right foot and stepped forward. Then, he stopped and looked around again.

"You are not in the haze yet." I told him, trying to hide a smile.

Ben turned around and faced me, feigning frustration. I could see the smile he was fighting though. "Listen, can't you just let me be the protective companion? I got an image to uphold here."

I put up my hands in surrender and we both laughed. "Lead the way, oh faithful companion." I told him.

Ben turned back around and began walking into the haze and I followed him. The air felt thick and greasy, but nothing happened. We kept walking. The oasis was visible on the horizon. We made our way to it with no mishaps, shaded the entire way by some mysterious and invisible force.

Yet again, this oasis looked identical to the other two. We walked to the pond and sat down on its edge to get a drink. Ben sat next me, on my right side, and we both dipped our hands in the water. After that first drink, I dipped my hand in the pond again, and splashed some water on my face and neck. Ben did the same, sighing as the cool water helped him relax.

"Well, that was new and different." Ben said once we had rested a bit. "I wonder what our new mythical beast friend is this time."

"I don't have the feeling like something is watching me like we did with the unicorns. And I don't see anything moving in the trees." I responded. "I guess we have to wait until they come introduce themselves."

Ben giggled. The sound of his giggle came from my left and was so strange, I turned to look at him. There he was, grinning like he thought this was the silliest thing in the world. But Ben hadn't moved since we sat down and I was sure he had sat down on my right side. Hadn't he? I turned to my right, and there was Ben, looking confused.

"Wait, how did you do that?" I asked.

"I didn't." Ben said. "That's not me."

I looked to my left again, and then back to my right. The Ben on my left kept giggling while the Ben on my right looked very perplexed. I jumped up and moved away from the pond. Both Bens watched me, without moving. The left Ben was still giggling.

"What is happening?" I paled, suddenly worried that this was some horrible trick and I would have to figure out which one was the real Ben and save his life, just like in the stupid movies I has been thinking about earlier.

The giggling Ben dissolved into a small furry animal about the size of a puppy, but with fur colorings like a raccoon. The Ben on the right, the real Ben, laughed this time.

"I've heard of these!" he exclaimed, laughing. "You are a tanuki, aren't you?"

The raccoon dog nodded. In a voice I assumed only I could understand, the animal introduced itself.

"My name is Porex, and yes, I am a tanuki. I shaded you from the haze."

"Well, thank you, Porex." I replied, after translating for Ben. "How did you do that? And how did you look like Ben?"

I continued translating for Ben as Porex told us about himself and his family. "We tanuki are tricksters and shapeshifters, but not in a bad way. We like to play harmless pranks, and you two looked like you could use a bit of a laugh. We also have the ability to stretch our skin like a golden bag. We can make them rather large, like a sail or a fishing net to help people, or trick them. I saw two gods walking towards our oasis. We haven't seen gods or humans or pretty much anyone else since the Floods, so I was curious and investigated. I overheard you talking about a haze that had harmed you before and decided to help. I stretched myself wide enough to make a bubble of safety around you until you reached the oasis." Porex paused for only a second. "Then I got bored and played a prank on you. Was it funny?"

Ben chuckled. "Yes, Porex. Now, that we know it was just harmless fun, your prank was a little funny. And thank you, by the way, for protecting us. That haze is dangerous stuff and we have no idea what it is or how it works yet."

The small animal stood up on his hind paws. "Would you like to meet the rest of us? My gaze is just passed the trees over here." Porex pointed one paw to the west as he spoke.

"Your what?" I asked.

"My gaze," Porex answered patiently. "A gaze is a group of tanuki, like a herd or flock."

"Oh, yeah, of course. We would love to meet your gaze. Lead the way." I held my arm out the way Porex had indicated and waited for him to lead us.

Ben and I follow Porex through the trees. When they opened onto a clearing, we were standing on top of a small hill. In the valley below, we saw a city, much like the city of Taikarlu. The city was surrounded by forests with a river running through it on one side. Porex ran down into the heart of the city, with Ben and me following closely behind.

The city looked like it had been inhabited by more than just the tanuki at one time, but had been abandoned a long while ago. I asked Porex about it as we walked.

"Before the Floods, gods and coordinators used to come to our city all the time." He told us. "Sometimes even humans, especially Buddhist monks, would come visit us. Other animals would come too. We were a pretty popular destination for vacations. It became a game among some of the gods. Were they really meeting their friends here, or was it the Tanuki playing a trick? Some gods thought it brought them luck if they were able guess correctly."

"I remember that." Ben exclaimed. "I never came here myself, but I remember others talking about it. They always said it was fun to gamble with a tanuki, but it would be frustrating when they cheated. One god even told me he was happy because he had won a bunch of games against the tanuki, but then when he tried to show me his bag full of money, it had all turned to leaves."

Porex laughed. "Yeah, that was always a good prank to pull on the gods. What would they care? It's not like they needed money or anything." Porex laughed a little bit more, but then turned somber. "But then the Floods happened and the gods stopped coming. Everyone stopped coming. We tried to go to the gods to ask them why they wouldn't come play with us anymore, but we couldn't find our way. We were lost and it wasn't a good trick."

"I'm sorry." I told Porex. "It really wasn't a good trick, but it wasn't the gods' fault. A human named Malachi broke Taikarlu. He made it so none of the mythical beasts could find the gods or the humans anymore because he was angry. He hid the Heka too."

While we had been talking, we had walked into the tanuki city. Several other tanukis had seen us and, curious, they had begun following us as we headed to the center of the city. They had been listening to our conversation with Porex.

"Is that why the Heka has felt so weak all this time?" an unfamiliar tanuki asked.

"Yes," Ben replied. "Hi, I'm Ben. What are all of your names?"

The tanukis all tried to answer at once. Ben looked at me to translate but I just shrugged.

"Hey, guys." I told them, "Ben can't understand you. I have to translate everything you say for him, and I can't do that if you all talk at once."

The tanukis started all apologizing at the same time and I just laughed. Ben arched his eyebrow as an unspoken question as to why I was laughing.

"They all just keep talking at the same time. They are even all apologizing for talking at the same time and promising not to do it again... but all of them are doing it at the same time." I replied. Ben smiled and shook his head.

"Herding cats?" he asked me.

"Yeah, something like that." I told him. I turned back to talk to the tanuki again. "How about we let Porex do the talking for everyone?" I suggested.

All the tanukis nodded their head in agreement and Porex excitedly started listing the names of everyone in attendance, and telling us who wasn't there too. "This is Crocatee, and Teadboon, and his wife Ponibia. Their son Wolvy is home babysitting his baby brother Little Terrmi. Over there are Hedgea, and her grandmother Krequo. Hedgea is engaged to Arache right there. Her mom and dad died a while ago, so she lives with her grandma now."

"Woah." I told Porex. "That's all still a lot to translate for Ben. I really, really would love to hear everyone's names and stuff. I would, but um, Ben and I are kinda in a time crunch." I wasn't sure how to get us to the point of why Ben and I were there without being insulting at the same time. The tanukis were so friendly, and I immediately liked them a lot. Porex was like an excited child.

Porex seemed to understand. "The Heka stuff, it is important, right?" He said. "I heard you talking in the Lost. You need to save it, right?"

"Yeah," Ben told Porex, now that I could effectively translate. "The Heka is trapped and Anna and I are going through the Wastes, what you called the Lost, I guess, and finding all of the oases. When we find one, we can connect it back to the others we already found and the city of Taikarlu. Each time we do, it breaks the Heka's prison just a little more."

"How can we help?" Porex asked, excitedly.

I smiled at him. "There is nothing you need to do, as far as I am aware, besides just believe us."

"Yeah," Ben added. "At least in the other oases, just Anna being in the mythical beasts' homes unlocked it."

"But her name isn't Anna." A tanuki from the back of the crowd said, somberly. All of the other tanukis sounded young. This one was different. She sounded older and wiser. "Your name isn't Anna. You can't win if you don't even know your own name." She repeated.

"What do you mean?" I asked. Here was yet another being, telling me that my name was important, and not what I thought it was. I walked through the gaze towards the wise tanuki.

Porex piped up. "That's Waalish. She is the oldest tanuki. The smartest and most cunning too."

I had reached Waalish and knelt down to look her in the eye.

"Nice to meet you, Waalish."

"It is an honor to meet you, AnnaBella Cain, heart of the Heka." Waalish replied.

I was stunned by her title for me. "Heart of the Heka?" I asked her. I lowered my voice, hoping to let just her hear me. "Is that my name?"

"No," Waalish shook her head. "I do not know your name, only that you are important to the Heka. Very important."

"How do you know that?" I pressed.

"I just do." Waalish replied. "I don't know why or how. I just feel it deep in my soul that you need to know your real name and that knowing that is the most important thing to fixing the Heka. More important than unlocking the oases. All of this, I just knew the minute I saw you, even though I did not know the Heka was trapped, or that you were here to free It until you said so."

"But I don't know my name." I whispered, a little scared.

Waalish climbed into my lap and snuggled against my face. "That is okay, for now." She told me. "Your name will come to you when it is ready. You found us, didn't you? You will find your name."

"Hey, Anna." Ben called out.

Waalish climbed off my lap to allow me to stand and walk back to Ben.

"What's up?" I asked him, trying to sound nonchalant. No, a small raccoon dog did not just almost make me cry, ok?

"So, Porex and I were talking," Ben started. I raised my eyebrows and he corrected himself. "Well, really, I was talking, in yes and no questions, and Porex shook his head in response. Anyway, Porex doesn't know what the haze stuff is either, but if Malachi was the one who broke the world, and the one to trap the Heka in the Wastes, he probably made the haze as a guard dog for the Heka's prison. Right, Porex?"

Ben and I looked at Porex, who was nodding that he agreed. So, Ben continued. "When Porex came out into the Wastes to spy on us, and then protect us from the haze, he wasn't hurt by it. He touched it, but it didn't hurt him like it did me. So, we figured, maybe if Porex came with us, he could do his golden bag trick anytime we ran into the haze stuff." Ben crossed his arms over his chest and smiled in a sort of self-satisfied way.

I looked over at Porex and he was standing the same way, arms crossed and a proud smile, nodding. It was almost comical how similar they looked.

"You sure, Porex?" I asked. "I mean, we know nothing about that haze. It may have been a fluke that you weren't hurt. I would hate to have something happen to you."

"I'm sure," Porex said confidently. "Besides, travelling to the different oases, meeting all the other mystical animals, would be fun. Who wouldn't want to be in an epic hero's tale, even if I am only the cute sidekick."

I laughed at his giddiness. Out of the gaze, I heard what had to be Porex's mother, shouting.

"Porex Kimura! How dare you decide to go on an epic adventure without asking!" I heard her shout.

Porex was crestfallen immediately, but Ben and I were having a hard time containing our laughter. I mean, honestly, a pouting raccoon dog is really cute and hard to take seriously.

"Aww, ma!" Porex whined. "But they need me, ma!"

"Wait." I said, stopping the argument. "Porex, how old are you?"

Porex stamped his foot. "I am one hundred and thirty-seven years old, and I can go on an epic adventure if I want to." He tried to look tough, jutting out his chin in determination, but his eyes betrayed him. He kept glancing over at his mother, then back at me, as if he was daring her to argue but also afraid she actually would.

"And at what age is a tanuki an adult?" I pushed.

Porex looked at the ground, sulking again. "One hundred and fifty." He moaned. "But it's not fair! Billobo wanted to go into the Lost at my age and you let him, Ma. Why can't I go play with the gods?"

I had been translating all of this to Ben, who was trying really, really hard not to laugh. But at that statement, he straightened right up.

"Oh no, Porex." Ben said, somberly. "This is not a game. Porex, look at me."

Porex turned to look at Ben, who knelt down to look the tanuki in the face. "This is not a game, Porex. This is dangerous." Ben sat on the ground and held out his right leg. He twisted it so the scar from the haze was visible.

"You see this, Porex?" Porex nodded, and Ben continued. "This is what that haze did to me. It hit me with an invisible whip coated with poison. I almost died. It took a whole flock of Caladrius and Anna to save me. Some of the Caladrius died saving me. This is most definitely not a game, do you understand?"

Porex nodded again, then turned to me. "Tell Ben I know it's not a game. It is serious, saving the Heka. And dangerous, but I still wanna come. Tell Ma to let me go? You can make her let me. I know you can."

"I'm sorry, Porex." I replied kindly. "I really am, but I don't think it a good idea. Ben and I are just teenagers, just like you. And I can't make your mom let you go any more than you can. And I wouldn't even if I could. Moms know stuff, you know. If she says no, we gotta listen to her." Porex looked really sad and made me feel bad.

"But," Ben said slowly. "If your mom is okay with it, we may have another, really important job you can do for us."

Porex looked up, hopefully. "Anything, just tell me. I can be helpful and do important jobs!"

I caught on to what Ben was going to say and continued for him. "If your mom is cool with it, we need someone to go to the land of the Caladrius. There should be a bunch of unicorns and gods moving between their forests, the Great Plains of the unicorns and the gods' city of Taikarlu by now. Someone needs to tell them that the city of the Tanuki has been unlocked."

Porex was so excited it seemed like his body was vibrating. "Yeah! I can do that."

"Only if your mom says it is okay," Ben reminded him, glancing at the tanuki who had yelled at Porex. The small raccoon dog mama seemed cross, but eventually sighed and waved at us.

"Fine, go. Get yourself Lost like Billobo, and I will have to come rescue you like I rescued him. Not that I don't have a ton of baking to do for your little sister's birthday party or anything..." The mama tanuki wandered off still muttering to herself.

Waalish spoke once the mama was out of earshot. "Ignore Dannii, Porex. Grandmama Waalish says you can go to the oasis of the Caladrius. Be safe. I will deal with your mother."

Porex was bouncing up and down like a puppy. "I can go? Yay, I can go! When should I go?" He kept looking between me and Ben.

"Go now." I told him, laughing.

And with that, Porex was off like a shot. He zoomed out of the city on all four paws, kicking up a trail of dust behind him. We heard him, saying, "On a mission to save the Heka, I'm doing my part. I'm a heroooo!" as he ran away.

Ben and I laughed at Porex and his happiness. When Porex was far enough away that he crossed the boundary where the oasis used to end, I stopped laughing. The pain from the Heka's cage tightening didn't catch me off guard this time, so I stayed alert and upright, but it took a lot of effort for me. Ben stopped laughing as well and looked at me. My face must have shown the pain I was feeling, because Ben looked concerned. I shook my head, ignoring how I felt and told Ben, in short huffs, that we should move on.

Chapter Four

Ben and Bella left the gaze of Tanuki and headed back to the oasis. Once again, they rested by the pond, sipping water and cooling themselves. With the pain of the cage getting smaller fading, they were both able to laugh at the antics of their small friend, Porex, again.

"Porex is a good little guy," Ben told Bella.

"Yeah," she replied. "He just wanted to help. The Tanuki seem like an interesting group. Are they all so young-like?"

Ben sat up straighter. "Nah. Some of them come off that way because of their size and cuteness level, but some of them are more like Waalish. You said she sounded wiser. There are some really ancient myths in the human realms about them, especially in like Japan, where they are lucky but also tricky. I had never met them before, so I can't tell you which way is more prevalent in reality. Human myths mess so much up so often, but this one I really don't know much about."

"Well, I think they are brave." Bella told him. "Porex was a little too brave though."

Ben and Bella continued to laugh. Eventually, though, their thoughts returned to their mission and the obstacles in their path. Their laughter trailed off as they focused on the tasks at hand.

"You know," Ben said, "even though he was a little goofy, Porex protected us from that haze. Before I realized he was just a kid, I thought maybe we didn't even need to figure out what that haze was anymore."

Bella sighed. "Yeah, but he was just a kid, and he could've gotten hurt because we didn't figure it out. We have to do this the right way, Ben. No short cuts that put other beings in danger."

Ben nodded, agreeing. Malachi's guard of the Wastes was too powerful to be played with, but at the same time the pair had no real idea how to figure out what it was and how to defeat it. If Bob hadn't killed Malachi, maybe he would have told them, they both thought to themselves.

But there was no use in wishing for what couldn't be changed. Bob did kill Malachi in a fit of anger and sadness, and there was no bringing Malachi back.

The two sat by the pond, their feet dangling in the water. Bella closed her eyes and laid back on the ground. Ben watched her, wishing he could relax like that. Too many thoughts swirled inside his head to let him, though. Thoughts about what would happen when they released the Heka.

Ben knew what it had been like when the Heka had walked among the gods in Its full power. It was amazing. Everything felt free and wonderful in a way Ben hadn't experienced in a long, long time. Ben missed that time, but he also remembered the trouble that came with the Heka walking among the gods. The fighting and power grabs, gods getting envious of other gods and stirring trouble amongst their believers, wars that lasted hundreds of years.

Bella didn't know what that time was really like, Ben thought. She got a small taste of it when Malachi got angry in front of the Commission, but that was just a tiny sliver of a taste. No one in that room had been at full power because the Heka hadn't been at full power. The gods had gotten a really nice setup going since the Floods receded. It wasn't perfect, but it wasn't the Chaos that had been before. What happened to the setup when everyone was back at full power and hungry for more again?

And what happened to Bella? Ben thought. He looked at her again. Bella had dozed off with her feet in the pond and the sunlight dappling through the trees, making her hair shine with streaks of auburn. Her face was relaxed in sleep, peaceful. Beautiful.

No. Ben pushed that thought away from him. He didn't know what was going to happen when they rescued the Heka, but he knew Bella was somehow connected to It. A god that connected to the Heka would not be just any old simple god, and Bella was not just a god. Bella was a human too.

Ben sat up straight, realizing he had just stumbled into probably the most important piece to this puzzle of Bella and the Heka. Bella was a god. The humans made her so. But she was also human, the first human body in Taikarlu ever. But she was more than that. She was also a coordinator. Bella had worked with her dad as a coordinator for a hundred years. Bella was all three: god, human, and coordinator.

There had been beings that were two of the three before. Children of gods and humans were common, just like children of coordinators and humans. Less common were the children of coordinators and gods, but there had been some. But never, never had there been someone who was all three. Ben knew that this had to be important but he wasn't sure why.

As he watched her, thinking this over, Bella shifted in her sleep, smiling. Even though she couldn't see him, Ben couldn't help but smile back at her. No, he admonished himself. Don't smile at her like that. Don't think of her like that. She is bigger than you, Ben told himself. She is bigger than everyone. So, she can't possibly have any sort of feelings for me.

Ben turned away from Bella's sleeping form. He had to protect her. That was his only job, not fall in love with her. Ben cursed under his breath and forced himself to stop thinking of Bella and focus on how to solve the problem with the haze.

But, in the human realm, a small tribe of people felt something in their faith shift. It was a new feeling, a pleasant one, and they made an offering to their god, Benahahminen, that his newfound love would be a success. And Ben never denied his worshippers anything.

When I woke up, Ben was no longer sitting next to me. I sat up and looked around to see if I could spot where he had wandered off to. I didn't see him at first, but knew he wouldn't have gone far. I waited patiently for him to return, letting my mind wander over the problem of the haze.

There hadn't been a haze issue between the city of Taikarlu and the unicorn oasis. But then again, I had been to the unicorn oasis before with Gavya and basically knew where I was going. Well, not really. I had needed to use the sand to guide me. I had used the sand to guide me and there was no haze, hmm. Was there a pattern there?

I thought back, trying to remember if the Wastes had felt wrong between the city and the unicorns, like it had in between the unicorns and the Caladrius and between the Caladrius and the tanuki. It seemed like that walk had been days ago, maybe even months ago. The stupid no-time problem in Taikarlu was messing with my head again. I tried to focus on how the Wastes had felt as we walked to the unicorns, but all I could remember was being so focused on guiding the sand. I really could not remember anything feeling off with the Wastes back then.

Well, that was a starting point, I guess. The Wastes were clean and there was no haze issue before we unlocked the first oasis. So, whatever it was, was probably turned on by that unlocking. We had been assuming it was a trap set by Malachi to prevent people from unlocking the Heka, but what if it wasn't? What if Malachi had nothing to do with it?

For thousands of years, people had attempted to go into the Wastes and find a way to navigate in it. Not only people, but the animals too. All three of the mythical beasts Ben and I had unlocked said the same thing that the gods in Taikarlu had. Any attempt to go through the Wastes, or Lost, or Barren Place, or Nothing, whatever they called it, led to that entity getting all turned around and ending up right back where they started. Not a single being had mentioned the Wastes feeling wrong or some type of haze attacking them. That was only something that had happened to Ben and me, and only happened after we had unlocked the first oasis.

Or was it? Ben hadn't actually felt the wrongness of the Wastes, like I had. He just accepted me saying it felt wrong, like he accepted all the other weird stuff I did. Ben hadn't felt the wrongness of the haze, only I had, but only Ben had been hurt by the haze and I hadn't. This was another clue.

I needed to talk to the Heka about this. Like a full-on discussion about it, not just both of us freaking out. And I needed Ben in on it, too. I had no idea if that was even possible, but we needed to make it happen, somehow. I couldn't keep having conversations with Ben and then relaying them to the Heka by feelings, or verbally when It decided to yank me to It, and then having to turn around and relay those conversations to Ben. The three of us needed to sit down together and figure out the haze issue before any of us moved any further.

"I am not willing to risk Ben getting hurt again," I said aloud. "And I am not willing to risk anyone else either," I added. I didn't know if the Heka could hear me, but I knew It could feel my feelings, so I hoped my determination on this point was clear enough for It to know what I was thinking.

Almost as if I had called for him, Ben came trotting back out of the woods toward the pond. He had something blue cupped in his hands, and was grinning.

"Blueberries!" Ben exclaimed when he sat down next to me. He put his hands out, and dropped the blueberries in my lap. "Eat."

I smiled, my mind preoccupied. "Thanks." I told him, but didn't start eating. "Ben, we need to…"

Ben shook his head. "Nope. Eat first, then talk. Remember, I am the faithful companion. I need to make sure your human body eats and sleeps and drinks. You told me that is the companion's job, right? So, let me do my job. Eat."

I rolled my eyes, but ate a few of the blueberries anyway. As I chewed, I offered one to Ben. He declined it, saying, "I ate some while you were sleeping." I knew this was a lie because I could feel the blueberry juice staining my tongue and teeth, and his mouth was completely free of blueberry stain. Not that I was looking at him mouth that closely, or anything.

I swallowed my mouthful, and told him. "Liar."

Ben breathed out hard. "Fine. I lied. But it doesn't matter anyway. I am fully a god. I don't need to eat. You have a human body. You need them more than I do, and since we did a dump and run on our packs, the only food we have is what can be foraged from the oases. You eat. I'm good."

I wanted to argue, but Ben had a point. I finished eating the blueberries by myself. Once I was done, I told Ben I had been thinking and that we needed to talk.

At the exact same time, Ben said, "So, I had a thought we should talk about."

Ben and I laughed. "You go first." He told me.

"No, mine might take a bit." I countered. "You go first."

"How might it 'take a bit,' Anna?" Ben asked me. I didn't even realize he had subtly swayed me into talking first until after I was finished telling him my thoughts.

"So, the haze is a problem, yeah?" I started. Ben nodded, indicating to me to continue. "We assume it is a trick from Malachi, but I have been thinking that we don't know that for sure. All we do know is that it only appeared after we unlocked the unicorn oasis."

"True." Ben agreed.

"I am not sure about a few things though," I added. "Can you actually feel the Wastes like I can? How they feel kind of dirty now?"

Ben thought for a moment. "Not really." He eventually answered. "I feel the not-rightness of the part you said was the haze, but the Wastes don't seem to be that way, and, honestly, the haze just makes me super nervous. It's not this dirty air feeling you keep talking about but more like a 'I really don't want to do this anymore' feeling."

I nodded. "That answers my second question. The Wastes feel normal, just the same as the oases, to you, and the haze feels uncomfortable rather than wrong?"

Ben thought for a moment, his head cocked to one side. "Pretty much. I mean, if I were to go off my own feelings, yeah. The Wastes never changed, not since we left Taikarlu. When we got to the first bit of the haze between the unicorns and the Caladrius, I felt really weird, like I wanted to turn and run back. You seemed super freaked out by it, though, so I think that made me freak out too."

Ben waited a beat, then continued. "If I am being really honest, I haven't felt the same at all since we went through the first haze. I have been more unsure of myself. Like, I am doubting myself a lot more now. But I can't be sure if that is from the haze itself or if it is just the natural feeling someone would get after being hurt like I was. I mean, I really, really want to help you and protect you, because it would suck if you got hurt and I don't know if I could live with myself if something happened to you. I really, um." Ben stopped talking, as if he had said more than he meant to.

"Yeah?" I encouraged him to continue.

Ben shook his head. "No, yeah. I, um, what I meant was that the self-doubt could be another haze thing, or could just be me."

I was pretty sure that was not where Ben had been going with what he was saying, but he seemed disinclined to say more, so I left it alone. I continued with telling him my idea. "What I am thinking is, if the haze was a Malachi thing, wouldn't it have been a problem between Taikarlu and the unicorns? And even if it was only activated after the unicorn oasis was unlocked, wouldn't the change in the Wastes be noticeable to anyone, not just me? I think the haze and the Wastes feeling wrong is a Heka problem, not a Malachi one."

"Why would the Heka be trying to prevent us from freeing It?" Ben asked. "It's dying and needs to be freed. Wouldn't It help us, not hinder us?"

"It would help me, not us." I told him. "I said it, way back with the Speaker in the Joint Commission room. I needed to do this alone. But then you offered to come with me and I didn't want to go alone, so I said yes. Maybe the problem is there are too many gods unlocking the Wastes, or something.

"I was thinking about, and I realize, the only one to be harmed by the haze was you. I can feel it and whatever, but I can also feel whatever the Heka is feeling, so if the Heka is trying to stop you from coming with me for some reason, then I would feel that pushback. Maybe, and I am not just saying this to try to get rid of you or because I think you are a liability or anything, Ben, but maybe the haze is really the Heka trying to stop you from coming on what was supposed to be a solo quest."

Ben thought about this before responding. "Maybe. But that is making a lot of assumptions. Just as many, or maybe more, than the thought that the haze is a guard dog put in place by Malachi to stop anyone from freeing the Heka."

"I know," I sighed. "Which is why I think the best thing we can do it talk to the Heka about it directly."

"You mean the best thing you can do, Anna." Ben replied.

"No." I said firmly. "I mean we, Ben. We need to talk to the Heka. Together. No more of this me traveling back and forth at the Heka's whim, relaying messages. I can't be the interpreter for you with the mythical animals and with the Heka anymore. Something has to give if we are going to survive this, and win. The Heka needs to come to us, when we need It, not me going to It when It wants."

"And how do you plan to force the creator of the entirety of existence to come to us when you call It, Anna?" Ben asked sarcastically, crossing his arms over his chest and raising one eyebrow.

"I don't know," I leaned back, resting on my hands, "but I have to try. We have to try. Otherwise, how the hell else are we going to figure out this haze issue and save It?"

Ben took a deep breath and blew it out slowly. He was shaking his head as if my idea was impossible. He stood up and started pacing. He rubbed his hands across his face, then spoke. "Okay," he finally relented. "What do we do?"

"Well, before we do anything, I think I should warn you about a few things." I looked up at him. "When I heard the Heka for the first time, in the Trials Arena, my dad was there. He said that when the Heka was talking to me, he kind of felt It like this overwhelming feeling. It was for me too, the first time. So, you should probably be ready to feel like the most impressive overwhelming, awesome power type thing. When I came back to, my dad was prostrate on the floor from It, and Dad doesn't bow down for anyone."

Ben nodded, "So, awe-inspiring power. Got it. What else?"

"I don't know if you will feel what I feel, like where we are when I am talking to the Heka," I continued, "but in case you do, it is pretty overwhelming as well. The first time, it was like being in the middle of a whole galaxy but not at the same time. Time was really, really fast and slow all at once. I remember realizing I could hear grass growing, everything was so loud. But at the same time, it was deafeningly quiet, if that makes sense to you."

"Yeah," Ben said. "Remember, I have always been a god. You were just a human when you first experienced that, but I was there when the Heka made the earth. I remember what it felt like to watch universes be born."

"Oh, right." I said, feeling awkward. I had put so much stock into me being the only one who could talk to the Heka now, that I forgot that Ben and the other gods had talked to the Heka before humans were even made. "Well, that universe in the head of a pin feeling has changed some. I can feel the walls of Its cage and still feel like I am in the middle of empty space. It is kind of disconcerting, and a little nauseating. Like, I sometimes feel sick to my stomach from it."

Ben nodded again. "Anything else you think I should know?" He didn't say this in a condescending way, but somehow it felt like it to me.

"No, not really, I guess." I told him, looking away.

Ben put his hands on his hips. "So, how do you want to try this? Summoning the Heka and including me in on the conversation?"

Suddenly, I felt very small. Ben was saying all the right things and wasn't doubting me, at least in his words. But still, I had this sudden feeling that he thought I was being dramatic and self-important. I had this urge to take back everything I had said and let him lead us. I didn't want to be in charge anymore, and some part of me thought that some part of Ben believed I shouldn't be either. He was the one who had been a god his whole life. I was just this interloping human who shouldn't have existed in the first place. What right did I have to think I knew more than him?

As if he picked up on my sudden burst of imposter syndrome, Ben sat down next to me and took my hand. "Anna," he said gently, "you may be the youngest god, seeing as you were just made a god recently, but that doesn't change the fact that you know a whole bunch of stuff none of the rest of us ever will. You may not have an organized religion that has been practiced by humans for millennia, but I have never had a conversation with the Heka in my mind to talk about our feelings. That is a you thing. Don't doubt it."

I took a ragged breath, blew it out, and finally risked looking at Ben again. His eyes seemed kinder than they had, more caring. Ben shifted, settling into his spot on the ground, but didn't let go of my hand.

"How do we contact the Heka?" he asked again.

I inhaled deeply one more time, before answering him, to steady my nerves. "Just keep holding my hand." I told Ben. "I am going to try to call It."

I closed my eyes and tried to find that warm and ice feeling that was my Heka power. I hadn't actually had to look for it in a long time. It was just there, always now it seemed. But for some reason, it seemed elusive. Ben's hand felt warm in mine. It was rough and calloused in spots, but also soft. His thumb was moving over mine and I had a hard time concentrating on anything but the sensation of it, of him.

I shook my head, gently, trying to rid my mind of thoughts of Ben and focus on thoughts of the Heka. I had never seen the Heka, so I could only imagine the feelings I had when in Its presence. It was hard to keep myself focused on a feeling, rather than the really clear image that my mind wanted to focus on.

I pulled my hand out of Ben's and opened my eyes, groaning.

"What happened?" Ben asked.

"Nothing." I lied. I shifted in my spot, pretending to get more comfortable. Internally, I admonished myself. Focus on the Heka, Bella. I held out my hand to Ben, who took it quickly. "Let me try again."

This time, I kept my thoughts on the Heka. I need you, Heka, I thought. Ben and I need to talk to you together.

"I'm here." The Heka replied.

"Woah." Ben breathed. I had made the connection with the Heka in that expanding universe but also caged in place, and Ben had joined us too.

"Hello, Benahahminen." The Heka said.

I could feel Ben's heart pounding. He was in awe of everything that he was experiencing. Even though my eyes were closed, I could see him. Well, not really see him like I would with my eyes open in reality, but I could sense him the same way I could sense the Heka in this place. I could feel his feelings, just like I could feel the Heka's. It was strange and odd and felt a little invasive. I wondered if he could feel my feelings too, like the Heka could? And would this last after we left the Heka? Would we maintain this connection like the Heka and I had? I hoped not. There were definitely things I was feeling that I did not want Ben to know about.

"Um, hello, I mean, um." Ben stumbled over his words, unsure how to properly address the supreme creator in this type of meeting.

"Relax, Ben." I told him. "The Heka isn't really that judgy."

I felt the Heka chuckle. "You want to talk about the haze."

"Yes," I replied. "I know that you said before the haze in the Wastes was a spot where you aren't, or can't be, or at least are blocked, but what are the chances it is you creating it?"

The Heka thought about this. "I don't think it is me." It finally responded. I felt Its doubt, though.

"You aren't sure." Ben said. It wasn't a question, more of an observation. Ben could feel the Heka's feelings here too.

"No." It replied. "I am not sure, but I do not think so."

"How can you not be sure?" Ben asked, curiously.

The Heka replied, "Bella and I are entangled in ways I cannot explain. This has made… changes."

"In ways you can't explain?" Ben asked. "You mean, you don't know how Bella and you are entangled?"

"Let me rephrase." The Heka replied, "In ways I won't explain, at least not right now. "

Ben muttered under his breath, "Thanks, so helpful."

I chuckled. "Welcome to my world."

Ben thought to himself, "So this is what Anna has to deal with when she talks to the Heka. No wonder she is always so stressed and confused. I gotta make sure to be kinder to her about that stuff." At first, I thought he said it out loud, but then I realized, no, I was right the first time. Ben thought that. In his head. And I heard his thoughts.

Ben? I thought in my mind. Ben? Can you hear me?

Ben seemed to not notice my calling him. Okay, so I can hear his thought but he can't hear mine. Good. I think.

An image of me sleeping next to the pond entered my head. Then I felt the longing. Oh, no. Oh, no no no. Nope, La Di La. I don't want to hear Ben's thoughts and memories. Nope. Focus on the Heka, I told myself. The Heka, not Ben. Not the way his hand feels in mine. Not the sensation of his thumb rubbing across mine. The Heka was talking, I needed to listen to It.

I cleared my throat. "What?"

The Heka repeated what It had been saying. "The haze may not be anyone's creation. Not mine or Malachi's. At least not a purposeful, separate creation."

Ben spoke up. "What does your cage feel like to you, Heka?"

"What do you mean?" It asked.

"I mean," Ben responded, "this is my first time here, but Anna was right how she described it to me. I feel like I am in this amazing, wide-open place. Like what it would feel like to float between two galaxies or something. But at the same time, I feel closed in."

The Heka nodded in understanding.

Ben continued. "But I am not an infinite being like you. Neither is Anna. So, infinity will feel weird to us. How does this space, this place, feel to you?"

"I feel," the Heka started, but then stopped. "I understand what you are asking Ben, but I have no words to explain it that would make it make any more sense to you. You have never been infinite, I have never not been. I do not know what it feels like to be a contained being normally."

"What about when you did inhabit a body?" I asked. "Before Malachi destroyed it?"

I had a sense of the Heka sitting back, pondering that. "Would that be containment?" It asked. "Being inside a body? I could leave that body any time I wanted. I could let pieces of me leave while others stayed, or leave it entirely. Gods and humans cannot do that. In death, humans leave their bodies, but they retain that contained feeling, as their souls and spirits still have a defined shape. I have never had a defined shape or size. I have never had to be in only one time or place. Except now."

We sat in silence, each of us thinking about what the Heka had said, trying to make sense of it in our own minds. I could feel everyone else's thoughts, the Heka's and Ben's, on top of my own. I tried to block them, but it was getting harder and harder to define what was my thoughts and what was someone else's.

An idea hit one of us. I am not sure which one of us knew it first, but Ben was the first one to speak it. "It's your body." He said quietly.

"My body." The Heka echoed.

"The cage is a body." Ben kept going, saying the thought that all three of us were sharing. "Not necessarily a physical body, per se. But it acts the same way as a body would for me and Anna or any other finite being. It contains you."

"Finite beings don't notice their cage," the Heka kept the thought going, "the way I don't notice my lack of boundaries. When you come into my space, you become aware of infinity. You suddenly can define it in a way finite beings shouldn't be able. My cage is the lack of infinity, a finiteness that an infinite being shouldn't be able to define."

I took over speaking our shared idea. "The haze is the edges of your cage. Malachi didn't create it any more than you did. It just is. Infinite beings shouldn't have edges. So, the fact that you do feels wrong, dirty. And because we are, as you put it, entangled, I can feel the edges the same as you can when I run into it. The oases are like doors that let you seep out into the infinity, so they feel better, cleaner. The Wastes are the inside the cage, kinda wrong but with open space. But the haze is the edge an infinite being should never have."

"Why did it hurt me?" Ben asked. "Why me and not you, Anna?"

"Because you are finite." The Heka answered him.

Ben shook his head. "But that doesn't make sense. Anna is finite too."

I felt the Heka close off from Ben a little. "It will. It doesn't now, but it will make sense soon." The Heka suddenly pulled back from Ben entirely and I knew he wasn't there, in the Heka's space, Its cage, with us anymore. I felt him in the physical world of Taikarlu let go of my hand. The Heka and I were alone. Ben was watching my physical body, but unable to spiritually rejoin us. He was disappointed at that, I could tell.

"Ben is right about one thing," the Heka said, pulling me away from my thoughts.

"What is he right about?" I asked.

"You are different." I was going to question that statement, but the Heka didn't let me speak. "While you were sleeping, he realized that you are all three, god, human and coordinator, and that this makes you special. He isn't going to tell you that, because he is not sure what it means and is afraid it will scare you or make you pull away from him."

"Why are you telling me, then?" I asked.

The Heka sighed. "Because you need to know. And because Ben needs you to know. He just doesn't know he needs you to know. Because you need to realize that you can keep Ben safe. Safe from the haze, but more importantly, safe from you."

"What do you mean, safe from me?" I said, defensively. "I wouldn't ever hurt Ben. I love," I cut myself off.

"Exactly." The Heka replied. "You didn't need to say it out loud for me to know. We can feel each other's feelings, remember?"

Oh, yeah. "What do I do?" I whispered. I don't know why I whispered.

"That's up to you." The Heka said. Then, It was gone.

The Heka was done talking. I was back in the physical realm. I didn't open my eyes though. I knew Ben was still sitting next to me, watching me. I could feel him there, in the physical sense, but I needed to find out if I could still hear him spiritually. Like I did with the Heka. Could I still hear his thoughts and feel his feelings?

I waited, trying to clear my mind of everything I was feeling and focus on feelings that were not mine. There was the Heka's feelings of being cramped and of wishing It could just tell me everything, but knowing It couldn't yet. Well, that was new. I always figured the Heka knew way more than It was letting on. I mean, It was the infinite creator. Of course, It knew things. But I hadn't really registered that It was actively hiding things about me from myself.

I mentally turned away from the Heka and tried to focus on Ben. The Heka was so powerful, I thought it would be hard to put Its feeling to the side, but actually it was surprisingly easy. And there were Ben's. He was looking at my lips, wondering what it would be like to kiss me. I wondered too.

Nope.

I really did not want to go there. I mean, I did, but no. Ugh, this sucked. The Heka is hiding things about me from me, even though I can feel everything It is feeling. Ben was hiding things about me from me, even though apparently now I could feel what he is feeling too.

And now this. Ben and I have feelings for each other. This was way too many feelings for one girl. I opened my eyes, hoping the Ben-me connection just needed time to fade, and really hoping that Ben could not feel my feelings, or even guess them.

"Wow." Ben said.

"Yeah." I replied, still trying to get my bearings. "It's a lot."

"You were not kidding." Ben whistled. "And you have done that how many times, now?"

I tried to count, but gave up. "A few." I finally said.

"And you haven't gone crazy yet?" Ben whistled again. "Yeah, I think you can just relay messages back and forth. I'm good at once."

"Ben," I said, trying to broach a topic I really didn't want to. He had a right to know I could feel his feelings, though. Especially with what I was feeling him feeling. And with what I was feeling back.

As if he knew what I was going to say, and he didn't want to discuss it either, he kept talking. "Well, that answers the question of what the haze is, but doesn't really help with what to do about it. I mean, the Heka didn't outright tell me, 'Go home, Ben," so there is that." Ben was babbling. As he babbled, he stood up and starting moving around. "We should probably get going, though. So many oases, so little time, right? I wonder what creature is next."

"Ben," I started again. I stood and followed him as he paced.

Now that I was standing, he instinctively moved toward the edge of the oasis, heading into the Wastes. He kept babbling, ignoring me. "There are so many mythical creatures. I mean, humans are really inventive. Some of the creatures were made by the Heka and became a myth to the humans, but some of them were added to the myths and then created by the Heka. Just like with the gods, it isn't always clear which came first. It's the whole chicken or the egg type of problem." Ben kept walking with me a few steps behind him. He was moving his hands as he talked, gesturing a lot. Occasionally, he turned around and walked backwards, looking at me, but then he would turn back, still talking the entire time. "Let me know if I am headed in the wrong direction, Anna. The jackalope. That's a great example. Humans made that one up, I am sure. Well, pretty sure. I mean it is a rather silly mythical creature. But then again, the jackalope has existed as long as I can remember. So, did humans make it up and the Heka created it, or did the Heka create it so that the humans could make it up? Chicken or the egg?"

"Ben," I tried a third time, with no more luck than the first two times.

Ben was still talking. I could tell he was afraid to stop talking.

"Most of the humans believe sirens and whatnot are human creations. Sailors made them up because they had never seen or heard whale song before, or something. But sirens are real and existed before humans did. I mean, they are wrong about what the siren song does, obviously, but when do humans ever get the full story right?"

I sighed. Did I keep trying to get his attention or do I give up and let him ramble? We were walking in the right direction through the Wastes, a kind of south-easterly way. I realized we were encircling the city of Taikarlu, and wondered what would happen when we closed the circle. I reached out and touched Ben on his arm, trying one last time to get his attention.

"Ben," I said softly.

All at once, Ben stopped walking. He turned around and pulled me into his arms. Without hesitating, he leaned down and kissed me. I had never had a boyfriend before, so I had never been kissed like that, and it was so unexpected, I had no idea how to act. Ben shifted, putting his arms more comfortably around me.

Suddenly, I was panicking. I didn't know how to kiss. What was I supposed to do? You can watch a hundred movies with people kissing in them, but it still didn't prepare you for the real thing. Especially when you were feeling your own emotions as well as the other person's. I was freaking out while Ben was very happy. Somewhere in there, I realized, was the Heka's feelings about this too, but I couldn't focus enough to sort out who was feeling what anymore.

Just as suddenly as he started kissing me, Ben stopped. He stepped back, away from me, and I realized that, even though I had been panicking, I hadn't wanted him to stop. I felt exposed without his arms around me. But then, I realized Ben was panicking. He was feeling like he had done something wrong. Really, really wrong.

Ben turned away from me and started walking through the Wastes. He was moving quickly and, in my shock of both him kissing me and then stopping kissing me, it took a minute for me to make my brain realize I needed to move to go after him.

"Ben," I called out, but he kept walking. Why did he have to have longer legs than me? I was almost running to catch up, but on the shifting sand of the Wastes, attempting to run ended up a futile exercise of slipping and falling while moving forward.

"Ben, stop!" I called out again. This time, Ben did stop but he didn't turn around and face me. I huffed as I caught up to him. "Why did you run away?" I asked him in between trying to catch my breath. "Why did you feel like you had done something very wrong?"

Ben turned around at this and looked at me sharply. Oops. "What do you mean why did I feel like I did something wrong?" he asked, putting a heavy inflection on the word 'feel'.

"I meant," I scrambled, "I meant to say why did you act. Not felt."

Ben narrowed his eyes. "How long have you been able to feel my feelings?" he asked me, sounding almost betrayed.

"I, um," I stammered as I tried to think of a way out of this. Shoot. I sighed. I looked down and told him the truth. "Since we went to the Heka together." Ben crossed his arms over his chest. "That's it, I swear."

Ben didn't believe me. "You have been able to feel the Heka's feelings for a whole lot longer."

"I know," I told him. "I think it has something to do with us going to It together. Anyway, you can't be mad at me. I tried to tell you, but you just kept rambling about sirens and jackalopes and chickens. And then you were kissing me."

Ben groaned and ran his hand through his hair. I could feel his emotions were all mixed up. Part of him was frustrated and upset. But another part didn't care and just wanted to kiss me again. There was another feeling there too, but I didn't understand it. Ben opened his mouth, as if he was going to say something, but then thought better of it. He turned around, paced for a few steps, then turned back, opened his mouth, closed it and then paced again. He did this a few times before eventually just sitting down on the sand with his head in his hands.

"You know what I am feeling, so I can't even figure out what to say." He moaned.

I sat next to him, and spoke softly. "Just say what you want. Your feelings are just as confused as mine are."

"You're confused?" Ben asked. "That's not, I mean, you're not angry at me?"

Surprised, I asked him, "Why would I be mad at you?"

"Because," he started to say, then he groaned again. "Because I can feel your feelings too." Ben admitted, ashamed.

Oh. Ohhh. "And you felt me panicking when you kissed me." I nodded, understanding.

"Yeah," Ben admitted. "I had been talking and talking, trying to convince myself that me feeling you having, you know, feelings for me, was all in my head. But then you touched my arm and it was just so overwhelming. All I could think about was you. I assumed it was so strong because you were feeling the same way, but then I felt you panic. And then I started panicking because you were panicking. And," Ben rubbed his face again, "and this is all just too confusing."

I snorted. "At least you only have to deal with your feelings and mine. I get to feel yours, mine, and the Heka's. Two teenagers and an infinite being's feelings all swirled together? Now, that is confusing." I paused, thinking. "Unless, you can feel the Heka's feelings too?"

Ben shook his head. "No, I don't think so. Just you."

"I think," I started slowly. "I think maybe, we just need to take a step back. We both know that I," I took a deep breath. Don't stop now, Bella. "That I have feelings for you. And we both know that you have feelings for me. We are both concerned about all the other stuff going on with the haze, and the Heka, and the different mythical animals, and all of that. And then on top of all that is the mysterious crap with my name and stuff the Heka knows but won't tell me. It's a lot."

"A whole lot." Ben agreed.

"Yeah," I continued. "And I am a human, god and coordinator all stuck in a seventeen-year-old's brain and you are a millions of years old god stuck in a… wait, how old are you supposed to be?"

Ben looked confused. "Also seventeen. When did you figure out the god coordinator human thing?"

I waved his question away. "The Heka told me after It booted you out. Not important. Well, yes important, but not right now. So, we are two seventeen-year-olds with a whole lot more going on than the average seventeen-year-old. Hormones are probably still a thing for you and definitely still a thing for me."

Ben snorted and glanced at me then looked away. "Definitely still a thing for me."

I blushed. I felt him think I was beautiful in that half of a second he looked at me. Then I felt him blush because he felt me blush. Suddenly, I wanted him to kiss me again. Or he wanted to kiss me. Or he wanted me to want him to kiss me. Or. "Oh, hell." I said.

I stood up and walked away from Ben. I understood what he meant about it all being so overwhelming. There was no way for me to separate what I wanted and felt from what he wanted and felt. Ben's and my feelings had become as entangled as the Heka's and mine had been. Until I could figure out what was really me, what was Ben and what was the Heka, I really, really didn't want to do anything with any of these feelings.

"So, we won't." Ben said. I turned back to ask him what he meant, but I knew. "Anna, I like you. I know I do because I felt that long before we met with the Heka and got all this," Ben waved his hand around in the air as if he was stirring an imaginary pot, "stuff mixed up. But what I also know is that I only want to act on that if you do too. If you do, not if my feelings for you are making you think you have feelings for me too, and especially not if the Heka is trying to be a little matchmaker or something in your brain without your consent."

Ben took a deep breath in, stood and continued talking. "You have a ton of crap on your plate. I should help you carry it all, not become another thing for you to worry about. So, I am taking us off the table. It's a non-issue. There are no feelings, no wanting to kiss, or whatever, until this ends and we only feel our own feelings again."

"What if it never ends?" I asked. "What if it is permanent, that we can feel each other's feelings?"

"Then we will deal with it once we know that for certain." Ben said a whole lot more confidently than I knew he felt. "Besides, I am almost positive it is just a temporary after-effect of being around the Heka."

Ben was bluffing entirely, and we both knew that. Even so, I decided to bluff with him. "Good." I tried to sound light-hearted. "Great. On to the next problem. We still need to go to the next oasis and help whoever is waiting for us there. Preferably without you almost dying when we brush up against the edge of the Heka's cage."

"Yup," Ben said, faking it as much as me. "Lead the way, Anna." He held out his arm as if holding open an imaginary door for me, and I walked past him, keeping to a southeasterly direction. When I passed by, Ben held his breath and waited a moment, then followed behind me. I pretended not to notice that he stayed at least an arm's length away from me as we walked. There was going to be a lot of pretending in the near future.

We continued to walk towards where the clean feeling of the oasis was, and I kept my senses sharp for any hint of the greasy uncleanness from the haze. I finally felt it just as the oasis came into view at the edge of the horizon.

"Stop." I told Ben. "The haze is right in front of us."

"What should we do?" Ben asked me.

"If the haze is the edge of the Heka's cage," I said, thinking out loud, "then we must be at the outer most boundary between the unlocked places and the locked places. Taikarlu is to the north, unlocked. The tanukis are to the northwest, unlocked. We don't have anything to the east or south unlocked yet, so there is no way to just walk around it."

"What if you shield me?" Ben suggested. "Like you did when we first came to Taikarlu together. You used your Heka to shield me and Albert and Nummi to test if your human body could be protected from the effects of so much Heka power in one place. As far as I know, you are still shielding your own body."

I had forgotten that I was doing that. Holding the shield had become just second nature. I closed my eyes to remember what that shield felt like. I found it, that shimmery cloth floating just an inch outside of my skin. I plucked at it to see if it would stretch. It did, and I pulled it wider, throwing the extra fabric over Ben.

Immediately, a bunch of thoughts that weren't mine were bouncing around in my head. Is her hair more auburn or gold in the sunlight? I wish I could get some of that chicken from that one restaurant on 5th street. What was it called again? That young man is at my idol again, asking for help to be a better hunter. I wish he would bring me something better than bananas. I gotta remember to tell Albert about the tanuki. He will think Porex was hilarious.

Then there was a lot of screaming. At first, I thought it was inside my head, but then I realized it wasn't. Ben was screaming. I opened my eyes to see him clutching either side of his head and writhing in pain on the ground. He was kicking the sand and screaming worse than he had after the invisible whip hit him.

"Pull it back!" he panted between screams. "I can't! Pull it back!"

I grabbed the fabric of my protection shield and snapped it back to my frame. Ben stopped screaming but he continued to lay on the ground, panting. I ran to him and kneeled next to his heaving frame. "I'm sorry!" I told him, unsure what had happened or what I should do.

Ben laid there, panting, for several more minutes. His breathing slowly became more even and less ragged and he stopped clutching his head. When he tried to sit up, I reached out to help him, but he shrugged away from my hand as if it burned him. He sat up, resting his arms on his legs, still breathing hard. His arms and legs were trembling like he had just ran a marathon. Then he looked at me.

"Is it like that all the time?" Ben asked. "Inside your head?"

"What do you mean?" There wasn't anything but my thoughts inside my head. Well, my thoughts, the Heka's feelings and now, Ben's.

"All that noise." Ben wheezed. "It was like everyone in the whole world was talking at once. All the gods and animals too. It was so loud. I could hear everything everybody was thinking and feeling, not just the stuff they were saying out loud."

"I don't think that was my head, Ben." I told him. "I haven't ever heard all that."

"It wasn't so much hearing it." He tried to explain. "It was a feeling, like how I could feel what you were feeling and it sounded like you were talking inside my head. Except it was just so many people. All their thoughts and feelings and memories. I could tell if they were hurting, and if that hurt was physical like a broken leg or mental like they were sad or something. I could tell if they were happy too, or angry, or whatever they thought or felt. And then it was just overwhelming. I couldn't separate one person from another one because there were just too many of them."

Ben hung his head again, still trying to catch his breath and stop trembling. I couldn't understand what had happened. When I extending the fabric of the shield to protect him, it was like his mind had become one with mine. But I don't know whose mind he became one with because what he was describing wasn't what was inside my head.

I stood up and walked away from Ben. It was my turn to start pacing. What had gone wrong? Was this what the Heka meant when It said I needed to keep Ben safe from me? The Heka had said I could keep him safe from me, though. I had to figure out what Ben had tapped into when he had access to my mind.

Then it dawned on me. When I could hear Ben's mind, I could hear his worshippers just like he could. I didn't have any worshippers for Ben to hear. But my mind wasn't the only mind in my head. I was connected to the Heka, and the Heka was connected to everything and everyone. Even from Its prison, It was still connected.

But that didn't explain why Ben heard all that when I didn't. Unless I did and didn't realize it. My connection, my entanglement with the Heka came on slowly. When Ben mingled his mind with mine under the shield, he would have gotten all of my mind and the Heka's all at once. He hadn't had time to protect himself like I would have.

He hadn't had any warning that he needed to because the last time he was under my shield, I had done it differently. I hadn't known my Heka could do anything and was still operating under the idea that my Heka workings needed to be based on my coordinator job of telling truths. I had been thinking of making a shield of truth, to protect the truth of everyone's body. This time, I had just picked up my shield and thrown it over Ben and pulled him into my shield, my truth. My truth now included the Heka's thoughts and feelings, and maybe it meant the Heka's hearing too.

Could I hear everything the Heka heard? I sat down in the sand, far away from Ben just in case. In case of what, I didn't know, but just in case. I crossed my legs to get comfortable and closed my eyes and tried to relax. I held my shield for my physical body against the physical power of the Heka, but tried to consciously let go of everything else.

No more pushing this to the side and not thinking about it. No more forgetting about things until I had time to deal with it properly. I let it all flow.

At first, all I thought about was Ben. I thought about kissing him, and his beautiful golden eyes. I wanted to stop thinking about that, but I forced myself to let go and think about whatever came to mind. Then all the problems bubbled up. The haze, the Heka, the mystical animals. I realized I could hear them, the animals at all the oases. I could hear the excitement of the unicorns. The foals were scampering all over the Great Plains, happy in the presence of the gods and the other animals again.

Then I could hear the gods. Nummi thought that the tanuki were interesting. He and Waalish were discussing the advantages of being able to shapeshift, but inside, Nummi was worried about Ben. Ben had been his pretend grandson for so long that Nummi was having a hard time letting go of that humanistic protector feeling.

The humans. Oh man, there are so many humans. Their voices started mingling inside my head. I couldn't separate one conversation from another. Then the non-mystical animals in the human realms chimed in. Spring was coming soon for some of them. Others were preparing for the upcoming winter. There were other beings that I didn't recognize there too, talking and thinking, loving and hurting, all inside my head. Were they aliens from different planets? Or gods I hadn't met yet? I didn't know. Their worries were fascinating. I could listen to them all day.

Then it was all gone, all of them, and all I could feel was Ben's lips on mine. I wasn't panicking this time. His lips were warm and soft and gone too quickly.

"Better?" Ben asked me softly.

I opened my eyes and Ben was sitting very close to me. He was sitting directly in front of me, his knees just barely touching mine. "What happened?" I breathed.

"You were lost in them, Anna." Ben replied. "You were lost in the world of other people, in the voices you hear because of the Heka."

"How did you know?" But I knew how he knew.

Ben tapped my knee with one finger, very gently. "Because you were disappearing. You were disappearing from my mind. I couldn't feel your feelings anymore."

I was having a very hard time focusing on anything besides Ben's finger. "Did you feel everyone else instead?"

Ben stopped tapping my knee and scooted back so he wasn't so close anymore. "No." He replied, with a very forced casualness.

"No. I just didn't feel you. I thought about slapping you, to break the spell you were under, but..." He stopped.

I understood. He wanted to kiss me again and this gave him an excuse to. He was worried I would be mad. He still wasn't sure I had wanted him to kiss me the first time and didn't like the fact that he had, in his way of thinking, taken advantage of me this time. I wanted to tell him that he didn't, but I knew he wouldn't listen. In his mind, he was still convinced that I only had feelings for him because of his feelings for me, or the Heka, and I had no way to prove to him that wasn't true. Honestly, I had no way to prove it to myself either.

I cleared my throat, and tried to force the same casualness he had. "I didn't know that was all there in my head."

"I think it is the Heka," he replied. "Not you."

"I'm sorry." I told Ben. "I'm sorry that hurt you."

"How were you to know?" Ben nonchalantly pulled himself up to standing. "But that does means that you shielding me won't work. What's our next idea?"

I stood as well, not nearly as gracefully as Ben did. My body felt too close and too restricting after letting my mind be so open. I thought about the issue out loud, listing what we knew, hoping to spark an idea. "You can't just walk into the haze because your finiteness will make you get hurt. I can't envelope you in a shield, because then the Heka's mind will be open to you and Its infiniteness will break your mind. A tanuki can stretch its skin as a shield and protect you from the edge of the Heka's cage, but we don't have a tanuki here to help us."

"That about sums it up," Ben spun around on one foot and pointed at me, kicking his other foot through the sand. "You have the entirety of existence within your mind, Anna. Find a new idea, any new idea."

"Oh sure," I told him sarcastically. "You discover that my mind contains the thoughts of millions seconds before I do, and it almost kills you, but you expect me to be able to filter through all that noise and just, what? Find the one random genius who has the perfect solution to our problem with a snap of my fingers? Why don't I cover you with my shield again and you try it?"

Ben held up his hands in surrender. "No, thank you," he drawled.

I laughed. This was impossible. It was like trying to untie the Gordian Knot while pushing Sisyphus' boulder up the hill. I started pacing and thinking out loud again. "So, the haze hurts you because it is the edge of the Heka's cage, and the cage is a finite thing trying to contain an infinite being."

"That is the way I understood it," Ben replied. "It only hurts me and not you because I am finite. For all that I am a god, I am finite in a way the Heka isn't. You have a connection with the Heka, or have mingled with It somehow, so you have a touch of the infinite and the edge of the cage doesn't bother you because of that touch of infiniteness."

I pondered this a little more. "Porex didn't get hurt touching the edge of the cage either. He had made himself into the golden bag and didn't get hurt."

"He was a finite being in an infinite body. Tanukis can spread their skins as large as they need to, essentially infinitely." Ben added. "You and the Heka are infinite contained in the finite. Porex was finite contained in the infinite. But I am finite contained in the finite. So, the cage's edge hurts me."

I nodded. "You have to contain both the infinite and the finite for the cage's edge to not hurt you. But how exactly does the edge of the cage hurt you because you are not at least a little infinite?"

Ben started pacing with me, both us of trying to understand this problem. An idea started brewing in me. "What if the cage itself isn't the problem? What if it is the Heka inside that cage that is the problem?"

"The Heka said It wasn't hurting me," Ben countered.

"The Heka said It didn't think It was making the haze, not that It wasn't hurting you." I corrected. "I have learned you have to be kind of literal, but very allegorical at the same time, with the Heka. It didn't create the haze. The edges of the cage Malachi made and put the Heka into made the haze. The Heka, though, really wants to escape that cage. Like I already told you, the cage pinches and hurts. The smaller the cage gets, the more It hurts. And worse than that, the act of an infinite being stuck in a finite space is literally killing the Heka. The Heka is straining against the cage's hold on It, straining to break out to survive."

Ben's eyes lit up. He figured out where I was going with this and took over talking. "The Heka, in Its infiniteness, pushes up against the finite boundary of the cage, and the cage strains against the Heka. When you touch the cage, nothing happens because you are already too full of Heka. When Porex touched the cage, he was using an infinite amount of the Heka and so he too felt too full. But little old me, the finite god of a tiny tribe of humans, has space to spare. Or at least the Heka mistakenly thinks so when I touch Its cage, and It tries to come into my space. But as a finite being, I am already using all of my space for myself. Any physics teacher will tell you; two objects cannot exist in the same space at the same time, therefore I get ripped apart."

"Yes!" I agreed excitedly. "All we need to do is tell the Heka this and It can stop trying to expand into your space. Then, you'll be fine."

"No, I won't, Anna." Ben shook his head, sadly. "The Heka can't stop trying to take up more space. It is infinite. Infinity cannot stop itself stretching into forever. If there is space, the Heka will try to occupy it. It can't tell what is space inside the cage versus space inside me. If the Heka was free, instead of caged up, It could expand everywhere including inside me because infinity can be big as well as small. But once contained, the Heka cannot control if It is big or small, tall or short. It can't control Its shape anymore. Malachi created a physics paradox when he put the Heka in that box. One that can only be solved by the Heka being freed again."

"Or It dies." I added.

"But we won't let that one happen." Ben said. "We will solve this and save It."

I sighed and plunked down on the sand again. "Yeah, we just have to figure out how to make you infinite."

I felt the idea hit Ben's brain. He got so excited all at once, I knew he had cracked the problem. "We don't need to make me infinite. We just need to make me contain something infinite, or seem to contain something infinite, so the Heka is tricked into thinking there is no space for It inside me."

I had been really excited based on feeling Ben's excitement at his idea. Once he spoke it out loud though, I realized it wasn't actually an idea as much as just a different way to state the problem. And I told him so.

"All you did was say what I just said using different words." I complained. "We need to make you infinite or at least seem infinite."

Ben shook his head, disagreeing. "No, we need to make me contain something infinite. That is where what you and I said are different. We don't need to make me infinite, just contain something else that is infinite."

"I still don't see a difference," I admitted.

Ben mumbled, "How do I make you understand what I mean?" He kept mumbling under his breath, writing imaginary letters in the air, as if he was thinking. "I got it. Okay, Anna," he started again, "think of this like a game. Can you list off all the things you know are infinite?"

I didn't think this would help, but I decided to play along. "Well, the Heka is infinite, a tanuki's golden bag," I started.

"Yes, we know those. What else?" he pushed.

I tried to think. "Math is infinite."

"Math?" Ben asked. "What do you mean?"

Here I am, in the land of the gods, and I am just now finding out my teacher was right when he told me 'you will too use this in real life.' "Ugh, I hate that Mr. Gomez was right. Remember geometry? Pi is infinite, numbers are infinite, lines are infinite, that stuff?"

Ben groaned. "Ugh, not more math. Ok, let's rule that stuff out as the solution because," Ben shuddered, "ugh."

"There was a poem we read in ninth grade Lit class that said the power of the human mind is infinite. Like, it is infinitely creative, infinitely beautiful, infinitely emotional. You know, all that poetic type stuff." I said.

Ben thought about that. "Do you think a god's mind would contain the same infiniteness that a human mind would?"

"I dunno, maybe." I answered. "I mean, probably not the way we need because then your mind being infinite would have already protected you."

"True," Ben said, dejectedly. Ben ran his hand through his hair again in frustration. I found myself watching Ben as he moved around. Ben was tall, almost a foot taller than me, and muscular. If not for the splash burn marks all over his arms and legs, he would be the perfect actor for any main role in a sappy teen movie. Before I knew better, I thought his scars were from a car accident, but now I knew that they were actually caused by a fight with a bi-headed, poisonous snake.

Ben had long, flowing, jet-black hair that went past his waist and golden-brown eyes that twinkled when he smiled. I had muddy brown hair that couldn't decide if it was curly or not, and my eyes were either blue or green, or some combination of both, depending on my Heka use. He always looked at ease back in the human realm in his signature t-shirt over a long sleeve shirt and athletic pants, and still did in his tank top and short here in Taikarlu. Whereas my short, slightly pudgy frame looked almost blobish in my normal attire of loose-fitting t-shirt and jeans, with the humans or here. I suddenly wondered what Ben could ever see in me. I wasn't beautiful like him. Maybe he had it backwards and our feeling each other's feelings wasn't making me think I was in love with him when I wasn't, but making him think he was in love with me when he wasn't.

Ben stopped moving. He became utterly still. "Think that again," he said.

My face burned with embarrassment at what I had been thinking. I did not want to think it again, knowing he was listening.

"Anna," Ben said, embarrassment in his voice too. I wasn't sure if he was actually embarrassed too or just feeling mine. "Think that again, please. I think it is important."

I lowered my eyes and thought again. Ben is beautiful. Maybe it isn't me feeling his feelings and not being in love with him. Maybe he is only feeling my feelings for him and he isn't in love with me.

"Love," Ben whispered. "Love is infinite."

"No, its not." I argued. "Do you know how many people in love get divorced or break up? Like, just look our high school. More than half the kids' parents were divorced, and how many people did we know who hooked up, swearing they would love each other forever, only to break up the next week and be in love again by the weekend."

"That's not love." Ben countered. "Not real love, not true love. I mean that been married for seventy years and are still each other's best friends love. Like that jumping in front of a bullet to save them love."

I snorted. "Do you think that type of forever love is even real anymore?"

Ben shook his head. "It doesn't matter if it is real anymore or not. We just need the Heka, or really the Heka's infiniteness, to think it is."

I was skeptical. "So, we are going to pretend that you are so full of the infinite power of love that there is no room inside you for any more of the Heka? You told me gods don't have love like that, that they are more like teenagers. What will make you so different to be so consumed by love?"

"Except when it is destiny," Ben reminded me. "Gods like to love 'em and lose 'em unless their love is predestined, or part of a myth cycle, remember?"

"Still doesn't answer my question," I complained. "You don't have a myth about loving someone." I started drawing lines in the sand in front of me, hoping it would help me think.

Ben was standing a few steps away from me, shifting his weight from foot to foot as we talked, but he turned and paced a few steps away. He started scratching his head nervously and looked back at me. Timidly, he started, "Well, um, about that?"

I stopped my finger mid-design and didn't move. "What?" I asked. He was feeling embarrassed and I was suspicious of that feeling.

"You remember how you saw my memories and kind of saw me watching you sleep next to the pond?" Ben was choosing his words very carefully. I looked up at him through narrowed eyes, indicating for him to go on. He finished in a rush. "Well, my worshippers kinda sorta felt me feeling some feelings for you and they kinda sorta shipped us."

I repeated myself, more incredulous this time. "What?"

Ben sighed. "My worshippers felt me falling in love with you and created a brand-new myth where we fall in love and then they made offerings to our happiness. They shipped us, you know, relation-shipped us. They kinda made us destined for each other."

"What!" I said for the third time. I was not as angry as I probably sounded but I was definitely surprised.

Ben shrugged, throwing his hands in the air. "I didn't mean for them to do that. They just kinda did."

I picked up a handful of sand and threw it, groaning. "Ugh, so you mean this whole time, I have been worrying about whether you really did like me or if I was going crazy and that you could feel all my super embarrassing feelings and you knew that we were destined for each other the whole time?!"

Ben rushed back over towards me and knelt down, close to me but not too close. "No, no, no. It's not like that. I mean, yeah, my worshippers making a myth up makes it more likely that we would get together, but it doesn't mean that we have to. We still have free will and everything."

I stared at Ben, completely unsure how I felt at that moment. Part of me was angry he didn't tell me about this. Another part of me was relieved. And yet another part of me was nervous. "But I thought if two gods loving each other was in a myth, then they were stuck with each other."

"No," Ben corrected, settling into the sand. He pulled his legs to sit cross-legged on the other side of my sand drawing. With one finger, he continued my designs while he spoke. "Think of it like Fury. The more the people told stories about my dog, Fury, the more often he was around with me. When they stopped, Fury just kind of disappeared. Love myths are the same, but opposite. The more two gods buy into the love myth, and allow it, the more often the people will talk about it and the stronger it becomes. If worshippers create a love myth and those two gods really aren't into it, the two gods just don't hang out for a while and it's like the worshippers forget that story and it all goes away."

"So, the more you and I hang out and act like we are in love, the stronger that destiny becomes. But if we decide we don't want it, we can make it go away. We still get a choice." I said, making sure I understood. This god stuff was complicated.

"Exactly," Ben smiled. "And right now, that works to our advantage. If we feed into the love myth, then the infinity of love will be all over me and the Heka won't think It has found space It can fill when I touch Its cage in the haze. If, later, we decide we really don't want the love myth, we just stop hanging out for a while and it will eventually go away."

"Wait," I sat up straight, and lowered my eyebrows, suspicious again. "Just how long is a while?"

Ben looked at the sand and mumbled something.

"Say that again," I commanded. "I didn't quite catch that."

A little louder, Ben replied, "Like a thousand years, or so."

I jumped up so fast I kicked sand in Ben's face. "A thousand years?!" I shrieked.

"Anna, Anna." Ben stood up, brushing sand out of his mouth and hair. "You have to remember," Ben ran his hands up and down his chest. "Immortal. I am immortal, and my guess is you are immortal now too. A thousand years is nothing to us."

I realized he was probably right, that I overreacted, forgetting that immortality thing. I had been a coordinator for a hundred years and it didn't even really feel that long. It would probably suck to spend a thousand years away from my only friend, but it really wouldn't be that long to someone like him. Or me. I didn't want to admit I knew I had reacted in a human way, so still pretended to be a little angry.

"Fine," I said, crossing my arms over my chest. "How do we convince the Heka that just saw us like five minutes ago that we are somehow now magically in an infinite love?"

Ben looked at me. Not just like one person looking at another, but he really looked at me. I don't know why but the anger I was pretending to still hold disappeared really quickly. My mouth went dry and my heart sped up. Suddenly, I was nervous.

Ben took a few steps towards me, and my heart kicked up faster. He kept looking at me as he, ever so slowly inched closer and closer until he was standing right in front of me. I had to tilt my head back to keep looking at his face. Man, Ben is really tall.

We stood that way, Ben and I, looking at each other for a very long time. Maybe thirty seconds, but it was a really long thirty seconds. Finally, Ben leaned down and whispered in my ear.

"That's how." He said.

Ben twitched like he was going to stand back up straight then changed his mind. Then he whispered, "Oh, and by the way, you're wrong. You are absolutely beautiful." Ben actually did stand up straight and stepped back this time. I would have thought that those thirty seconds had not had the effect on him the same way it had me, except he kept wiping his hands on his pants because they were too sweaty. That, and the fact that his mind was racing with a million feelings the same way mine was.

O. Kay. Then. I took a deep breath and turned to the haze. This whole time it had been right next to us, but I had completely forgotten about it. Looking towards it again, its greasy wrongness crept over me. I turned back to Ben and held out my hand.

Ben looked at me quizzically like he didn't know what I wanted. I held my hand out again, saying, "Nothing for it but to try, right?"

Ben stepped forward and grabbed my hand tightly. At first, I ignored how good it felt, his hand in mine, but then realized I probably should focus on that feeling rather than ignore it. I started walking forward. I could feel Ben getting nervous after a few steps and stopped.

"Just focus on me, okay?" I reminded him, then added. "And maybe, stay behind me, looking at me and thinking of me."

Ben nodded and we started walking again. I could feel when the haze actually touched him. Ben inwardly grimaced at the feeling of the haze washing over him. But it did just wash over him. Step by step, very slowly, we moved through the haze towards the oasis.

And nothing happened. It took forever but was over before I knew it at the same time. The haze's wrongness faded as the scrubby brush of the edge of the oasis slowly turned into the forest that had become so familiar and comforting to us.

When we reached the pond, Ben and I both exhaled audibly. Ben let go of my hand and, looking at it, I noticed he had been squeezing it so tightly that he left imprints of his fingers on mine. I watched as the blood circulation returned to my hand and the marks faded. When I looked up, I realized Ben had been watching my hand too, fascinated.

I held up my hand for him to see, showing him the palm then the back, as the last tinges of marks faded. "Yup," I said, trying to break the tension. "Still a human body. Blood flow and all."

Ben patted himself, feeling over his arms and legs. "Still a god body," he chuckled, "an uninjured one to boot."

"That's a step in the right direction," I joked back. I was honestly relieved, and a little surprised, that our plan had worked. I could feel that Ben was covering up his relief too. It's interesting that, even though we both knew that we could feel each other's feelings, we still hid our emotions as if we were embarrassed by them, I thought idly. There was a philosophical question in there somewhere, but just then, I didn't worry about trying to answer it. Instead, I let myself enjoy our success.

Ben kicked off his socks and boots and dove headlong into the pond, swam a few feet under the water, then bobbed up, shaking his head. His long hair stuck to his face and he pushed it back with his hands, smiling. I smiled back at him, took off my shoes and socks and joined him in the cool water. I didn't get in as dramatically as Ben, choosing instead to just slide into the pond, dip beneath the waterline and come back up quickly.

Ben and I casually swam around the pond, enjoying a well-deserved break. Yeah, it had taken us way too long to move from the last oasis to this one. And yeah, it took way too long to figure out the issue of the haze, but the Heka would just have to be okay waiting for five more minutes while we relaxed. If we kept going as we had been, stressed and tense and overworked, either Ben or I, or both, were bound to make a mistake. And mistakes at this point could be fatal for me, for Ben, or potentially for the Heka. A fatal mistake for the Heka meant a fatal mistake for the whole of creation. A break to swim and relax would keep us sharp, I reasoned.

I floated in the pond, my eyes closed, enjoying the interplay between the cool water on my back and the warm sun coming in through between treetops on my face. Suddenly, I felt a great big splash of water on my face. I opened my eyes and rolled over to swim rather than float.

"I don't want to horse around, Ben." I told him, assuming he had splashed me playfully. "Can we just relax for five more minutes, then get back to work."

Ben looked at me innocently. "I thought you had splashed me."

I was about to counter when something plunked into the water between Ben and me, splashing both of us. We both looked around to find out where whatever it was had come from. Another plunk and more water splashed, then another. It seemed like whatever was hitting the water was falling from the sky.

I looked up and saw a flock of birds flying overhead. We were being pelted from something those birds were throwing at us. The birds' aim seemed to get better as small stones were falling from the sky in rapidly growing amounts, and getting closer and closer to actually hitting us.

"Run!" Ben yelled, pointing towards the cave that we knew was near the pond in the other oases.

I scrambled out of the pond, grabbed my shoes and booked it towards the cave. Ben followed right behind me. Neither of us stopped to put on our shoes, but just ran barefoot, yelping when we stepped on sharp stones or when the birds' ammunition got too close.

The cave was exactly where we thought it would be. I darted inside the mouth of the cave and stopped to catch my breath. Ben was only seconds behind me. He waited patiently for me to recover, not needing things like oxygen, then asked "What in the heck was their problem?"

I shook my head, still a little winded. "I don't know. Did you get a good enough look at them to tell what they are?"

"No," Ben replied. He walked to the edge of the mouth of the cave and peered out at the sky. "It's some type of small bird, that's all I know."

"Helpful." I rolled my eyes. "Are they still flying overhead and throwing things?"

Ben looked up again. "Flying, yes. Throwing, no." He walked back into the cave and sat along the wall, pulling his shoes on.

I sat on the opposite side of the cave and did the same. "Maybe we go back out there and look again?"

"And get hit with tiny flying rocks?" Ben asked sarcastically. "No, thank you."

"Well, if those birds are the mythical beasts we need to talk to to unlock the oasis, we are going to have to go back out there at some point." I countered.

Ben looked at me, skeptical. I rolled my eyes and pushed myself off the cave wall to stand up. "Fine, I'll go, ya big baby."

I walked to the mouth of the cave and glanced out. The birds were flying in circles around in the sky. There were so many of them that the ever-present sun was almost blotted out and I couldn't see where one bird ended and another started. I stepped out of the cave, watching them.

Immediately, tiny little pebbles started falling out of the sky and bouncing off the ground very close to me.

"Hey!" I yelled up at the birds. "I just wanna talk to you. No need to attack me!"

Part of the swarm of birds broke out of the flocks' circling pattern and angled their flight downward. They came very close to the ground, then at the last second pulled out of their dive to fly mere feet above the oasis floor, dodging between trees in groups of two or three. More and more birds followed the first birds until the entire flock was circling around through the trees, out into the Wastes and then back towards the cave, where they flew back up above the treetops.

The birds circled and circled this way, flying down in between the trees, and then back up to the sky, then back down again. I watched as they performed this acrobatic flying, trying to determine what an individual bird looked like and why they were doing this.

I realized that the reason I thought I couldn't tell the difference between one bird and the next was because each bird had three heads. As the birds dipped into the trees and flew close to the ground, one of the three heads would try to pick up a small pebble in its beak. Sometimes, they missed and or didn't find a good enough pebble, and the bird would have to circle again for a second try. The next time it dipped down, a different head would pick up the pebble. The birds were circling and circling until each head had found and managed to pick up a pebble with its beak and then that bird would stay among the treetops as its flock mates attempted to gather pebbles.

Slowly, the number of birds flying near the ground became less and less with each circling. Finally, the last few bird heads had gathered pebbles in their beaks and all the birds stayed up above the trees. I waited, knowing they were planning their next assault. As the pebbles started raining down again, I ducked back into the cave.

"They have three heads on each bird," I informed Ben. "Ring any bells?"

Ben tilted his head, thinking, then shrugged. "Not really. There are a lot of mythical animals from a lot of different cultures throughout time. I don't know all of them."

"Well, these ones don't seem very friendly." I kept one ear out for the sound of the pebbles hitting the ground. As the plunks and patter of falling pebbles lessened, I tentatively stepped outside the cave once again.

"Hey," I called out to the birds as they started flying in the formation to collect pebbles again. "Hey! You're stuck, aren't you? I can help!"

The swirling flock of birds changed their pattern. They flew in figure eights above the trees for a few moments, then suddenly dived towards the ground in front of me. My experience with the Caladrius made me think that the entire flock of birds, which seemed to number in the thousands, was going to land directly in front of me. I held my ground, but inside, I was worried about that many obviously not happy birds coming to talk to me.

I was shocked when what landed was not a thousand birds but just one. The bird was small. It could have likely fit in the palm of my hand, with mostly brown feathers. It seemed to resemble a small eagle or other bird of prey, except its eyes were black rather than yellow. All six of them. The three heads seemed to move independently of each other, each one looking this way and that, barely missing bumping into each other with their small beaks. The beaks on the two outside heads still held pebbles, while the middle head didn't. It was this head that spoke.

"Why did you trap us here?" It asked angrily.

I crouched down, resting my arms on me knees to be more at the bird's height. "I didn't." I replied, "I was not the one who trapped you."

The three heads all looked at me as if they doubted my statement. The middle head responded, "If you didn't, who did? We were free to roam, going everywhere and traveling amongst all the people in the land. Then suddenly we weren't and could find our way to no one. Then, you appear, after ages of fighting to leave this cursed land, and you want us to believe that you were not the one who cursed it? Why should we trust you?"

This was new to me. At the other three oases, the mystical beasts seemed to immediately recognize who I was and why I was there. None of them doubted my motives, so I had not had to convince any of them that what I was telling them was true. They just trusted me.

"Ben?" I called out, keeping my eye on the bird. "Can you come here?"

Ben casually walked out of the cave and spotted the bird on the ground. "Oh hey, whose your friend?"

The middle head replied viciously. "She is no friend of ours."

Ben cocked one eyebrow at me in question, and I shrugged in response, forgetting he probably couldn't understand it.

"They seem to be under the impression that we trapped them in this oasis" I informed him.

"Not him," the bird replied, "just you. You have the taint of the Heka on you. Who else but the Heka would have the power to break the world like this? To lock up the ababil without our consent?"

Ah, I thought. The picture gets a little clearer. "It is not the Heka who is doing this, but the Heka who is the victim of this." I tried to explain. "What happened for you during the Floods?"

The middle head seemed as if it was going to get angry again, but the left head dropped its pebble and knocked its beak into the middle head to silence it. Then, it spoke. "What harm is there in telling her this? Either she is the cause and already knows, or she isn't and could possibly help. Either way, we have nothing to lose."

The middle head grumbled something quietly, which the left head ignored. The left head turned toward me and spoke again, "We flew and flew and found nowhere to land. When we were close to death from hunger and exhaustion, the land suddenly reappeared. We landed to eat and rest, then flew again. We wanted to go to Taikarlu to ask the gods what had happened, but could not leave this place. No matter how hard we tried, we could not pass the boundaries of this place. We could see sand everywhere, but could not fly over it. It was like the world had shrunk to just this place, like the human realms and the lands of the gods were gone."

I nodded my head, understanding. "That was the way it was for many mythical beasts."

The right head dropped its pebble and interrupted me. "We are not mythical! We are real and belong in the world of the humans, protecting them and hunting what would harm our people."

I lowered my eyes and put my hand over my heart. "I apologize. I never meant to insinuate that you weren't real. I only meant that, to the humans who have been isolated from beings such as yourself for so long, you have become a myth. They have forgotten you are real and that once upon a time you, and other animals like you, walked among them."

The left head spoke this time. "The humans have forgotten us?" It asked, forlorn.

"Unfortunately, yes." I told it. "It has been thousands of years that you have been trapped here. You and many others. Ben and I have already seen the unicorns, Caladrius and tanuki, and helped them regain their freedom. They were trapped, similar to you, in oases similar to this one. We believe there are at least six more places just like this yet to visit and help."

"Help with what?" The middle head asked, skeptically.

"And why does your companion not speak?" Asked the left head.

Oh, right. I looked up at Ben, who was watching me with a blank face. He hadn't understood any of this except my responses. He was probably very confused. I responded to the left head before filling Ben in.

"He doesn't understand you the way I do." I told them. "Like you said, I am tainted, as you put it, with the Heka. That lets me understand you. Ben isn't. I will have to translate what you say for him. Is it okay if I take a moment and fill him in on what we have already discussed? Then I can answer all of your questions, with Ben's help. He knows more about the gods than I do."

The three bird heads conferred with each other quietly for a minute, then the middle head nodded in agreement. I quickly filled in Ben.

Ben took over explaining everything to the bird, giving them an abbreviated version of the story. "The Heka is trapped, that is what caused the Floods. The Heka was moved into a cage, made up of the sands you saw that we gods called the Wastes, and the Floods went away. The Wastes separated everyone from each other. Now, the Heka is dying because It cannot survive in such a limited cage, and Anna and I are on a mission to unlock the oases that are scattered throughout the Wastes in an attempt to free the Heka. For some reason, Anna has the ability to connect with the Heka and find the oases to help out their inhabitants, free them. Each time she does, though, the Heka's cage gets smaller, but, we believe, also weaker."

"How do you go about unlocking the oasis?" The left head asked. I remembered now to keep translating all of this for Ben.

I answered this time. "Mostly, it seems, I just need to learn about the inhabitants of the oasis, be shown around their home and then let them know what happened. Then, they are able to leave their lands and connect with the other lands I have already freed. At least, that's what I think is happening."

The right head looked skeptical again, or as skeptical as a bird could look. "So, we tell you all about us and show you our home and magically you free us from this prison? How do we know if we give you all this information, you won't use it to harm us more?"

I didn't know how to react to this. The ababil was afraid we would harm them? More than they already were by being locked away? I looked over to Ben to see if he had any ideas. He looked as confused as I felt, so there was no help there.

I had been crouching, my elbows resting on my knees, as I talked to the ababil. My toes were going numb so, as I thought, I sat down, crossed my legs, and stretched my back. I slowly twisted my back, first to the right then to the left, bracing my hands on my knees to pull my stretch deeper, cracking my spine and releasing the tension from my sore muscles. Then I slowly tilted my head to each side, doing the same for my neck. All the while, I was thinking. How do I convince them we are here to help?

Finally, I just ask them. "Ben and I, we are here to help. How can I prove that to you?"

The three heads seemed to confer with each other. Each head made tiny squawks and chirps, and the middle one looked left then right again as if looking at each head as it voiced an opinion.

The left head finally spoke out loud. "We cannot think of any way you could prove yourself. I want to believe you, that you are here to help, but the others do not."

"The others?" I asked. "You mean your middle and right head?" I had already picked up on the idea that the three heads were independent of each other in thought but was hoping they would make it clearer exactly how independent they of each other they were.

The left head seemed to ruffle its feathers. Interestingly, only some of the body of the bird's feathers ruffled in a random pattern, dispelling the idea that each head controlled one specific segment of the bird body. "No. I mean all of us." He replied.

Ben sat down next to me, asking, "All of us? Who is all of us? Do you mean the whole flock?" Ben looked at the empty skies. "And where did the rest of the ababil birds go?"

"We are the flock." The left head responded. The middle head was swaying, as if it was trying to decide whether it would peck the left head to make it stop speaking. "We can be one bird or a legion, depending on what the humans need. We have become the many to protect a mosque, defeating an army of elephants, and also have been just a few, guarding travelers on a pilgrimage, or just one single bird as a companion to someone lonely. What is needed we can be."

An idea formed in my brain. "How do you know what the humans will need, protection-wise?" I asked.

"I do not know," the left head replied, "we just know. It is almost a feeling, like hearing a prayer, or a wish, and when that person's motivations are pure and true, we fulfil that need."

"So, if I were to wish for a protector for the ababil," Ben said, "for Anna to come to the ababil and be their source of freedom, you would be able to tell that I am being pure in my motivations, right? Then you would trust Anna?"

The left head turned to the other two, conferred with them again, then spoke. "We would trust you. If we could sense your purity of heart, then we would trust you. Her, I do not know. No one has ever prayed for the ababil to trust someone else before. But then again, the ababil has never had a reason to not trust someone's intentions before."

"Do you realize," Ben said slowly, "that you are trusting Anna right now?"

The three heads cocked to the side in unison, showing their confusion. So, Ben continued explaining. "Anna is translating what you are saying to me. She could be translating differently than what you are actually saying, but you are trusting, based on my answers, that she isn't. Why not?"

The three heads conferred again. This time, the right head spoke up. "We had not considered that she would be lying to you. But you are right, she could be as she translates. I do not think she is, though. Your answers seem to follow what we are saying properly."

"If you can trust her with that much, and believe in my honest intentions, then can't you believe she is here to help like she says she is?" Ben asked.

The three heads conferred again, this time taking much longer to respond. We watched as the left and right head seemed to argue with the middle head. The middle head snapped out with its beak against the other two, who deflected its attacks and continued chirping and squawking. Finally, the middle head hung down in a sign of defeat.

When it raised up again, the middle head sighed, asking, "What do you need from us to free us from this captivity?"

"I am not sure what more I need. For the others, I only had to learn about them and them learn about me to make them capable of leaving the oasis. I have learned about you and, unless you have a hidden land somewhere past the oasis, I know about your lands already." I answered. "Can you separate and have another ababil see if it can leave the oasis?"

As I watched, the three headed bird both stood still and flew off at the same time. They didn't separate like splitting cells, just seemed to suddenly be in two places at once. We waited quietly until the second ababil returned and combined with the one on the ground just as effortlessly as it had separated.

"We cannot." The middle head stated, almost haughtily.

"Hmm." I tried to think of what we had missed. The other mythical beasts had been freed so easily, I never considered what I was actually doing to free them. There must have been some action I, or they, had taken without being aware we were doing it, that was actually the key to unlocking the oasis. Something I, or they, had not done here.

I closed my eyes and tried to remember my actions at each of the other three oases. I heard Ben chuckle. "Shh," I told him. "I am thinking. What happened at the other oases that didn't happen here?"

Ben kept chuckling. "Here it is again. The question you have been wrangling with this whole time. What's your name?"

I opened my eyes and gave Ben a hard look. "What does that have to do with anything?" I complained. "I need to figure out how to help the ababil, not what my name should be."

Ben shook his head. "No. Not you. The ababil." He pointed to the bird. "They need to say your name. At every other oasis, someone said your full name. They haven't."

"We do not know her full name, only that you call her Anna." The middle head said.

When I translated this to Ben, he again shook his head. "Yes, you do. You know her name even if neither of us ever said it. The Caladrius and that elder tanuki knew it without you or me ever saying it." Ben turned to me. "I think they have to know, and say your name, Anna. When they trust you as they once trusted the Heka, then they know and can say your name. I think that is what is missing. I think that is the key."

The ababil looked from me to Ben and back again. The middle head cried out, frustrated. "How are we supposed to know her name without you telling us?"

Ben scootched closer to the bird. He put out his hands, palms up. "Do you trust me? Do you believe my intentions are pure and honorable?"

The two outer heads nodded agreeing, but the middle head did not.

Looking directly at the middle head, Ben asked, "Why do you not trust me? Can't you feel my motives? Isn't that what you said, you just know like it is a prayer or a wish? I am praying for you to trust me, to trust her. I am praying with everything I have to the Heka that you believe we want to help you and would never harm you."

Suddenly, half the bird jerked, like it was trying to move but was stuck. The left head turned to the middle head. "Let me move to him. I trust him."

The middle head shook itself violently. "We cannot trust anyone! The Heka is gone. It abandoned us. Praying to It is worthless. I cannot trust him."

Quietly, Ben repeated what we had told them. "It did not abandon you. The Heka was tricked and has been locked away. It wants to get free, to come back to all of Its creation and help them again, but It can't. The Heka has always been there for you, until It was taken away and couldn't. Now It needs you to be there for It."

Both the right and left heads looked at the middle head. After a moment, the bird hopped forward, fluttered upward and landed on one of Ben's outstretched hands. Ben lifted the bird gently so that all three heads could look at him, eye to eye.

"Anna and I are here to free you, so that you can help us free the Heka." He said calmly. "What is Anna's name?"

The bird ruffled all of its feathers. The three heads all bowed down and closed their eyes. Ben closed his as well. I watched them sit there, the three heads and Ben, eyes closed, with Ben sitting calmly and the birds ruffling its feathers over and over as if it was shuddering. Finally, after what felt like hours, but in reality was only a few minutes, all eight eyes opened.

"AnnaBella Cain." The middle head whispered. "AnnaBella Cain."

Then the ababil exploded. Where there had only been one bird in Ben's hand, thousands took flight. Soaring and gliding, swooping and diving, the flock swirled in the air. They reached the treetops and flew in every direction. With that many birds all flying at once, it should have looked chaotic, but instead it looked beautiful, like a dance.

For a while, Ben and I sat quietly, watching the ababil. Soon, though, we noticed that even though none of the ababil landed back on the ground, the skies were clearing. The ababil were flying away in every direction and not turning back. After a few more moments, there were no more ababil left that we could see. At the same time, I felt that now familiar pinch and burn as the Heka's cage grew smaller and more constricting.

The oasis had been unlocked, I knew, and they had left the air over the oasis, freed.

I turned to Ben. "My name." It was more of a question than a statement.

"You name." Ben repeated. "It has been the question and the answer all along."

I opened my mouth to say something more, but couldn't figure out how to put my thoughts into words. Why? Why my name? Why me? It all kept coming back to my name and my questions, but I still hadn't found the answer to either. Now Ben made it sound like my name was both, somehow.

Ben tilted his head to one side. "You know," he said ponderously, "the Caladrius said that you might be 'tainted' after helping to heal me, and the ababil said that you were 'tainted' by the Heka. It is interesting that they both used that word: tainted."

"Great." I replied sarcastically. "now, along with everything else, I have to worry about being tainted."

"At least we know how to actually unlock the oases?" Ben offered. "That's one answer."

"But why is that how the oases are unlock?" I asked him. "Why did Malachi make my name, which by the way was not made my name until thousands of years after he hid the Heka, how we unlock Its cage?"

Ben didn't say anything. He stood up, brushed off the seat of his shorts, and slowly walked over to the pond. Kneeling at the side of the water, he used his hands to scoop up some water and drank. After he was satiated, he stood up again, dried his hands by running them through his hair, and looked at me.

"I don't think he did." Ben finally answered me. "Or, at least he didn't do it intentionally. I think… I think there is something going on here that Malachi never intended to happen at all."

"What is going on here, then?" I asked, still sitting.

Ben shook his head, and walked over to me. He offered me his hand and I grasped it, using his strength to help me stand. Once I was standing, Ben didn't let go of my hand. He kept holding it, rubbing his thumb in small circles caressingly. He looked into my eyes. "I have an idea, but I don't want to say it. I think, if I am right, that this is something you have to figure out on your own. Way back when we were in the Joint Commission room, you said you thought this was something you had to do alone, meaning this journey to unlock the oases. I think you were right about needing to do something alone, but were wrong about what it was. You have to figure out what your name is and why it matters, why it is the key, alone."

Ben stopped speaking for a moment. He watched me digest what he was saying, still staring into my eyes. For a moment, I felt his emotions change. He had been feeling very serious, a special sort of seriousness that made him seem even more godlike to me. That seriousness was replaced with some other feeling I couldn't quite figure out.

Ben's eyes were a golden color. This close, though, I could see small flecks of green and black in his irises. As I watched, trying to figure out what this new feeling he had was, Ben's pupils dilated. He sighed, and broke eye contact with me and dropped my hand. Suddenly the mysterious feeling was gone, shrouded as if Ben was forcibly pushing it down, and his seriousness returned.

"I think," Ben started again, "I think that this thing with your name is the most important part of everything we are doing. And I can't help you with it."

I stood still, watching Ben slowly move away from me, feeling bereft. I had heard what Ben said but didn't really process it. I hadn't wanted him to let go of my hand. I hadn't wanted him to look away. I shuddered a breath and convinced myself to let it go. Move on.

We needed to keep going and find the six other mythical beasts oases, I reminded myself.

Chapter Five

Ben and AnnaBella did not speak to each other any further as they left the ababil oasis. AnnaBella picked a direction, still a south-easternly one. The pair were moving around Taikarlu in a circular pattern. They were hoping that if they completed the full circle around Taikarlu, they would have reached all the oases by the time they ended up back with the unicorns. What they would have to do after that, they weren't sure and didn't discuss.

Both Ben and AnnaBella walked while deep in thought. AnnaBella tried not to feel worried about the things she could not answer, but her mind raced with thoughts about them anyway. Her name, she knew, was the biggest question she had. Names are important, she reasoned in her mind. A name encapsulates everything about a person, the things known and the things unknown.

My name is who I am, she thought. *It has always been AnnaBella Cain. Anna with Mom and Bella with Dad, and everyone else just called me one, the other, or both depending on my relationship with them. Now my name is something else, something I don't know but apparently everyone else has guessed. How can my name mean 'me' if I don't know it.*

Ben did not think about AnnaBella's name. Instead, he thought about her hands, her face, her smile. He thought about how little she smiled and how much he wished he could help her smile more.

The two continued walking through the Wastes, not paying attention to where they were or where they were going. Neither of them noticed when the haze that signaled the edge of the cage appeared on the horizon.

My thoughts had distracted me for so long that I didn't realize how far Ben and I had walked until I felt a greasy uneasiness envelope me. I stopped in my tracks, realizing that I had walked right into the edge of the Heka's cage without even noticing.

Ben was a few steps behind me. I turned back toward him, calling out his name. "Ben! Stop!" I tried to run out of the haze toward him but wasn't fast enough.

Ben had been swinging his arms lazily as he walked, his eyes downward, looking at the sand. He had been following my footprints. His right hand swung forward into the haze as he looked up at me.

It happened so quickly, neither Ben nor I realized it had happened at first. As I pushed my feet against the shifting sand, trying to move toward him inch by inch, I watched his face.

At first, he looked just how you would expect someone to when they had been deep in thought and you disturbed their reverie. Then, he was surprised. By the time I had forced my feet to find traction and was actually able to run to his side, the surprise had turned to absolute agony.

Ben screamed and pulled his right hand to his chest, cradling it with his left hand. Blood welled from between his fingers and dripped onto the sand. The blood pooled there momentarily and then seeped down in the moisture-deprived ground, leaving only a dark stain.

I reached Ben's side right as he fell to his knees, still screaming. Dropping beside him, I pulled on his left hand.

"Show me!" I demanded. "Let me see. How bad is it?"

Ben moved his left hand so I could see the injured right one. His entire body was trembling as he wheezed and small whimpers of pain escaped from him. I took his right hand into mine. The pinky finger was completely gone.

I grabbed his right wrist and shoved his arm as far above his head as I could get him to stretch. "Keep it above your heart!" I said, panicking. Then I bent over in the sand, brushing the desert floor, pushing sand one way and another. "Where is it? Where's the finger? We can reattach it…"

"Anna," Ben panted, pulling his arm down again.

I looked at him and grabbed his arm, thrusting it into the air again. "No, keep it up so you don't bleed to death!" I looked back at the sand, intent on finding his amputated finger.

"Anna," Ben said again, his voice cracking from the pain.

Finally, I looked at him. He had pulled his right arm down to his chest and was cradling it with his left again.

"Not. Human." Ben wheezed.

This stopped me. I had forgotten that Ben is not human. He wasn't in a human body. Ben was a spirit of a god. I sat down fully in the sand next to him, unsure how to help an injured spirit of a god. Last time this happened, I had just run towards the next oasis, and the Caladrius had helped us. But I looked out at the horizon and the next oasis wasn't even on the horizon yet. The area of haze around the oasis was bigger than it had been before. There was no way I could drag him bleeding and in pain to the safety of that place this time, especially since I didn't know if there would be help there like there just happened to be before.

This meant I had to come up with a way to help Ben on my own, and I had no idea what to do. How was he even bleeding? Could he bleed out and die, or would it be something else for him? He was obviously in pain, so something was happening, just like with his leg before. But what would happen because of the injury, I suddenly didn't know.

Ben spoke again, still strained. "Heal me."

"How?" I asked him. I was panicking and I could feel Ben's pain, but somehow, I didn't feel panic from him, only a sense of urgency.

Ben tried to slow his panting breath, but failed. "Heka," was all he said.

Use my Heka, I assumed he meant. Gingerly, I took his left hand from his right and pulled his right hand into both of mine and placed it on my lap. As I moved the injured hand, Ben grimaced and bit his lip to not cry out in pain. He was pale and sweating. I looked at his hand in my lap. The spot where the pinky finger should have been was bleeding, the blood staining my clothes and skin, and the edges of the tattered skin were just starting to show a tinge of green from the god-poison.

There was no time for me to try and figure out how the body mechanics of a spirit being worked right now. Right now, I had to fix him and just hope I did it right. I took the injured hand into both of mine again, trying to be careful and not cause Ben more pain. I wrapped my fingers around his hand tightly and closed my eyes. Taking a steadying breath, and pushing down the panic, I felt for my Heka and pushed It into his hand with everything I had. The cut felt dirty, greasy like the haze did. In my mind, I looked for all of the greasiness and wiped it away.

Ben audibly sucked air through his teeth. I knew I was hurting him more, feeling that pain both through our connection and through my Heka, but I has no choice but to continue. Once I could feel no more of the greasiness, I bent all of my will on healing him. I had no idea what to actually do, so I just held his hand as tightly as I could and pushed at it with my Heka, wanting above anything else in the world for it to not be hurt anymore.

Ben let out a high-pitched scream and then fainted, falling to the sand. I took my hands away from his and looked at the injury. The finger was still missing, but the skin had pulled itself up around the remaining stump and knitted itself together. He was no longer bleeding and there was no green tinge to the skin anymore.

Gently, I set down Ben's hand, sat down and pulled his head into my lap. He was still unconscious. I brushed sand from his forehead, where it had stuck to his sweaty skin. Slowly, his color returned to normal and his eyes opened.

"Hey." I said quietly.

"Hey." Ben replied, his voice hoarse.

"Does it still hurt?" I asked.

Ben thought for a moment. I saw the fingers on his right hand curl into a fist and then relax.

"Not hurt," he answered me, "just sore." Slowly, Ben shifted to sit up.

"I couldn't," I started to say, "your finger. I didn't. It's, um, it's gone." I stammered.

Ben looked down at his hand. "Yeah," he replied.

I looked at the sand. "I'm sorry I didn't fix it right."

Ben sighed. "How did you not fix it right?"

I looked back up at him, then back to the sand. "I mean, your finger is gone. I didn't fix it."

Ben chuckled. "Oh yeah, you just stopped me from bleeding to death, but couldn't reattach a finger you couldn't find. You think I'm gonna, what? Be angry about it? Anna, don't be so hard on yourself. You literally have magically healed someone, what? Two times now? Are you supposed to be perfect after only having done it once before this?"

"But." I started to say. I looked at Ben, and, even though he was obviously still a little pale and shaky, his eyes were glinting as he smiled. He was laughing at me. I had been freaking out and now he was laughing at me. Angrily, I told him, "Don't laugh. I had no idea what I was doing and was scared I would actually make things worse! And now, you are missing a finger. A god is missing a finger!" I threw my hands up in the air in frustration. "How am I to know what kind of havoc that will cause?"

Ben took both my hands and put them in his lap, holding them with his one good hand. "Anna, it probably will cause a few interesting new stories among my worshippers when they find out about it. That's all." I could not understand this calmness he felt, when everything felt so crazy to me.

I pulled my hands out of his, and dug them into the sand. "Well, how was I supposed to know that? I couldn't even figure out if you were able to bleed to death as a spirit god thing." I picked up handfuls of sand and threw them down harshly. "I hate knowing nothing about the stuff everyone else knows."

"Anna." Ben replied kindly. When I wouldn't look at him, he grabbed my chin and pulled my face up. When I looked him in the eye, he said my name again, softer. "Anna, you do know things. You know things no one else knows at all. You know the Heka, and It gives you everything you need to know. You knew how to heal me, didn't you?"

"No," I told Ben. "I didn't. I just guessed and threw all my Heka at it, hoping it would work."

"No, you didn't." Ben countered. "You didn't throw your Heka at it, but The Heka at it."

I eyed Ben suspiciously. "What's the difference?"

"The difference," Ben said, "was that, had you just used your Heka, nothing would have happened. I am not your worshipper and you are not my creator. You cannot perform miracles on me. Gods worship the Heka the same way humans worship a god. I am the Heka's worshipper and the Heka is my creator. Only the Heka can perform a miracle on a god."

"I don't understand what you are saying, Ben." I told him.

Ben sighed. "Okay, let me try to explain this. You know that gods can do miracles for their worshippers, right? But can't do miracles for other gods' worshippers."

"Right." I agreed. "Before the Heka went missing, they could but not anymore."

Ben continued. "No. that's where you misunderstand. At the beginning of everything, gods could only do miracles and stuff for their own worshippers. They could show their power to other gods' worshippers and those that hadn't chosen a god, but they could not directly hurt or help other gods' people. After the Heka disappeared, gods were even more limited. They could only do anything at all, any sign of power or miracle or whatever, to their own worshippers or the undecided that they were trying to get to worship them."

I nodded. "Makes sense."

"Right." Ben said. "Now, the gods worship the Heka the same way the humans worship a god. Before and after the Chaos, War, Floods, all of that. Some have always worshipped It and still do. Some gods worshipped before that stuff happened and don't anymore, becoming like the human undecided because of the Heka being missing and all that. Some gods rebelled and caused the Chaos and whatever.

"Anyway, for the gods, it is the same as for the humans. If you worship the Heka, the Heka could do miracles for you. It wasn't very often a god needed a miracle or something, because we are gods and it is really hard for us to get hurt and impossible to get sick and stuff. But if something happened, and a god needed a miracle, the Heka could do it. Other gods couldn't do a miracle for the god in need because that god who needed it wasn't their worshipper. So, you cannot have done a miracle and fixed my hand. My hand shouldn't have been able to be hurt that badly in the first place, but that, as we are discovering, is a different issue. It was, and I would have died."

"Try not to think about the hows and whys of a god that is only a spirit getting injured and bleeding in a way that could have killed me, because that doesn't make sense to me either. We both have to just accept that whatever Malachi did does not fall into the realm of normal for god stuff. I mean, he trapped the Heka. None of this is anywhere near 'normal.' But you did heal my hand. I am not your worshipper and you healed my hand. So, there are only two possible ways this happened. One: you didn't heal me, but tapped into the Heka and allowed It to heal me through you. Or, two…" Ben let his voice trail off.

"Or two?" I pushed.

Ben shook his head again. "I don't know or two." He lied. I know he lied. "I don't remember or two."

I debated for a moment whether to push more, make him say what he didn't want to, and decided against it. The feelings Ben had now told me that even if I did push the issue, he would deny knowing anything more. He was warring with something in his own mind, whether or not to tell me, whether or not something was true. I understood how confusing that could be, especially when you weren't alone in your own head, as we weren't. So, I let him be. He would either figure stuff out and tell me, or not. And if he chose not, I would probably figure it out eventually anyway since it is really hard to hide things from someone who always knows what you are feeling.

So, I changed the conversation. "We need to find a better way." I told him.

Distracted with his own thoughts, Ben asked, "A better way for what?"

"For this," I waved a hand at him. "If we are both going to be distracted and trying really hard to think our thoughts privately, while also being able to know what each other is feeling, we have to find a better way to protect you against the haze that will try to kill you if we

110

are just the least little bit not paying attention. Plus, I have a feeling the haze is getting bigger the more oases we unlock. Soon, we may leave one oasis and directly enter the haze and only leave it when we get to the next one."

Ben nodded, agreeing. "Well, then, what do we do? The only thing we know of that stops the edges of the Heka's cage from hurting me is making me seem filled with the infiniteness of love, our supposed love for each other. How do we do that without having to think about it all the time?"

I thought for a moment. Most humans demonstrated their absolute love for each other by getting married. Not that getting married definitely meant that their love was real or infinite, but people whose love was real and infinite definitely usually got married, as long as it was legal for them to. I knew that there was absolutely no way I was marrying Ben just to keep him safe from the haze, but maybe there was some part of a marriage ceremony, or a marriage itself, that we could borrow to use as a talisman for him.

"You have an idea?" Ben asked. "I can kinda feel that you do, but it seems sort of watered down."

"Yeah," I replied slowly. "I kind of do, maybe. We need to make you a talisman that stands for our love. Like, how two humans give each other rings when they get married and that represents their love for each other." I explained, but then added in a rush, "But, without the getting married part."

"Hmm." Ben answered. "A talisman? What could we use as a talisman?"

I felt something pushing at the back of my mind. It was an idea but I didn't think it was my idea. I tried to relax and let it come to me, the way thoughts from the Heka usually did, but it was hard. So much had happened so quickly and I still was trying to settle from the panic of Ben being injured and healing, never mind finding a solution to this newest problem.

As Ben and I thought, I kept finding myself distracted. I would try to think of a solution, or allow the Heka to feed me one, but would end up staring at Ben's neck above his tank top. The tank top itself was damp with dark patches where his hand had bled on it, but that wasn't what was drawing my eye. More specifically, it was the hollow of his throat that was visible over the collar of his tank top. No matter how many times I shook my head and looked away, I kept finding my gaze drawn back to him.

Finally, I gave up fighting it and just watched him. Most of the time, with humans, you would notice the hollow of their throat twitch

111

with their heartbeat and breathing, but Ben's was utterly still. There was something about that spot. I kept staring, hoping whatever it was would become clear.

Eventually, I realized that Ben was watching me watch him. My cheeks grew hot as I blushed. I could feel his amusement at my blushing as well as all the other feeling he felt watching me. Among the expected ones was a curiosity.

"What are you curious about?" I asked him, desperately wishing he would look away from me.

"I am curious," Ben explained, "because I have no idea what you are feeling."

"You can't feel my feelings anymore?" I said, hoping that maybe whatever had caused this connection between us was finally fading.

"No, I can." He replied, dashing my hopes. "You are very embarrassed right now and I would know that even if you weren't completely red to your ears. But I couldn't tell what you were feeling while you stared at my neck. It was like you were not the one staring at me. Your mind was one place and your eyes were another."

"Oh," I said, trying to not blush harder at being teased about blushing.

"So, what were you thinking?" Ben asked again.

Taking a deep breath to try to stop being embarrassed and red, I told him. "I wasn't, well kind of. I was trying to think of a way to make a talisman for you, but I kept getting distracted. Like there was something I should have known, or some idea I was having, but I couldn't make it actually form. It has something to do with your neck though. That's all I know."

"Do you think maybe it is the Heka having an idea instead of you?" Ben asked.

I nodded. "That's what I thought, but the more I tried to relax and let It tell me the idea, the more I seemed to just space out looking at you."

"No," Ben said. "You were not spacing out. You were feeling a whole bunch of stuff, but none of it was spacing out."

I looked at Ben quizzically. Now, he knows my feelings better than I do? "So, if I wasn't spacing out, what was I feeling, Ben?" I asked him, pretending to be affronted.

Ben just raised his eyebrows at me and smiled. Then he blushed a little. Oh, yeah. That. The feeling both of us kept having, didn't want to think about having, but had to because those feelings were the only way to protect Ben from the haze. I rolled my eyes. Why couldn't I have just had a normal crush on a guy like other seventeen-year-olds?

Oh yeah, because some human decided I get to be a god. Well, that and a whole other bunch of nonsense happening that made everything in my life way more complicated.

Ben took my hand. Initially, he had reached out to take my hand with his right hand. At the last moment, though, he switched and used his left. He felt embarrassed and a little nervous when he made the switch.

"Is your right hand still bothering you?" I asked him.

"No," he replied looking away.

"Then why did you…" I started to ask, but I felt him suddenly feeling very self-conscious, like he suddenly didn't feel good enough anymore. I reached out my free hand to take his injured one, and clasped it firmly. Then, I removed my other hand from his hold and touched a burn mark on his left arm. "You know, none of these scars make you less than in any way to me, right?"

Ben looked back at me. He was unsure if he could believe me.

"Hey," I told him softly, "you weren't actually in the Trials Arena with me, so you don't know what we did there. I do, though, and I am pretty sure it is close to the truth of how things were in the myth that your people believe. You were amazing and brave and smart and cunning; all the things I have seen you be when we were supposedly human and all the things you have been walking through the Wastes with me. The burns, and your hand, they are marks of that bravery. I like them and wouldn't want you to change."

Ben took a deep breath and let it out shakily. He looked down and shook his head, smiling almost sarcastically. I knew he didn't believe me. Still holding his hand and touching the scar on his arm, I leaned over and kissed him. Ben was surprised at first, I knew, but then I felt him relax and kissed me back.

As we ended the kiss and I leaned back away from him, I could still feel his lips on mine. I touched my lips, tracing that feeling, and an idea formed. It was definitely not mine, but I let it form anyway.

"I have an idea," I told Ben, "or really, the Heka has an idea."

Ben nodded. "Okay, whatever it is, let's try it."

I took my hands away from Ben and sat up straight. Ben copied my actions. I closed my eyes and focused all of my Heka on how I felt about Ben. I tried not to shy away from my feelings, even though I knew Ben could feel me feeling them. It made it difficult to focus on how much I liked him, how beautiful I thought he was and how nice it was to kiss him, but I forced myself to not be embarrassed or suppress anything.

Eventually, my feelings for Ben became intermingled with my

feelings of the Heka. I opened my eyes and leaned over, kissing Ben on the hollow of his neck. On the exact spot my eyes had been drawn to. As I kissed him, I pushed all of those feelings, both the ones for Ben and my Heka, into that spot.

Ben hissed slightly. I drew back from him and looked where I had kissed. There was a small red spot on his skin. It faded quickly. I looked at Ben's face.

"Did you burn me with your lips?" he asked.

"No." I told him. "It was red, but it faded. I think that I marked you. I don't know. It was an idea from the Heka. Mark you with my feelings and the Heka mixed. Like a talisman, but just part of you now."

"So, now what?" Ben asked. "Am I just, what, branded by your Heka with the infinity that is love and can walk through the haze, right next to the Heka's cage, and nothing will happen?" He sounded incredulous. "It's that simple?"

I shrugged. "Maybe. I don't know. Like I said, it wasn't my idea."

Ben stood and held his hands out wide. "Well, I guess if it was the Heka's idea, we should just go ahead and try it. What's the worst that happens? I lose another finger and you heal me again, right?"

I could tell Ben was not as mad or disbelieving as he sounded. He was actually scared. Scared that it wouldn't work or that it would, I couldn't tell. Either way, it didn't mean his tone hurt me any less. Ben felt my hurt, I was sure of it, because he suddenly felt remorseful.

"Ugh." Ben exclaimed, running his hands through his hair. He had messed up the ponytail ages ago, jumping in and out of the pond at different oases and with all the running and fainting and whatever. But this final pulling at it made the hair tie come loose completely. It fell into the sand.

I reached over and picked up the hair tie. Dusting it off, I stood and pulled on Ben's shoulder to make him turn around. With his back to me, I used my fingers as combs and pulled his hair neatly together and put the hair tie in it, tighter this time to his neck.

As I fixed his hair, I talked. "You know, I've said this to you and you've said this to me a bunch of times before, but I think we both forget it. This isn't easy, what we are doing. I mean, how could it be? You keep getting hurt. I have a million questions I can't answer. The Heka is freaking out and dying. And through all of this, we can't even be alone inside our own heads. It's enough to drive anyone nuts.

"Add in a little teenage romance, and we are gonna blow our stacks occasionally, right? It's just bound to happen. I mean, if the creator of everything, everywhere gets to lose Its cool once in a while, why should we think we have to stay calm all the time?"

I patted Ben's back to let him know I had finished straightening his hair and he turned back around to face me. As he looked at me, I kept talking. "I know you were more scared than upset, and I know you are sorry you snapped. I forgive you. But only as long as you promise that the next time I go off the handle a little, you will forgive me again too."

Ben smiled slightly, and looked up at the sky, sighing. He looked back at me, saying, "Of course, I will. And you will forgive me, then I will forgive you, and we will both forgive the Heka."

I chuckled, happy to see him being silly again. "Now, do you want to try the Heka's idea? Since I already branded you and everything?"

Ben nodded his agreement. "As long as this time I know it is coming, I think maybe I could pull back fast enough so the cage won't hurt me too badly." I felt him add the "I hope" part even though he didn't say it out loud.

I walked to the edge of the haze and waited. Ben came and stood next to me, a bundle of nerves. The muscles in his jaw were twitching from how tense he was. Slowly, he reached out his right hand to cross the threshold into the haze.

Nothing happened. I looked from Ben's hand to his face. He gave no sign, internally or externally, of feeling pain. Ben crept forward a step, allowing his arm to enter the haze. Still, nothing happened. He kept creeping forward until, finally, his whole body was inside the haze.

"Anything?" I asked.

Ben shook his head. "It feels weird. Like oily. Like maybe I used too much lotion and my skin is sticky with it. But it doesn't hurt and no appendages are falling off."

"Well, that is definitely a good start." I breathed a sigh of relief. "I can't see the next oasis, so I think we still have a ways to go."

Ben nodded. "Let's get going, then."

The two of us started walking again. We chatted, mostly to not worry about how long the talisman would work and what we would do if it stopped working suddenly. We talked about nothing in particular, just idle chatter like we used to during lunch at school. The only difference this time was some of that idle chatter included things like the different gem patters on the unicorn horns we had seen and whether or not the ababil could stay separated for a long time and what happens when all the birds eat and then come back together as one. Would they feel bloated or do they only each eat a little so that they aren't overfull?

We walked for long enough that I started to feel tired and wanted to take a break. Before I could tell Ben, I noticed that the ground seemed to be sloping upward rather than continuing to be flat. The further we went, the more the ground sloped upward, getting firmer, and the more shoots of grass I could see poking up between the sand.

Before long, the upward slope became too difficult to walk normally. Ben and I seemed to be bending over and used our hands more often than not to brace ourselves. Luckily, the ground had become somewhat completely solid by this time and we were not having a problem with the sand sliding around under our feet. Eventually, we could see the top of what was shaping up to be a rather tall hill. We crested the top and looked down over the fields below.

The tall hill sloped down into other, smaller gently rolling hills, covered with grass and heather, that ended in a field of tall, swaying grass dotted with yellow and white flowers. To one side of the open field was a barn that used to be green. Further through the field was a silver metal building.

"I know this place," I said. "It's Area One, where Dad took me for the Trial Arenas. How did we end up here?"

Ben stood with his hands on his hips, surveying the field below. "I told you, all the parts of Taikarlu used to be connected until the floods and the Wastes. We just unlocked enough of the Wastes to reach Area One."

"Do you think we need to do something to unlock this place?" I asked. "Would there be a mythical beast here for us to help?"

Ben shook his head. "No. Probably just someplace to pass through on our journey." He started walking and I followed him.

I spent most of our time walking down the hill looking at the barn. It seemed like so long ago that Dad first brought me here. Yet, it really hadn't been. He brought me here in June, and last I knew a human calendar date, it was sometime in November. Only six months ago in real time, assuming Ben and I hadn't been going through the Wastes for longer than a few days, or weeks at the most.

We made it down the hills and walked through the field. The insects were buzzing around, much like they were the first time I was here. We passed the bronze plaque that described the place, the one I had read the first time. I glanced at it briefly as we walked by, but didn't look too long. I knew that, inside the barn that housed the Trials Arena, there was another plaque. That one had the rule that no humans were allowed to use the Trials, the rule that had started so much of this trouble. That plaque held the key piece to my father's lie, to my punishment, and to how that last six months were also a hundred years.

I picked up my pace, wanting to leave this beautiful place with bad memories behind. As we passed the metal building, I overtook

Ben. I kept walking, telling myself not to look back at the Trials Arena. I wasn't mad at Dad anymore for his lie, I reminded myself. It was the Heka's fault, not his, and the Heka had a pretty good reason for what It did. I almost believed me.

Area One faded from the landscape the way it arrived. The grass got shorter and was only visible in clumps, while the ground softened and became grittier. Eventually, there was no more grass at all and the ground was back to shifting sand.

I let myself look back then. The buildings were just dots on the horizon and Ben, right behind me, had a look of concern.

"You okay?" Ben asked.

"Yeah." I told him, turning back around to see where I was going rather than where I had come from. "Just some not so great memories of that place."

"Okay," he said, almost unsure. "I'm here if you want to talk."

I waved him off and then pointed to the horizon. The next oasis finally came into view on the horizon. Ben and I both picked up the pace, moving quickly to it.

As we walked into the oasis, everything seemed exactly the same as it had in the last four. In the center was the deep pond formed by water flowing from somewhere inside the cave to the left. Ben and I wandered around the oasis, walking through the trees, in and out of the cave, and to the distant edges of the larger tree growth, before meeting back up by the pond.

"This oasis seems smaller than the other ones." Ben said.

I nodded in agreement. The area where the oasis stood was smaller, with its grove of trees and detritus on the ground sparser here than they had been in other places. "I wonder if that has something to do with the mythical beast that resides here."

"Well, let's see." Ben rambled. "We have seen two types of birds, with their home in the sky, and the unicorns that are horse-like and live on rolling hills and pastures, and one small creature that lives in cities and the woods. We haven't seen anything aquatic or anything that thrives in the cold. Mythical beasts can live in any type of area humans live in, so I am guessing eventually we will see places like that."

"Well, I don't see any evidence of habitation in this oasis at all." I told him. "Maybe I don't see it because this animal is aquatic and is in the pond? It wouldn't care about the whole oasis's size then, just the size of the pond."

Ben shook his head. "No," he countered, "if that was the case, I would assume the pond would be much bigger than it normally is, not just the oasis smaller."

I slipped off my shoes and socks and walked to the edge of the pond. "I'm going to check it out anyway." I told Ben, then dipped into the water. I took a giant breath and dived under the water, keeping my eyes open.

As I looked around, all I saw were the normal tiny fish that had been in every pond at every oasis. Small and very curious, but not afraid of humans, the tiny silver-streaked fish swam right up to me, inspecting me and nibbling gently at my clothes and skin. I swam around, looking for signs of any other animals, but by the time I needed to come up for air, I hadn't seen any.

I climbed out of the pond and put my socks and shoes back on. I told Ben what I found, or really, didn't find.

He paced a few steps with his hands on his hips and grunted. "Didn't think so."

"What if it is hiding, the way the unicorns did at first?" I posed.

Ben grunted again. "Then we wait, I guess. The unicorns eventually showed themselves to us. Whoever this is will too."

"You're right." I said. "I think I am going to go rustle up something to eat." I walked away from Ben, towards the outer reaches of the oasis where the blueberry shrubs had been in the other lands. I found the bushes and picked the fruit, eating some and saving some to bring back to the pond with me.

As I searched for the best blueberries, I heard a faint noise behind me. I turned and looked out over the Wastes, but didn't see anything. I chalked it up to an overstressed imagination and went back to eating.

The noise happened again, and this time I knew it wasn't my imagination. I didn't turn around, but did stop picking the blueberries. I kept listening and resisted the urge to look over my shoulder into the desert.

There it was, the noise a third time. Slowly, I turned around and caught sight of something dipping just below the sand. As casually as I could make myself, I walked back to the pond.

"Hey Ben," I said, still feigning casualness. He would read on my emotions that I was not casual. I did not want whatever was in the sand to know it had been spotted yet, though. "Can you come help me with the blueberries?"

Ben had been kneeling down, examining what looked to me like a pile of dirt on the ground. He looked up at me, confusion on his face. I tried to impress on him with my face and my emotions to stay cool, act like it was nothing. Ben cocked one eyebrow up, and, in response, I tilted my head back the way I had come from and raised both my eyebrows.

Understanding finally registered with Ben and he stood up. "Yeah, sure, Anna. Coming."

The two of us slowly walked back to the blueberry bushes. Once there, I turned my back to the Wastes and pretended to pick at the bushes. Ben copies my movements,

"There is something moving in the Wastes." I whispered. "Every time I look, it vanishes below the sand. But I can hear it moving and caught just a glimpse of it."

Ben walked nonchalantly around to the other side of the bush, pretending to be picking berries from that side. He kept his head down, but raised his eyes to look over the bush and past me into the desert. "A desert-dweller. Hmm." He murmured.

We stood there, being as silent as we could, pretending to be engrossed in picking berries for some time. I heard the sound again, a kind of slippery sound, as if silk was rubbing against sandpaper.

"There!" Ben whispered harshly. "I saw it. Some sort of snake, but it was moving strangely. It came out of the sand for only a moment, then ducked below it again."

"Could you tell what it was, even a guess?" I asked.

Ben shook his head once, moving only slightly. "No. The movement seems familiar, the interesting way it slithered on the sand, but I can't place where from."

I groaned silently. The waiting was infuriating. Finally, I gave up and turned toward the sand. Standing at the edge of the oasis, as close to the shifting sands as I could get without actually leaving the firmer ground, I knelt down and tapped the sand.

"Hello?" I said loudly but calmly. "Who is there? We won't bite, you can come out."

The sand shifted in way the seemed purposeful. Two heads, very close to one another popped out of the sand.

"You don't bite," one of the heads spoke.

"But we just might," said the other head.

Quickly, I stood up and took a step back towards the oasis. Ben came up next to me.

"What did they say?" He asked, still whispering.

I spoke clearly so the heads could hear me. "They threatened to bite me." I told Ben. "Well, not really threatened but more like teased that they could."

Ben spoke loudly now. "We are not here to do any harm, and we would hope that you wouldn't do any harm to us. Come out of the sand so we can have a proper conversation." Quietly, to me, he continued. "We haven't encountered a carnivore yet. These might eat

119

meat and see us as prey."

I nodded curtly. I hadn't thought about the fact that some of the mythical animals might eat humans, or meat in general. I should have though. I met several such animals in the Trials Arena. My mind thought back to the possessed carnivore horses that the king in one of the tests had owned and I shivered. I hoped that we wouldn't have to meet up with anything that dangerous.

The two heads slithered out of the sand awkwardly. As their body become free of the sand, their erratic movements made more sense. They were one snake with one body and two heads. Not like the type I had helped Ben fight off in the Trials Arena, with multiple heads on the top of one body. Instead, there was one body with a head at either end and neither end was the tail. They moved as if the head at one end controlled half the body and the head at the other end controlled the other half, and they didn't always agree on where to go.

Ben whispered in my ear again. "I know these. They are called amphisbaena. They eat ants mostly, hence their sometimes being called 'mother of ants,' but they are also scavengers, eating carrion. In the Greek myths, they were born out of blood that dripped from Medusa's head after Perseus defeated her. They followed armies and would eat the fallen soldiers. They are one of the mythical reasons why soldiers don't like to leave fallen comrades behind after a battle."

I listened to Ben while I watched the snake come closer to the oasis. It stopped just a few steps away from the boundary between the oasis and the Wastes. Without looking away from the snake, I asked Ben, "How do we proceed then? Do you think they would actually bite us if they eat carrion or ants? Do they have poison or anything?"

Out of the corner of my eye, I saw Ben shake his head slightly. "Whether they are poisonous or not is up to interpretation. Some myths say yes, some no. So, no clue if these ones are or not. Pretty sure they won't actually bite, but I wouldn't put too much stock in that. The tales tell of their uses, in medicine and whatnot, but not about how easy they are to capture or kill." I could feel Ben felt irritated. He hid it when he talked, but it was there in the background of his feelings.

Great. I bent down again, perching myself on my toes. I wanted to appear inviting and friendly but also be able to move quickly if the amphisbaena decided to not play nice.

"Hello," I repeated. "I am Anna and this is Ben. Just so you know, I can hear and understand you but Ben can't. I will have to translate for him what you say. Is that okay with you?"

The two heads looked at each other, then both said, "That is fine by us, although what you would need to talk to us about, we don't know."

I gave the amphisbaena a quick rundown of what we knew, Malachi's actions, the Heka being trapped and creating the Wastes, and our desire to free It. "We have already freed the unicorns, Caladrius, tanuki and ababil. Would you like to tell us a little about yourselves and what happened for you after the Flood?"

The amphisbaena hissed. The left head spoke first. "The Flood was an awful time."

"Too wet, too wet." Intoned the right head.

"This desert is wonderful now though." Said the left head.

"Why would we want to be freed from it?" Asked the right.

Ben and I looked at each other. "You like the Wastes?" Ben asked, surprised.

"Yes," both heads hissed.

"The desert is warm," said the right head.

"The sand is soft," said the left.

"Don't you feel, well, limited?" I asked the amphisbaena. "You used to follow human armies? Don't you miss that?"

The two heads looked at each other. "No," they hissed together.

"Are you sure?" Ben asked. "Maybe the other amphisbaenas do and would want to be freed. Are there more of you? Can you ask them?" He said all of this slightly sharper than I would have expected, the irritation he felt bleeding into his words, even though there was no reason for him to be irritated that I could tell.

"Yes," said the right head.

"No," said the left.

I shook my head. "Wait. Which of you are answering which question?"

The right head spoke again. "Yes, there are more of us."

Then the left spoke. "No, we will not ask them if they feel differently."

"Why not?" I asked.

"Because they don't." both heads stated.

The right head continued. "We are fine in the desert."

"There are plenty of ants in the oasis to eat," said the left.

"We can hide in the sand," said the right.

"And we keep company only with ourselves, not each other," said the left.

"Solitary animals," I told Ben. "Well, as solitary as something with two independent heads can get." I thought Ben would laugh at that, thinking it was funny, but instead he just rolled his eyes.

I turned back to the amphisbaena and explained the situation

121

better. "I know you are happy with things as they are, and we definitely do not want you to leave your home if you are happy here. But if we do not unlock your oasis, we cannot free the Heka from the cage Malachi put It in. If we don't free It, the Heka will die from being in captivity."

The right head interrupted me. "The Heka cannot die"

"Since It was not born," the left head continued.

"No," I told them. "That is not true. The Heka can die. What do you think happens to an infinite being when you put It in a finite space?"

The amphisbaena seemed to think on that for a moment.

"If the Heka dies," the right head stated.

"Then we all die," the left head finished.

"You see our conundrum." I agreed. "I would love to skip over this oasis and let you be if you are happy where you are, but I can't. If you want to survive, which I am sure you do, we have to unlock your oasis. You don't have to leave after we do. I am pretty sure you don't. But we must unlock it."

Both heads of the amphisbaena nodded, or seemed to at least.

"We shall be freed then," said the right head.

"Free to stay exactly as we are," said the left.

"If that is what you want," Ben told them curtly. "All you need to do is say Anna's name."

The amphisbaena heads looked at each other. "Anna," they said in unison.

I chuckled slightly and rubbed my face. So right, yet so wrong. "No," I told them. "You have to say my full name."

"But you have not told us it," the right head complained.

"How can we say what we do not know?" the left added.

"Use the Heka to figure out her name," Ben tried to explain.

"But the Heka is trapped." The right head seemed as if it was whining.

The left head whined as well, "How can we use It if It is trapped?"

"Oy," Ben mutter under his breath. "This is harder to explain than I thought it would be." He shook his head, and tried again. "The Heka is trapped, but the Heka power is still somewhat available. You know, the lifeforce part of Its power. You still have access to that. Use that lifeforce part of the Heka and try to see if you instinctually know Anna's name."

"Why don't you just tell us?" the right head asked.

I looked up at Ben and he looked down at me. Could it really be that simple? Did they have to figure it out themselves or could we just tell them? All the other mythical beasts had figured it out themselves, hadn't they? Or had we told some of them?

The amphisbaena made a hissing sound that seemed almost like a laugh. They laughed at our confusion.

"You don't even know what you are doing," the left head spoke.

"But you expect us to trust you?" asked the right head.

"And do as you say," the left head continued.

"To be free when we don't want to be," the right head finished. The two heads looked at each other and hiss laughed again.

I rolled my eyes. "AnnaBella Cain. My name is AnnaBella Cain."

Ben put a hand on my shoulder as if to stop me. "We don't know," he started.

I interrupted him, softly saying, "You're right. We don't know. They know we don't know. They know and don't care either. So, maybe we just chalk this one up as whatever, do the bare minimum and move on. They don't want to leave anyway, and we can't make them."

Ben shrugged and kicked at the ground. I could tell he thought I had just made a mistake telling them my name, but just he just muttered, "Whatever."

I looked back at the amphisbaena and asked them, "Will you please say my name and then at least attempt to leave the area you were stuck in after the Flood? For the Heka if not for me?"

The two head nodded, and the right head said, "AnnaBella."

The left head said, "Cain."

The amphisbaena put both its heads down and dug in the sand. Then it sunk its body beneath the floor of the Wastes and disappeared.

I grunted and leaned back to sit on my bottom, frustrated at that whole interaction but glad I could relax now.

"How do we know if it worked?" Ben asked.

I twisted to look at him. "I will feel the Heka's cage get smaller."

"And if you don't?" Ben said.

"If I don't," I repeated, "we find another amphisbaena and try again."

"Fun," Ben mutter sarcastically and he walked away, back towards the pond.

I watched him walk away and actively tried to read his emotions. What was his problem? I could tell he was frustrated about something, and slightly pissed off. But since I couldn't read his thoughts, just emotions, I couldn't tell about what.

I stood up and followed him to the pond. He stood at the edge of the water with his hands in his pockets, staring down at his reflection.

"Alright," I told him, standing a few feet away. I crossed my arms over my chest and tapping on foot. "We need to talk. What was that all about?"

Ben didn't look up. "What was what?" he asked, feigning ignorance.

"That," I said, "that being rude to the amphisbaena, being annoyed with me. What's going on Ben?"

Ben didn't speak. He stood there, still staring at his reflection, shifting his weight from one foot to another.

I sighed. "Ben, I know you are frustrated. I can feel it."

Ben whipped around and stomped towards me. "That is the problem," he growled, pointing at me. "That right there. You know what I am feeling all the time. I know what you are feeling all the time. I'm sick of it. Can't I just have a few private thoughts?"

I stepped back and put my hands up defensively. "I'm sorry. It's not my fault, so don't blame me."

Ben shook his head, pacing. "Yeah, well, I know it isn't. But I am tired of it. We have to find a way to stop it. Put up a barrier or something between my feelings and yours. I hate that you feel everything I am and I can't make it stop."

I threw up my hands in frustration. "Well, it's not a walk in the park for me either, you know." I countered. "I have no privacy at all, between you feeling my feelings and the Heka knowing my thoughts. Hell, I have a hard time knowing if what I am thinking is me, you or the Heka most of the time. I would love to be alone in my head, but even if I get you out, I still don't get to be alone in the one place I should be."

"Oh, right." Ben sneered. "I forgot. Anna always has to have it harder than everyone else. You know my feelings, so you know that everything you feel is worse than what I feel. I could never have something just as difficult or maybe more difficult than you do, because I am just a lowly god while you are god, coordinator and human with a Heka connection. You're the top of everything, including struggles."

"Hey!" I shouted back. "I never said that."

Bet turned towards me, pointing at me accusatorily. "But you felt it. Don't deny that, because you know it is true. I felt you feel that."

I rolled my eyes at Ben. "Right, you felt me feel that. Because you are an expert at interpreting feelings without their accompanying thoughts. You know exactly what I am thinking and feeling, right? Then what am I thinking now?" I asked him. In my head, I thought that Ben was being a jerk for no reason. He could feel my anger, obviously, and I felt his. But neither of us could tell each other's thought, I knew.

We stood there staring at each other, angry, but not saying anything for a long time. I told myself I was waiting for him to admit he had no idea what I was thinking and that he had gotten angry at my feelings, that he misinterpreted because of his own self-consciousness, rather than my actual thoughts. But honestly, I was questioning myself. Did I actually think I had it worse than anyone else? Did I downplay how hard some of this stuff might be on Ben? I didn't think so, but somehow, I felt guilty anyway.

As I warred with my own emotions, feeling angry and guilty and frustrated and confused, I felt Ben warring with his emotions as well. I tried really hard not to notice what emotions he was having, both to give him space and because I was scared of what those emotions might be.

Then I realized Ben and I have had this fight before. I plopped down on the floor of the oasis and hung my head in my hands, my eyes closed. We couldn't keep doing this. We couldn't keep having the same argument, the same fight, over and over and still expect to save the Heka. How could we possibly work together if we couldn't trust each other and be okay with each other knowing our emotions? Something had to change.

"Anna," Ben said suddenly, not in an angry way but surprised.

I looked up at him and realized that I couldn't see him. Oh. We were with the Heka, the both of us. Somehow, I had been so preoccupied I didn't notice. Or maybe I was just getting so used to being in the vast weirdness of Its presence that it didn't bother me anymore.

I sighed and waited for the Heka to say something. I expected that It had brought us both here to scold us for fighting again. I felt the Heka sigh heavily.

"I am not going to scold you." The Heka said to both of us. Ben must have thought the same thing.

"Then what do you want to tell us?" Ben asked.

"I don't want to tell you anything." The Heka replied. "I want you to tell me. What is going on?"

Ben and I glanced at each other, metaphorically. I let him speak first.

"We keep arguing because we can feel each other's feelings and it gets really confusing." He started. "I mean, there are things I don't want Anna knowing I feel. We aren't supposed to know the stuff about each other that we don't want to share. But we are forced to know it and, well, I guess being angry is the best way to hide an emotion I don't want Anna to know I am feeling, but getting angry means we argue and it doesn't help us any."

"You were getting angry to hide your other feelings?" I asked Ben.

"Yeah," he responded sheepishly. "I'm embarrassed by some of them. I don't want you knowing every time I feel…" Ben let his words trail off.

"Feel what?" The Heka asked him.

Ben sighed. "Every time I feel attracted to you, Anna." I could tell Ben's physical body was blushing.

The Heka responded before I could. "Why is that a problem? You both know you are attracted to each other, so why wouldn't you be comfortable knowing that?"

I answered this time. "You really haven't been around teenagers a lot, have you, Heka?" The Heka didn't respond so I kept talking. "These feelings are, well, new to us, to teenagers I mean. Ben and I, we aren't exactly teenagers, I know, but our minds are. And attraction, arousal, all of that, it's new to us. We get embarrassed by it because we don't know what we are doing and we don't really have any experience with, um," I cleared my throat, "With sex, and stuff, you know."

The Heka seemed to be pondering what I said. I could feel Ben's embarrassment along with my own. I tried to impress on the Heka these feelings that we both were having, letting It understand how difficult all of this, and this discussion about it, was for us. I wasn't sure how the Heka was interpreting my feelings, and Ben's vicariously through me, But hoped It would recognize why we kept having so many issues and come up with a way for Ben's and my mind to become separate again.

Finally, the Heka spoke. "I thought that by allowing you to become a sort of hive mind, that you would function better, quicker. Apparently, I was wrong."

Ben answered. "I think maybe if Anna and I could have also known what each other was thinking, as most hive minds do, it would have worked slightly better. But only slightly."

"Yeah," I continued. "Humans, and I assume gods, are social creatures, but not that social. We like having the ability to have some privacy and make up our own minds about things. We aren't designed to have hive minds. So even if you had added the ability to know each other's thoughts, it probably would have ended badly anyway because we aren't used to that and don't like it when someone knows literally everything about us in that way."

The Heka listened to what we were saying, digesting the information. "I am sorry for causing you both to be uncomfortable. I did not foresee that, even though you are both gods in your own right, you are designed to act in humanistic ways. AnnaBella, especially, since she was until recently only human."

Both Ben and I hastily accepted the Heka's apology. Infinite being could make mistakes too, I reckoned.

"Can you undo it?" I asked. "This ability for Ben and I to feel each other's feelings?"

"I believe so." The Heka responded. "If I do, will you not argue and become upset anymore?"

"Not as much, I think." Ben replied. "Humans and gods still do argue sometimes under normal circumstances, so we probably will occasionally, but it will be a lot less."

The Heka seemed to nod Its head in understanding. "Then, yes, I will undo it."

I opened my physical eyes. Both Ben and I had been ejected from the Heka's presence.

"Well, that was fun." I said sarcastically.

"Yeah," Ben replied.

I tried to see if I could tell what Ben was feeling, but I couldn't. It seemed that the Heka made good on Its word. I was going to say something about it to Ben, but just then I felt the Heka's cage get smaller. I twisted my face from the pain of the pinching and burning.

"Hey," Ben said nicely, "you okay?"

"Yeah," I sighed. "Just the Heka's cage tightening. The amphisbaena must be freed now, not that it will change much for them."

"So, we can just tell them your name." Ben acknowledged. "They don't have to guess."

I nodded. "Hey, Ben?" I looked up at him from where I was seated on the ground.

"Yeah?" He asked, coming to sit down next to me.

"Now that we can't feel each other's feelings," I asked, "can you tell me what you were so desperate to hide that you acted like you were angry at me?" I looked down, scared of what he would say. "Or were you actually angry about that stuff? Do you really think I make it all about me?"

Ben shook his head. "No, I don't. I mean, yeah, sometimes I do, but that is probably me just being jealous or whatever. You talk to the Heka all the time. I knew the Heka, like when It walked around and stuff in an actual body, but still didn't really ever get to talk to It. And you get to have full on conversations with It anytime you want, even though you weren't even a god yet when you first did. Sometimes, I don't think you appreciate how cool that is."

I nodded, agreeing. "I think you're right. I get so caught up in how messed up all this stuff is and how little I know and how confused I am, I can forget how awesome the stuff I do know and can do is."

Ben continued as if I hadn't spoken. "What I was trying to hide, though, was how I feel about you. In the human realm, if we were actually just the teenagers that we appear to be, we would only be shyly flirting with each other right now. But in this situation, and with our feeling bonded like the Heka made them, we knew everything all at once. Then you kissed me and branded me with your Heka infused love to make a talisman to protect me. At first, it felt like a small burn on my skin, but it changed to make me feel like we were in the depths of eternal love. Love that had been going on for ages. Emotional love, spiritual love, as well as, you know, physical love. It was really weird to want to, you know, do things with you, to that level when we have basically only kissed a little. I was ashamed and embarrassed and afraid you would think it was me feeling that instead of the talisman making me feel it."

"So, you hid those feeling under anger." I said, understanding. That much feeling would be a lot for anyone.

"Yeah. Sorry." Ben said. He looked down at his feet and toyed with the ends of his shoelaces.

"Hey, it's okay." I told him. "I probably would have been freaked out if I had to feel all of that, plus my actual feelings, plus yours too. I mean, it's not the same as me feeling my feelings, yours and the Heka's, but it is similar enough that I understand how overwhelming it would be. But we don't have to worry about that anymore. You get to just feel your own feelings now."

"And the talisman." Ben corrected me.

"You can still feel that?" I asked.

Ben seemed to think about it, then answered. "Not as strongly now, but yeah. Maybe it just feels less because I don't have your feelings mixed in too."

"Or maybe the talisman is wearing off," I replied, worried. "If it is, then you could be in danger the next time you touch the haze."

Ben was still looking at his shoes, playing with his shoestrings. A lot of emotions seemed to cross his face, but I couldn't feel any of them anymore so I didn't know what they were.

"Maybe," he finally said, "maybe you ought to, you know, redo

128

it." His voice cracked a little as he spoke, as if he was nervous. "Just in case."

With only my own feelings in my head, well mine and the Heka's, who was making a point to blissfully not be paying attention currently, I got very nervous about redoing the talisman. I knew I should, for safety's sake, but I was timid about kissing Ben in that way again. I looked down at my legs folded in front of me and copied Ben's actions of playing with my shoelaces. It didn't help distract me from my nerves.

"You're nervous." Ben finally said. It was not a question.

"How do you know?" I asked, afraid that the Heka had only half fixed the issue.

Ben chuckled. "It's not that. I can't feel your feelings anymore. It's something I learned back in school. When you get nervous, your mouth twitches."

I looked at him. "How do you know that?"

Ben smiled. "Playing poker with you. It's your tell."

I thought back to all the times Ben and I had played cards in advanced biology when there was a substitute teacher. The substitutes never knew enough about biology to teach a real lesson, so they just let us do whatever we wanted as long as we didn't get too rowdy. I smiled.

"That's how you won so much." I fake complained. "You won so many lunches and snacks off of me that way. I feel cheated."

"Hey," Ben said mockingly defensive. "If you hadn't been trying to bluff so often, I wouldn't have learned your tell so well."

We both laughed. I felt calmer, not as anxious after laughing.

Ben looked down at his shoelaces again, then back up at me. More seriously, he told me, "I am going to kiss you." When I seemed startled by that statement, he kept talking. "You have to kiss me. That's how you did it before. But, like I said, I know you are nervous about it. So, instead of you having to just dive into kissing my neck, I am going to kiss you first. Break the ice."

Before I could respond, Ben leaned over and kissed me gently on the lips. I knew that, to make the talisman brand work, I had to use my Heka to impart a serious idea of infinite love into my kiss. I tried not to think about that and just enjoy Ben kissing me.

Without me trying, Heka power, my Heka not the Heka, seemed to well up as we kissed. Ben leaned closer to me, lightly putting his hands on my knees as he deepened the kiss. Without breaking contact, I scootched over and climbed to sit in Ben's lap. He wrapped his arms around me as I did so, pulling me tighter towards him. I felt warm all over and the places where Ben and I were touching felt like there was static shocks running between us.

I pulled away from Ben's lips. He raised his head, giving me access to the hollow of his neck. I bent my head down and gently kissed him there, pushing all of my feelings and my Heka into the kiss.

Ben groaned, low in his throat. When I pulled away, I saw the red mark on his neck. I watched it fade into his skin. Ben used one hand to tip my chin up so I was looking at him again. He kissed me on the lips, a quick, gentle kiss, then let me go.

I was still sitting in his lap. Awkwardly, I climbed out of his arms and sat back down on the floor of the oasis. I looked at my shoes, just like he had, to hide my embarrassment.

Ben inhaled loudly. "So, we get to do that after unlocking every oasis, huh?"

I looked at him askance. "Get to or have to?"

Ben smiled and took my hand. "Get to," he replied. "Definitely get to."

Chapter Six

With half of the oases unlocked, and the mythical beasts they contained free, the cage was getting very small. It did more than cause a slight pinching and burning sensation, but cause insufferable amounts of pain. It was hard to think with the walls closed in so tightly.

AnnaBella noticed, as she and Ben began to move out of the fifth oasis into the Wastes that things were quieter inside her head than they had been. She mentioned this to Ben, who shrugged it off as probably Anna just getting accustomed to not feeling Ben's feelings anymore.

In reality, Ben worried about this quietness too. "The Heka seemed much more reserved when we talked to It this time, though, didn't It?" He asked.

AnnaBella agreed. Neither one voiced their concerns out loud, though. But they did pick up their pace, urgency making them put more effort into moving from this oasis to the next without delay. There had already been so many delays.

With the edges of the cage smaller, ironically the haze became bigger. AnnaBella and Ben entered the haze only a few moments after they left the fifth oasis. Ben's talisman of love and Heka held off the damaging effects of him bumping against the cage's edges, but did not prevent either of them from feeling the wrongness that cage wrought.

Even Ben, who had initially only known the sense of the haze through his connection with Anna and as a tiny almost shiver in his own will to keep going, now could feel the full effect of the haze. The tightening of the cage left the greasy, tainted air having a physically bitter taste and smell, as well as making any who approached feel queasy and desiring to run the opposite way.

In the unlocked sections of Taikarlu, the gods, coordinators, humans and mythical beasts were enjoying associating with each other. All but the amphisbaenas, who were quite happy to be left alone in their now not-Wastes desert, of course. Even they could feel the haze within the Wastes and avoided coming close to it.

But Ben and AnnaBella had no choice. They steeled themselves against the sensation of the cage's edges rubbing against them and continued walking. All they could do is hope they would get the second half of the oases done in time.

Ben and I had been walking east through the Wastes for some time. The haze had been surrounding us for most of the journey. Walking had become excruciatingly hard because the haze's effects had become so strong. No matter what I did, I could feel its greasiness clinging to my skin and felt nauseated.

When we first entered the Haze, Ben had almost been sick. He had asked me if that was what I had felt all along and I had told him it wasn't.

"The haze has gotten a lot stronger." I said. "It used to be small and only appear right before we entered the new oasis, just a little spot of wrongness, but now? Now it is filling up almost the entire Wastes and just feels so sickening. Like, I want to run back to the amphisbaenas' oasis. They were kind of mean and really didn't want us around, but I would prefer that to this." I gestured around as if showing him the haze.

"If this is what we are feeling," Ben posed, "then what is the Heka feeling?"

"I don't know," I told Ben honestly. "It seems really quiet. Almost too quiet. That is making me more nervous than the haze is."

Ben agreed and picked up the pace. I followed suit and soon, we were both moving as quickly as we could through the unstable sand. Any attempts to go faster, to run, would have actually slowed us down as our feet sank into the sands. We would have potentially risked an injury, like a twisted ankle or something. Or, at least, I risked it. I still wasn't sure how much Ben could or couldn't be injured in this place without it being the work of the haze.

So, we walked as fast as we could, putting all of our effort into straining our eyes towards the horizon, hoping for a sight of the upcoming oasis. We walked due east this time. Half the circle around the city of Taikarlu was completed, as well as half the oases. I wanted to feel good about having made it this far already, but something told me to not think of it as 'already' but 'so late.' I had the overwhelming sense that we were running behind and wouldn't make it to the Heka in time.

Finally, Ben pointed to something glinting on the horizon. The other oases hadn't glinted like that. Or at least, hadn't that I had noticed. I wondered what was making the air shimmer that way, and what it meant for our goal to unlock it.

As we had every other time, Ben and I entered the oasis and headed straight for the center where the cave and pond were located. This oasis was different, like I had thought. Instead of the pond being a small pool in the center of the oasis, it was huge and took up most of the oasis' territory.

"Must be water-based." Ben muttered, thinking aloud. I could tell he was running through a list of all the mythical beasts he knew that lived in the water in his head.

Throwing any sort of caution to the wind because of the pressure that there just wasn't any time, I stripped off my shoes and socks and immediately sat at the edge of the oversized pond. I rolled up my pants legs and dangled my feet in the water.

Ben was about to tell me not to do that, but was cut off as a figure in the middle of the pond popped its head above the water line. The head looked very human-like.

At first it was only one head, just floating above the water, looking at us. Quickly, though, several other heads popped up. Within a few minutes, there were ten heads, all with very feminine type, human features, long, shiny golden hair, bright blue eyes, and pale skin. From what I could see of them, apparently they were all naked, or at least not wearing any tops.

"Um, hi." I said, slightly unsure of myself. I had not been expecting something so human looking. "I'm Anna and this is Ben. He won't be able to understand you, so do you mind if I translate for him?" This is going to become my standard greeting, I thought.

"Hello," the first head who had broken above the water said. "My name is Eilidh, and Benahahminen should be able to understand us, although I understand why you would think he couldn't."

I turned to Ben and he nodded. He could understand them. Of course, he could. They knew his full god name without us telling them. Maybe they would know my name instinctively too, and make this super easy on us.

"Hello," Ben replied. "Can I ask you to say your name again? And could you clarify, is that your name or the name of what you are?"

The being smiled brightly, moving closer to the edge of the pond. "Of course." She replied. "Thank you for asking. My name is Eilidh. I am a naiad."

I tested her name once to make sure I had the pronunciation

right. "A-lee, am I saying that right?"

Eilidh smiled again. "That was close enough for your tongue, AnnaBella Cain."

Well, that solves the 'what is my name' issue. I started to say "What is a naiad?" but at the same moment Ben spoke.

"Naiad, that's a water nymph, right?" he asked, answering my question.

Eilidh kept smiling and nodded. "That's right, Benahahminen. We are what many call a water nymph." Eilidh has reached the edge of the pond and braced her arms on the shore. This lifted her further out of the water and made it very clear that she definitely was naked.

Ben and I both turned away from her, trying not to look. As we glanced around everywhere but at Eilidh, the other naiads swam up to the shoreline. Some of them leaned against it as Eilidh was and others climbed out fully to sit on the ground, their very human looking legs still in the water, much like mine were. And they were all, definitely, definitely, all completely naked.

They were also very human looking, exactly human looking and beautiful. Had I been anywhere else, I would have mistaken them for just a group of human females skinny dipping. I looked over at Ben and saw he had given up trying to look away modestly. I gently slapped on his shoulder and scowled at him.

He turned to me, surprised. "What?" Ben asked innocently. He must have seen my displeasure at his ogling on my face. "Anna, they are naiads, not humans. Plus, I am a god, not human either. This is nothing. Stop trying to use human morals in a not human interaction. Literally, no one here, not even you, are human so the things we do and accept doing will be different."

"If that's true, why did you look away at first?" I knew we hadn't really said anything about what our relationship was, but somehow, I felt like if I branded him with my Heka infused love, that made me at least akin to a girlfriend, discussion or no discussion. I really didn't want Ben looking at perfectly beautiful women naked. Yes, I admitted to myself, I was jealous, but can you blame me?

Ben didn't answer me. Instead, he scratched the back of his head and looked away from both me and the naiads. Sensing my discomfort, though, the naiads slid back in the water. Those who hadn't gotten completely out lowered themselves so nothing more was visible than if they were wearing bikinis. I knew Ben was actually right, and that I couldn't force human standards on them. Especially not when those human standards weren't the same everywhere for the humans even. It was my own morals that had to change to fit where I was, not the naiads that had to change in their own home to mine. It didn't make it any less uncomfortable for me and I appreciated their gesture.

Eilidh spoke again, pretending that interaction between me and Ben had not happened. "Water nymphs are bound to their water homes. We cannot leave this pond. Before the Flood, our waters were connected to every pond in every oasis, as well as to the river in the city of Taikarlu. Our waters were everywhere. During the Flood, we actually were very happy at first. With everything flooded, it was like all the realms everywhere became our home. But then we realized how the gods and humans were troubled, and no longer were happy. When the waters receded, we were stuck in this pond, no longer connected to any others or to Taikarlu, the gods or the humans."

"How did you know Ben's name, and mine for that matter?" I asked.

Another naiad answered. "Naiads are able to see the future." She explained. "My name is Sorcha, by the way."

Ben and I both said hello to Sorcha, making sure to correctly pronounce her name as Sord-huh, not Sorsha.

Sorcha continued, after flashing us a brilliant smile. "We have known, since the Floods receded and the Wastes appeared, that you two would come eventually. We knew you would come to save the Heka from Its imprisonment. We also know that, now that you have arrived, just the mere fact that Eilidh said your name, means that our landlocked pond should be open again to Taikarlu and the other oases you have already visited."

"Wow," Ben whistled. "You made this one very easy for us. Usually, we have to do a lot more legwork to get to this point."

Eilidh smiled yet again. The naiads seemed particularly happy and friendly. Almost too happy and friendly. Something in me started to wonder if there was a trick in this somehow. I thought about myths I had read about water and land nymphs when I was still a human and remembered something about them being dangerous. Water nymphs would lead men astray with their beauty, making them follow the nymph into the water without realizing they were, and then the men would drown. Did I need to have my guard up? Or was this the part the humans got wrong?

I noticed some of the naiads towards the back of the group swim away. I asked Eilidh where they were going.

"Since all of the needs of unlocking this oasis are already fulfilled, they are headed to the west, where our pond should now extend into a river and lead them towards the other unlocked areas. They are going to join the gods in Taikarlu and let them know you have made it this far."

"Oh." I replied. This seemed way too simple after everything else we had been through up to this point. Why couldn't I just take the easy win? Why was I doubting it?

Ben had started talking to Sorcha and a few other naiads who had swam closer to the edges of the pond. Eilidh swam up towards me.

"AnnaBella Cain, I do need to speak with you." She said.

I still was sitting at the edge of the water with my legs dangling in. Eilidh pulled herself up and sat on the edge with me. I made a pint of looking her in the face and telling myself not to even notice she was naked.

"There are things coming you should be aware of," Eilidh said softly to me. "The Heka's cage? It is hurting It quite badly. The Heka is very weak, and will not last much longer so I have to make this quick."

I nodded. "I know. I feel It getting weaker."

Eilidh tilted her head to one side. "That's right, you are connected with It already."

"What do I need to know, Eilidh?" I asked her.

Eilidh straightened again, becoming very serious. "There are four more oases to unlock. The haze will try to stop you. You cannot let it. You cannot let it even slow you down. If Ben falls behind, you must leave him, no matter what you feel for him now. The future is not perfectly clear at this moment. There is a chance you will not make it to the Heka on time."

"What do you mean? I thought you could see the future?" I asked.

Eilidh sighed. "Normally, we can. But something as big as this? It is difficult to see. When Malachi was deciding what to do, before he broke the world, we could see that he had a choice, many choices. We could see the many outcomes possible, like branches of a tree. Each decision he had to make led to a different outcome. But then, we could see all the new, different outcomes possible."

Eilidh sighed again, a sense of weariness creeping into her voice. "But this? This is where all visions of the future end. All of them, and they always have ended here, at the moment you enter the tenth oasis. Every choice made, every action Malachi took, you took, the gods took, even the Heka took, ended with you entering that last oasis and the visions going dark. There are two possible outcomes: you arrive in time to save the Heka, or you don't. What happens after either, we cannot tell."

I thought about what Eilidh was telling me. "If everything, every vision of the future goes dark at that specific moment, do you think it means I fail? The Heka dies, and we all die? Am I doing all of this just to fail at the end?"

"No." Eilidh said more forcefully than I think she intended. "At least, that is what we naiads have been telling ourselves. The future doesn't go dark because everything ends, but just because it is so unknown and unknowable." Eilidh paused, not sure she wanted to continue, but forced herself to. "But I think it may be that we are fooling ourselves. I am scared that we may just be lying to ourselves in our hope. This terrifies me. The Heka is not supposed to be able to die. What Malachi did, it was so wrong. I have nightmares about the non-existence that follows in the wake of the Heka's death. What will it be like for us, those moments between the Heka's death and ours? This is the stuff of my nightmares."

Eilidh turned and took my hands into hers. "Please, AnnaBella, promise me you will do whatever you can to reach the Heka in time. Even if it means abandoning Benahahminen."

I looked at Eilidh, having forgotten about her naked body, forgotten everything but what she was telling me. Abandon Ben? Could I really do that if I had to? I thought about the Heka. I felt It shift in Its cage, pinched and worn and so very, very tired. Yes, I would abandon Ben for the Heka. But only if I absolutely had to.

"I promise." I told Eilidh, sounding more confident than I felt.

Eilidh nodded, releasing my hands. "Then you should get on your way. Oh, and don't forget as you travel, to think about it. What is your name?"

With that Eilidh dove back into the water. The other naiads followed her, all of the disappearing beneath the water.

I watched the water long after they were gone. Great, I thought, no pressure. And thanks for the reminder about the name thing.

Ben walked over to me, smiling. "Well, that was easy. Should we refresh my talisman and hit the road?"

I looked at Ben. He had no idea that I had just agreed to abandon him, to sacrifice our feelings for each other for the sake of the Heka. I could not imagine giving him any sort of passionate kiss right now.

Instead, I deflected. "It has been such a short time here. I doubt it wore off yet. Let's risk it and see." I turned away from Ben and began walking in a north-easterly direction towards the outer edges of the oasis. In my rush to avoid Ben, I forgot about the other problem with the Heka's cage.

In the other oases, as soon as I had realized what would happen, I had been preparing myself to feel the burning pinch of the Heka's cage getting smaller as soon as someone, anyone said my full name.

This time, I forgot to prepare myself. I wasn't anticipating the pain, so I wasn't ready when it came.

I screamed as the feeling of being compressed washed over me. It was no longer like a bad sunburn, like my skin was just a little too tight and hurt to move. I felt the full force of the Heka's pain, as if it was me in the cage, not It. The walls pushed down on my skin, cutting me like razor blades everywhere. I collapsed on the oasis floor, my eyes shut tight, my body curled up in a ball. I knew this was happening only in my mind, only because I was connected to the Heka, but it felt so real. I couldn't breathe. There was no room to expand my lungs. Every muscle was on fire and my head felt like it was in a vice grip.

"Please," I felt the Heka plead. "Take this from me."

"I can't." I panted, trying to push the pain away, trying to remember my real body, not the Heka's.

"I cannot do this anymore." The Heka whispered. "Either take it from me or let me die." I could feel the Heka so closely, it was like we shared one skin. It really couldn't take much more, but this close to It, I didn't have the ability to give It hope, to encourage It to keep fighting. I wanted to run away. I wanted to escape and cut my connection with It, so I didn't have to feel this pain anymore.

But I knew if I did, the Heka would die. Eilidh's words echoed in my mind. "What will it be like for us, in those moments between the Heka's death and ours?" Humans and gods and coordinators and mythical beings and every other sentient being, and maybe even the non-sentient ones, may be finite, but we exist in the infinite that is the Heka. Our entire existence fits inside Its infiniteness. What would we all feel the moment that infiniteness collapses? Probably something much worse than what the Heka was feeling now.

So, I tried to be brave. In my mind, I reached out my hand to the Heka. I could feel the moment It grabbed on. "Give it to me," I told It. "Give me as much of the pain as you need. I will carry it for you."

All of this was symbolic, inside my head, not real. Or at least, that is what I convinced myself. I couldn't really be holding the hand of an infinite being with no physical body, so I couldn't really be draining some of Its pain away. I didn't really feel anything.

Whether or not it really was happening, I felt the Heka sigh. Its pain decreased enough that It could handle what was left, at least for a little while. I opened my eyes and sat up. I could still feel the pressure on me, the tightness squeezing me just enough that it felt difficult to breath. I reminded myself that it wasn't real pain. There was nothing stopping me from taking a full breath, and I didn't need to breathe anyway.

I looked for Ben. He was standing next to me, in shock.

"How long was I out?" I asked.

"You, um…" Ben stuttered. "A second or two, not long. You screamed, like really screamed, Anna. I… I don't think it was actually you screaming I heard but…"

I cut him off. I didn't want to hear that he had heard the Heka screaming through me. That would mean it was all real, physically real, and I actually was being suffocated the way it felt. I could only maintain it, and help the Heka, if I believed my lie that it wasn't real. So, I cut Ben off.

"Don't." I told him sharply. I forced myself to stand. Once I was upright, I closed my eyes and tried to settle myself within the new feeling of my compressed body. I opened my eyes and looked at Ben. "We need to go."

I started walking again, north-east. Ben was following me, trying to say something, but I blocked out his voice. Hopefully, I could get used to carrying this weight, this pain, for the Heka soon and explain it to Ben. But for now, he would just have to understand it was taking everything in me just to keep moving.

Chapter Seven

AnnaBella Cain kept trudging through the Wastes. Her physical body trembled at the burden it carried, but Annabella would not be stopped. The haze had come over her and Ben very quickly, but AnnaBella had shoved the thoughts the haze created to the side, refusing to allow herself to be distracted.

Ben watched Bella from a few paces behind. He was worried about her. Her arms and legs seemed to tremble as she walked. Sweat glistened on her forehead and a dark patch of sweat appeared on the back of her shirt. She wasn't talking to him and he had long since given up trying to force her to.

When they reached the haze, Ben had fought hard to ignore the queasiness and self-doubt that crept over him. He continued to watch Bella, and his worry increased when she stepped into the haze without showing even the slightest acknowledgement. *She doesn't even seem as if she would notice if the talisman hadn't worked,* he thought. *I wish I could still feel her feelings now, then at least I would have some idea why this change in her happened.*

Ben had seen Bella's reaction to the Heka's cage getting smaller after they has unlocked the naiads' oasis. Bella had screamed and shook, collapsing on the ground. But she never lost consciousness. Ben had heard a yell come from her that was not her own voice. The yell had the force of the Heka within it, a pained Heka, a suffering Heka, and that scared him even more than Bella's actions after that pain had subsided. Or after Bella stopped allowing the pain to control her, Ben countered within himself. There was a part of him that believed Bella was now taking on some of the Heka's pain in order to help It survive until they could make it to It.

Ben knew Bella was strong, but deep in his heart, he worried the most about if she was strong enough. What happened, he thought, if she wasn't strong enough to keep going from oasis to oasis, unlocking them, and carrying the Heka's pain? What happened if she faltered? What happened if she failed? Ben knew this was a burden he could not help Bella carry. This was hers, and hers alone. But he promised himself, as the waves of greasy nausea stole over him, that no matter what the haze tried to make him feel, no matter how badly he wanted to give up, turn and run, he was going to do what he could to help her.

I noticed the change in the way the Wastes appeared shortly before I noticed the seventh oasis on the horizon. The sun was still bright in a cloudless sky, but the temperature started dropping and the sand began to firm up much sooner than it had at the other oases. The temperature kept dropping too. I wasn't sure if this change was because of the haze being so present in this area of the Wastes or if it had something to do with the occupant of the next oasis. I just kept walking and figured that I would know when I got there.

Ben was still trailing behind me, his mouth twisted into a worried frown. He was worried about me, I knew, but there was nothing I could do to stop him from worrying. Especially because I was worried about me too. I couldn't make my muscles stop twitching, no matter how much I tried to convinced myself that the pain I was feeling wasn't physically real, just metaphorical.

As we got closer to the oasis and the scrub brush started becoming denser and taller, I noticed that, in between the plants, there were clumps of snow. The scrubby plants turned to evergreens and grew larger. The branches of the evergreens began to have a dusting of snow on them, and the closer we got to the middle of the oasis, the colder I felt. My muscles began to tremble from the cold as well as the pain.

Finally, Ben reached out and grabbed my arm, stopping me.

"Anna," he said. "you're freezing." His breath was hanging in the air like ice crystals.

I tried to speak, but realized my teeth were chattering. I brought my arms up to rub them.

Ben swung an arm around me, pulling me close. "Come on," he said. "I'm taking you into the cave. We can start a fire and you... you need to rest."

I didn't fight him. As we walked past the pond, I noticed that it was frozen solid. Ben stopped only momentarily, glancing at the pond, then continued guiding me to the cave.

Once he had me inside and seated, Ben took off back out of the cave. He was only gone for a few minutes. When he returned, he had a stack of wood in his arms. He placed the wood near me, in a neat pile, and proceeded to attempt to start a fire. Ben struggled with rubbing two sticks together. I wondered why he didn't use his Heka to start the fire.

After watching him struggle for a few moments, I gathered the energy and moved next to him. I closed my eyes and tried to find the warmth over cold that was my Heka power. There was a whole lot of cold, but not a lot of warmth. I tugged at what little I could find and pushed it toward the wood. It smoked slightly.

Ben bent down and blew on the baby embers. Finally, they caught fire and Ben shifted the wood until he had a nice small blaze going. I put my hands toward the flames and warmed myself. Ben curled up next to me, wrapping himself around me. As a god who wasn't affect by the weather, he felt gloriously warm.

Now warm and exhausted, I felt my eyelids droop. I didn't know if the pain I was holding for the Heka would return to It if I fell asleep so I fought to stay awake. Ben noticed me getting sleepy.

"Hey," he said gently. "before you sleep, I need you to eat." Ben pulled a few berries from his pocket. He must have picked them as he looked for dry wood. He held them out in his hand and I took them from him, eating as he requested.

He sighed and shifted so he was sitting behind me. Then he pulled me onto his lap and wrapped his arms around me. I snuggled against him, trying to be as close to his warmth and the fire's as I could.

Once we were settled, Ben spoke again, still softly. "You are taking some of the Heka's pain, aren't you?"

I nodded against his chest.

"Why?" he asked. He wasn't admonishing me or upset, but sounded more curious and concerned.

Finally, I spoke. "Because It would die if I didn't. The cage is too tight."

Ben sighed again, a long sigh. "Anna, you're still in a human body. You can't do everything. You're going to kill yourself before you even get to the Heka."

I shook my head, refusing to accept that.

Ben leaned back from me and grabbed my chin with his hand to force me to look up at him. "Yes," he said firmly, "you will. You are exhausted and cold and starving. Besides those berries I just gave you, when is the last time you had something to eat?"

I tried to look away from him. I couldn't remember eating anything besides a handful of blueberries for a long time.

Ben gave up, growling softly. He let go of my chin. I tucked my head back down and leaned back into his chest. "Go to sleep, Anna." He finally said to me.

I was going to argue that I couldn't sleep, that I didn't know what would happen to the Heka if I did. Plus, we were running out of time. We needed to find the mythical beast that lived in this frozen oasis, free it and move on. I was going to say all that, but I didn't. Instead, I fell asleep.

I opened my eyes sometime later and found myself alone in the cave. Ben must have moved me to the cave floor and left to try to find me some real food. He must have been successful too, because there was the meat of a rabbit roasting over the fire. I poked at the meat with a stick and saw the juices were running mostly clear.

Suddenly, I realized I was ravenous. I pulled the spit off the fire and bit into the meat. It was plain, obviously, but still tasted so good. Hunger is very much the best sauce. I ate the meat until I felt full, and then leaned back against the cave wall.

The fire had made it fairly comfortable inside the cave, and most of the smoke seemed to be funneling out the mouth of the cave, so it was both warm and bright. As I sat, I realized I wasn't feeling the pain from the Heka's cage anymore.

I sat bolt upright, panicking, and reached out to the Heka. It was still there, in Its cage. It shocked me how fast I could connect with It without going to the universe dying and being born place anymore. The Heka seemed to be doing as well as It had been before I went to sleep, maybe even a little better, so I stopped worrying.

I leaned back against the cave wall and was just going to relax when Ben came into the cave. He was walking very slowly, and backwards.

"Ben?" I questioned him. "What are you doing?"

"Shh." He whispered, shaking a hand at me without taking his eyes off of the cave entrance. "An amorak."

"A what?" I had never heard of an amorak before, but assumed it was probably our mythical beast.

Finally, Ben stepped out of visual line with the opening of the cave and faced me. "An amorak. They are kind of like a dire wolf, except they hunt alone rather than in packs and are much, much bigger." Ben noted the half-eaten rabbit meat and smiled. "Feel better after a rest and some food?"

"Yeah," I told him dismissively. "These amorak, what exactly is it that they hunt alone?"

Ben knelt down by the fire and cleaned up the mess I had left of rabbit meat and drippings. "Amoraks usually hunt hunters, ones silly enough to go out by themselves."

I sat up again. "Like you just did. Is the amorak hunting you?"

Ben looked up at me. He stood, wiped his hands on his shorts and smiled. "Yeah, probably."

"And you're not freaking out?" I asked, freaking out again.

"Nope," Ben replied. He walked over and sat down next to me. "Because now I am not alone. Plus, we want the amorak to come in here. You need to talk to it, don't you?"

Oh yeah. There had been mythical beasts at other oases that were annoyed by us or untrusting of us, but this was the first one actively hunting us as prey. I knew it had to happen at some point. Still, it made me nervous.

As we sat and watched the cave entrance, I saw first one paw and then another paw pad their way into the cave. Based on the sizes of those paws, the amorak was mammoth. I wiped my hands on my jeans to dry the sweat gathering there, and sat up further. The amorak sniffed, then walked the rest of the way into the cave.

It was huge, about the size of a lion. Maybe bigger. I've never seen a lion up close, a normal one anyway. The amorak walked into the cave and began pacing around. It looked at us but never came closer, eyeing the fire.

The beast had all the distinctive markings of a wolf. It had dark fur along its back that slowly changed to a more yellowish color along its sides, with two small fluffy ears that stood straight up and twitched as they picked up sounds. The amorak's mouth hung slightly open, its red tongue and sharp, carnivore teeth visible as it panted in the warm cave. It looked at me through the fire and its eyes were bright yellow.

I felt flustered at its size and the fact that would definitely probably eat me if it could, but I tried to say my now normal opening line. "Hi, um, my name is Anna and this is Ben. He probably won't understand you but I will. Is it, um, okay if I translate for you?"

The amorak kept staring at me and didn't respond, so I kept talking. "We came here to help you. You are stuck in this oasis, right? And have been since the Flood? Well, the Heka was trapped and it broke Taikarlu. All the mythical animals, such as... um, such as yourself were locked into oases in a large desert we call the Wastes. Now, we are going around to unlock all these oases, free they mythical beasts, which in turn will free the Heka. Any, um, do you have any questions?"

I waited, holding my breath. The amorak kept staring. I was starting to wonder if it couldn't speak when it finally responded.

"I am Kylo." The amorak said. Its voice was gruff and deep. "I do not care if you tell the other human what I am saying."

When I translated what Kylo said to Ben, he cleared his throat and spoke up. "Actually, I am not a human but a god. Benahahminen is my full name, I doubt you would have heard of me. I was only ever a minor…"

I poked Ben with my elbow and whispered out of the side of mouth. "Do not annoy the carnivore who could potentially eat us." I hissed.

Ben quieted down and Kylo continued speaking. "The Floods were horrible," he growled. "But afterwards, no one came to hunt my lands anymore."

"Yeah," I replied "Everyone was stuck in their own places."

"This area was fine," Kylo continued, "but out there, the sand was too hot. I could not leave."

"Do you want to leave?" Ben asked.

Kylo growled again. "Of course, I want to leave! There is nothing to hunt here. Only small game and plants. Nothing fit for an amorak to eat. I hunt hunters, not prey."

"Are there more of you here? Ben said you are a solitary hunter, and this oasis does not look very big." I asked.

Kylo shook his head. "It is just me. There were more but the space was too small. We fought. I am the last."

"The last amorak in this oasis or the last amorak anywhere?" Ben asked.

Ben seemed to be doing a very good job at saying all the wrong things because Kylo growled at him again. "I don't know! How could I know if there are others elsewhere if I cannot go elsewhere?"

"Good point," Ben muttered under his breath. I elbowed him again to tell him to shut up.

Kylo began to pace again, this time seeming much more restless. "You say you know how to let me be free of this place." He snapped. "Tell me how!"

Kylo's nervous pacing made me even more nervous, so I shifted to the side a bit to keep the fire in between us. Kylo seemed like he did not want to get close to the fire, like any wolf, and I used that to my advantage.

"Do you, by chance, happen to know my name?" I asked him.

"You told me it was Anna." Kylo said, then shook out his fur, like a dog freshly out of a bath. "But I do not think that is right."

"What do you think it is?" Ben asked, ignoring me side-eyeing him for talking again.

Kylo paced and shook his fur. His hackles raised up and he shook again. "Can't you just tell me?" he snarled.

"AnnaBella Cain," I told the amorak immediately. I could tell he was getting frustrated with this conversation and I didn't not want to see what happened if Kylo went from frustrated to actually angry.

"AnnaBella Cain," Kylo repeated. The amorak paced back and forth again on the other side of the fire. "AnnaBella Cain. AnnaBella Cain!" He shouted. "Why is nothing happening?"

Ben opened his mouth, then glanced at me. "Maybe you should explain it. He doesn't seem to like me very much." Ben whispered.

I rolled my eyes. "Yeah, ya think?" I said quietly to Ben. Louder, I told Kylo, "You wouldn't notice the change from here. If you attempt to leave the oasis, it should be comfortable for you to do so now." I thought about where we were in relation to the Hills in the city of Taikarlu. The amorak would probably be most happy going to that snowy region, rather than any other unlocked land. "If you go north-west, you should enter the city of Taikarlu in the wintery part. The gods there should all be quite familiar with the concept of mythical beast returning by now and will help you find other amoraks, if they still exist."

Ben whispered to me again. "Maybe we should send a note with him or something. Let Gavya know what Kylo will want?"

I didn't get the chance to answer because Kylo growled again. "Should? Should! You are making a lot of assumptions, aren't you, AnnaBella Cain." Kylo's paced further and further around the fire, crossing the small rivulet that ran through the center of the cave and out to the frozen pond, slowly working his way closer to us. He seemed to be realizing that going around the fire, rather than through it, was an option. He kept bunching his muscles in his haunches and looking at Ben and I as if he was sizing up his next lunch.

I knew working with a carnivore that saw me as potential prey would be hard, but I didn't realize how hard. I thought about all the things I learned in scouts for dealing with wild animals. I thought I remembered that we had been told to seem bigger, louder, more of a threat, but that was for bears and only as a last-ditch effort because bears don't really want to eat people. I had no idea if these tactics would work on a predator who actually saw me as potential prey, especially one that been actively talking to me, but anything was worth a shot now.

I squared my shoulders and shifted the way I was sitting, slowly rising to my knees rather than sitting on my butt, trying to get myself into the most authoritative stance I could. I lifted my head and spoke as calmly but loudly, without actually yelling, as I could.

"Kylo," I started. I cleared my throat and lowered my voice an octave. "Kylo, I am not making assumptions." Kylo stopped pacing and shook his fur. His hackles went down slightly, so I continued talking. "I am telling you, a mythical animal, what the Heka wants you to do. Go north-west out of the oasis. Run until you find the Hills section of the city of Taikarlu. Find Gavya at the Annex. She will help you look for more amoraks, but only if you eat no one along the way, even if they appear to be a lone hunter. Gavya will also find you an appropriate food source. I will give you a note to explain it since she will not understand you."

It was only at this moment that I realized I had nothing to write a note on, or with for that matter. "Ben," I slumped down and whispered out of the side of my mouth. "How do I write a note to Gavya? I don't have paper or a pen?"

Ben made a face, as if stumped. Then said "Oh. Hmm, never mind."

"What?" I asked him. The amorak was still waiting, not pacing again, but definitely getting antsy.

"Well," Ben told me, "I saw some birch trees outside. You could peel their bark for paper and then use cinders as a pencil. But that means getting outside the cave, passed Kylo."

I sat back up and used my authoritative voice again. "Ben is going to come past you. He needs to go in the woods to get birch bark for paper. Let him by."

Kylo grumbled a little and padded a few steps away from the fire, making space for Ben to walk between them. Ben stood and walked around the fire. "Sure, make me walk right next to the behemoth wolf." As Ben passed between the fire and an Kylo's head, Kylo opened his mouth and made a sudden chomping noise. His teeth never got close to Ben at all, but Ben still jumped and walked faster out of the cave.

"Not nice, Kylo." I said shaking my head.

The amorak made a noise that sounded like a laugh. "But it was fun."

After waiting a few minutes for Ben to return, Kylo found a corner of the cave far away from the fire and curled up to lay on the floor. I almost laughed watching him do this. When he found the spot he wanted, Kylo had sniffed it, then turned in a circle a few times before laying down, just like a pet dog would have.

While we waited for Ben, I used a small twig not already on the fire to pull out a few coals. I set them to the side, separated from each other to cool. Hopefully, I would be able to whittle them into a familiar shape to write with,

Ben came back, walking into the cave slowly, his eyes on Kylo. Kylo only lifted his head slightly, looked at Ben, then laid back down. Still, Ben gave Kylo a wide berth.

"Here." Ben said, handing me several large pieces of birch bark. The outside of the bark was rough, but the inside was smooth and a whitish cream color. The bark curled around itself, meaning it could be rolled up like a scroll easily.

I picked up one of the now cooled pieces of coal and tried to write on the bark. It took several tries to get it right. At first, I pushed too hard and broke the bark and the coal. Then I pushed to gently and the coal markings just smudged across the page. My third try, I broke the birch bark while trying to unroll it. I kept trying though, and eventually was able to scratch out a short note.

> *Gavya, this is Kylo, an amorak. He believes he is the last of his kind. Can you help him see if he is wrong? Also, find him something to eat. He eats solitary hunters normally.*
> *Anna*

I rolled up the note and then rolled several of my test pieces around the one with the note on it. On the final outer covering, I wrote *Take me to Gavya at the Annex. I will not eat you.* Then, I stood and carefully approached Kylo.

"I have written the note for my friend in Taikarlu." I told him. "It is fragile and the words can smudge easily. How do you want to carry it?"

Kylo thought for a moment, then answered. "Can you tie it to my leg?"

I looked around for something to tie the note with and spied Ben's boots. The laces were long. "Give me your boots, Ben."

Ben looked at me quizzically and took off his boots. I walked back over to him. As both Kylo and Ben watched. I took the shoelaces out of the topmost eyelets on both boots and, using a sharp rock, cut the ends of the laces, leaving just enough for Ben to still tie them properly. I handed the boots back to Ben, who put them on while I tied the four pieces of string into one long string.

I walked back to Kylo. "Give me your front paw." Kylo extended his front right paw and I proceeded to tie the birch bark note high on the leg. "Try to keep this out of the snow or wet. When you reach Taikarlu, approach the first person you see, slowly. Do not growl or anything. Try to act like a domesticated dog."

Kylo growled at this, but I shook my head. "Nope, nuh uh, don't do that." I scolded. "You need their help, so you can't scare them. And you will scare them, just being so big and, well, predatory. Go up to the person, lay down gently, and hand them your paw. Keep doing this to person after person until one of them actually reads the outside of the note. Then, follow that person where they take you."

I had finished tying the note and Kylo stood, shaking himself. I jumped back a little, frightened by his sudden movement. When he stopped shaking, I looked at the note. It hadn't budged.

I stood up and walked back around the fire to Ben. "Good luck, Kylo. I hope Gavya can help you find other amoraks."

Kylo grumbled, and then bounded out of the cave. I moved over to the fire and started spreading it around, trying to knock down the flames.

Ben watched me. "What are you doing, Anna?" he asked.

"Putting out the fire. We need to get moving to the next oasis." I told him.

Ben put a hand on my shoulder. "Wait," he told me. "When Kylo leaves the oasis, the Heka's cage will get smaller. We should stay here until that happens. Last time…" Ben didn't have to finish saying what happened last time.

I sank back down and leaned against the wall of the cave. I closed my eyes and waited, bracing myself for the pain I knew was coming.

Outside the cave, we heard a wolf's howl. It was long and sad and lonely. At that same moment, the Heka's cage tightened forcefully around me. I tensed, trying to accept the pain my body wanted to run from. Ben sat next to me and wrapped his arm around my shoulder.

"Let it roll through you, Anna. Not into you but through." Ben said comfortingly.

He was trying to help, I knew, but the pain didn't go through. It compressed me on all sides, squeezed me until it felt like my ribs would break. My breathing came in small pants. I bit my lip trying not to scream. I felt the blood run down my chin as my teeth broke through the skin there.

"Scream if you need to, Anna." Ben said. "It's just me here. You can scream."

I leaned over, putting my head in Ben's lap and curled up my body. I tried to fight it, but a guttural howl, almost like Kylo's, escaped me. In the darkness behind my closed eyes, I could see the Heka pushing at the walls of Its cage, fighting to stop it shrinking. The Heka could barely move anymore, It was so weak.

Three more, I thought to myself and the Heka, only three more. I fought to settle the pain over me like a cloak rather than let it overtake

149

me. I needed to finish those three more. The walls of the cage finally stopped shrinking and I was able to find some semblance of control over what I was feeling.

In my head, I reached out gingerly to the Heka. It reached back without actually making contact. It was still alive, but just barely.

I opened my eyes and struggled to sit up. I was still trembling. Ben helped me and I looked at him. "We are running out of time." I told him, my voice weak and hoarse.

Ben nodded. "I know. We are two steps behind, always."

Ben helped me lean against the wall and then stood. He finished putting out the fire, scooping handfuls of water from the rivulet running through the cave to douse the last embers. Then he turned to me.

"Are you ready to walk?" He asked.

I nodded yes, lying. Ben put out his hand and I grasped it. He pulled me up, and then put his arm back around me.

"Lean on me." Ben told me. "We may walk slowly, but we will make it."

I nodded again. The pain has settled to a constant pressure. We walked out of the cave and left the oasis this way, me leaning into Ben for support.

At the edge of the oasis, Ben stopped and glanced at me, questioningly.

"North-east." I told him. We oriented ourselves towards the worst of the bad-feeling Wastes and started walking. The haze started almost immediately after we left the oasis boundaries.

Even in my pain and weakness, I remembered that we had never refreshed Ben's talisman. I glanced up at him. His face was set, determined, the muscles in his jaw jumping slightly, but he showed no signs of pain from brushing against the edges of the cage.

That's good, I thought. I don't think I would have the power to draw up my Heka and kiss him to refresh the talisman, anyway. We were just going to have to hope that it worked for the rest of the way through the Wastes and three more oases.

Chapter Eight

Ben and AnnaBella walked through the hazy Wastes toward the eighth oasis. They leaned on one another as they walked. There was no chance of moving quickly now. Bella was carrying too much of the pain for the Heka to move at anything but a crawl.

While they walked, Ben chattered to distract Bella. He told her stories from his people, his worshippers, and ones from his time living in the human realms with Mari, Nummi, and Albert. Bella asked questions sporadically, showing that she was listening as well as she could. Ben kept the stories lighthearted and fun.

"So, then," Ben said, with a smile, "the shaman told the woman, 'You don't eat the seeds, you plant them'." Ben listened to Bella laugh, liking the sound of it. He shrugged his shoulders, moving Bella's arm that was draped around them back into a comfortable place. He loosened his grip around her waist and pulled her standing more upright.

Bella stopped walking, and looked at him. "Ben?" she said, out of the blue.

"What, Anna," he replied gently.

"How does the Heka feel to you?" Bella asked.

Ben thought. "The Heka usually feels like power, like I can do anything. It's not been as strong since the Floods, which you already know, but…"

Bella interrupted him. "No, I mean how does It feel to you right now?"

"Oh," Ben responded. He looked inside himself for that which he had always associated with his Heka power. Bella described it as a warmth over cold feeling in the pit of her stomach, but Ben had always seemed it as more like a dog, chained up in his mind, but ready to break free at a word. That dog was whimpering now, rather than flexing with power.

"It seems hurt," Ben finally answered. "Like It is cowering away from me. Instead of a familiar pet who loves me, It is like a wild thing cornered with a broken leg, ready to bite if It needs to but really unsure It could actually fight off any danger."

Bella nodded. "Can you make It do anything? Your Heka?"

Ben shook his head. "No, I don't think so. Maybe something small, but trying would be like forcing a wounded and starved animal to run laps, just wrong. I didn't use my Heka to light the fire back there in the cave because I worried that I would put too much pressure on It. You did, though. You used It."

"Yeah, I did." Bella responded. "It just seems like the Heka is just part of me. I know how far It can go, even now injured like you said. I can't separate It from me, both in Its pain and Its use."

'Something to think about," Ben said. "Why are you and the Heka so tied together, Anna? Even when It barely can move or think because of the pain, It is still linking Itself to you."

Bella did not respond to this but started walking again. In her mind, she knew that the Heka being so tied to her had something to do with what her name was, but she pushed those thoughts away. She had enough on her plate as it was.

Ben and I trudged through the Wastes. He half carried me for most of the way. The oasis had just come into view over the horizon when my legs finally felt strong enough to support me. We stopped and stretched, Ben easing sore muscles from helping me walk, while I convinced myself that I could keep moving under my own power, pain or no pain.

We started moving again, and, the closer we got to the oasis, the hotter and muggier it got. The scrubby plants quickly gave way to tall, dense trees, vines and flowers in a riot of colors. The air was so thick with damp that it felt like it was continually raining a fine mist. The sounds of wildlife echoed all around us with bird calls and cheeping, shrills and coos.

"The Amazon," I said. "I'd bet my hat."

"You don't have a hat," Ben replied.

I smiled weakly. "Then I have nothing to lose if I am wrong."

Ben and I followed our normal path towards the pond. As we walked, we looked around for evidence of whatever mythical beast we were there to help. There were so many animals in this oasis. I saw butterflies and spiders and snakes and birds in all shapes and colors. No other oasis had been this full of life. Any one of them could have been the mythical beast.

When we got to the pond, I looked down into the water. There were fish there, tons of them. In the other oases, there had only been the tiny fish that nibbled at you gently. Here, there were big fish and small fish, in all the same bright colors as the animals and flowers.

Ben leaned over to examine something in the muddy ground next to the pond. A foul smell, like rotten eggs floated toward me.

"Ugh, Ben!" I exclaimed.

He stood back up. "What?' He asked, his face the picture of innocence.

I plugged my nose with one hand. "I didn't know gods could fart. You're so gross."

Ben looked shocked. "I didn't. We can't. I mean, I could if I wanted to but I didn't." He insisted.

"Then, what is that awful smell?" I asked, my voice sounding nasally with my nose pinched shut.

Ben walked closer to me. I knew the moment he ran into the wall of the odor. He leaned back and waved a hand in front of his face as if to dispel it.

"Ugh." Ben gasped. "That is disgusting."

We both groaned and moved around, trying to find a direction away from the smell. It seemed to follow us.

I sniffed at myself, lifting my shirt to my nose. "Is it me? I know I haven't bathed in a while, but…"

Ben shook his head. "You probably smell." He looked at me apologetically. "No offense, but you are in a human body that sweats, but we have been around each other. We wouldn't suddenly notice your smell, but would be accustomed to it as it got worse. It has to be something in the oasis."

Ben walked back over to where he had been looking at the ground. "Come here." He told me. "I found this right before you smelled that. Maybe they have something to do with each other."

I walked over towards Ben and looked at what he was pointing to on the ground. It was a footprint. It looked almost human, maybe like an ape or something. Ben walked the way the footprints were going, following them.

"There seems to be a trail heading off in that direction." Ben pointed back the way we had come into the oasis.

I watched him follow them for a bit, but then knelt down and looked at the first footprint closer. Something was off about it. I looked in the opposite direction as Ben was going. There was a trail of footprints coming from that way, trailing around the pond away from the cave.

What was wrong with the footprints? Something in my mind told me there was a pattern I was missing. I looked at the footprint for a long time before it came to me.

I stood up quickly. A little too quickly. A dizzy spell hit me and I closed my eyes, waiting for it to pass. When it did, I called out to Ben.

"Hey, come here. I think you are wrong about this." I yelled.

Ben came trotting back to me. I knelt down and pointed at the edges of the footprint. "See this?"

Ben knelt down and looked, but came up empty. "I don't see anything but the footprint."

I pointed to the heel mark in the footprint. "See how deep the impression is from the heel?" Ben nodded, and I pointed to the toe marks. "Now, look how deep the toes are."

"The heel is deeper than the toes." Ben looked at me confused. "What does that mean?"

"Well," I said, sitting back on my haunches. "Either, this animal walks weirdly, striking the ground hard as it foot lands rather than using significant pressure to raise the foot up, which goes against most practical foot mechanics that we learned in biology, or it is walking backwards, the toes striking the ground first and the heel propelling the leg upward."

Ben's face lit up. "Or, its foot is on backwards!" Ben stood and started pacing excitedly. "A rather nasty odor, backwards feet, and a jungle home. I know what this is, Anna!"

I stood as well, my hands crossed over my chest. "What is it?"

Ben faced me, smiling broadly. "A mapinguary. They are mythical creatures that act as protectors of the Amazon. That would explain why there is so much wildlife here. The mapinguary would need a habitat that mimics the Amazon, plants and wildlife, to defend."

I nodded. "Wow, whatever Malachi did when he made these oases, it was really detailed to provide a perfect home for each animal."

Ben shook his head. "No, Anna. Malachi didn't make these oases. He just closed them off. The oases used to run continuously, one bumping right up to the other, with the edges being a mixture of both. Remember how Eilidh said their water used to run through every land? Each mythical animal had its own specific area, just as each god had their own specific area for their worshippers. They were all one big map over the land with no walls or anything separating them. You could physically walk from Valhalla to the amphisbaena's desert to the city of Taikarlu if you wanted. Before the Flood, you could go anywhere without the key and door system you know we use now.

Well, anywhere but Area Two if you were not a god. That was the only locked up place."

"Oh," I replied. "But, wait. Where would my lands be, then? If it was all mapped out, how would I, a new god, have lands for my worshippers' afterlives?"

Ben chuckled. "You just would. I mean, in all honesty, you probably do now, it is just empty since you haven't created anything. Just like time is wonky in Taikarlu, space is wonky. You should already know that. How do we know which direction we are moving without a compass or stars to follow?"

I opened my mouth, then closed it. I had never thought of that. I just did it.

"Exactly," Ben said. "The space in Taikarlu used to shrink and grow as much as needed when it needed to. Don't think of Taikarlu as part of Earth, which is fixed in a time-space type way. It is separate, a separate plane of existence connected to the human realm of Earth, the Milky Way galaxy in this universe. Taikarlu is sort of next to it, alongside it, but not really in it."

"So, I have lands somewhere in Taikarlu?" I asked. "New lands that are just sitting empty, waiting for me to decide how to use them?"

Ben put his hand on his hips. "More than likely. Unless, Malachi did something to stop it, I would say yes."

Huh. Interesting. I shook my head. While this was fascinating to learn, and definitely another reminder of the work I had to do as a new baby god when we finished saving the Heka, it was not important in the here and now. What was important was finding the mapinguary. I knelt down and looked at the footprints again.

"So, if their feet are on backwards," I said, following the trail of footprints around the pond with my eyes, "then the mapinguary did not come from that way, but went that way." I pointed the way I was looking.

"Yup," Ben agreed. "And the closer we get to it, the worse the smell will get. Warning, some myths say that the mapinguary's smell can cause a person to faint from its rancidness."

I stood and started walking, following the path of backwards footprints, but Ben spoke again. "Oh yeah, and you should probably know, mapinguaries are an ape-like animal with only one eye and two mouths. The second mouth is where the belly button should be."

"Thanks for that." I told Ben, then thought of a question. "Hey, Ben. I know this is completely off topic, but you mentioned belly buttons. I've never noticed. Do you have one? I mean, belly buttons come from the wound left when an umbilical cord falls off a mammal, but you aren't technically a mammal from a live birth."

Ben laughed and lifted his shirt, exposing his waist. Right in the perfect place was a small belly button. "Yeah, I have one. Don't ask me why or how, but I do. I always assumed it was just because we gods that shape our image in the familiar human shape copy everything exactly. We don't think about what we wouldn't actually have developed since we were created not born, don't need to nurse our young, or anything. We just created an exact replica of the humans that worship us."

We started walking again. I looked down at the footprints to follow the trail and Ben looked off into the jungle to watch for the mapinguary. We kept talking as we walked.

"So, what about gods like Shiva, who is somewhat human looking but blue and has too many arms, or Ganesh, that looks like an elephant?" I asked. "Do they have belly buttons?"

Ben shook his head. "I don't know. I don't exactly run around looking at other gods' stomachs. They do in pictures that Hindu people have drawn of them, as far as I remember."

I giggled and went back to following the footsteps. We circled around the pond, going the opposite direction of the cave. We hadn't gone this way in too many oases, so I wasn't sure what lay ahead.

Once we left the edge of the pond, the jungle oasis opened up into a massive, densely packed wooded area. The land seemed to rise and fall over gently sloping hills, but from our position, all we could see were trees, trees and more trees. At some points, the trees became so thick, laden with hanging vines and their bases covered with moss and flowers and smaller, bush-like plants, that it became hard to push through them. At these points, we would lose track of the footprints and Ben and I would spread out, searching the ground to find the trail.

All around us, we saw snakes clinging to tree branches and spider webs as big as out head, but none of these typical animals bothered us and we didn't bother them. The jungle was loud, a cacophony of sounds that, thankfully, hid the sounds of our walking. And always, there was the perpetual feeling that the air was so laden with water that instead of raining down, the raindrops just floated in the air, making it hot, sticky and miserable. I had expected that eventually I would be covered with mosquito bites, but nothing seemed to be biting today.

Finally, a small clearing opened up in the trees. Beyond it, I could see a shallow river snaking through the forest. At the edge of the water was a large ape, its back towards us. As Ben and I steeped carefully closer, the rotten egg smell got so bad my eyes started watering and I had to stifle a cough.

"Mapinguary." Ben whispered, pointing to the ape.

We stepped out from under the cover of the trees and stopped. The mapinguary seemed preoccupied with whatever it was doing and I didn't want to startle it, so I loudly cleared my throat.

The mapinguary turned around to face us. In its rather ape-like hands, it had a fish that was tangled in some vines. The mapinguary's eyes went wide as it registered that it was looking at two humanoids. It straightened up, standing on two legs, and was over seven feet tall. Its body was covered with dark, coarse hair from head to toe, except its face. It had one giant eye in the middle of its forehead, a nose and ears similar to a monkey, and two mouths. One mouth was in the normal place on its face and the other was exactly where Ben said it would be, in the abdomen where the belly button should have been. Both mouths were hanging open in surprise.

"Hello," I said, trying to convey that we were friendly and not a threat. "I'm Anna. This is Ben. Are you untangling that fish? We would love to talk to you but, please, finish helping the fish first."

The mapinguary looked from us, to the fish and then back to us. I gestured towards the fish that seemed to be flopping less and less in the mapinguary's hands. "Please," I repeated, "finish your work. We will wait."

"Th.. Thank you." The mapinguary stuttered from the mouth on its face, its voice a higher pitch than I imagined it would be.

I leaned my head towards Ben. "Could you understand that?" I asked in a voice just low enough for him to hear.

"No," Ben replied, "it just sounded like grunts."

I nodded. I hadn't been sure if something this similar to human would have spoken in a way Ben could understand, like the naiads had.

The mapinguary turned back to the water and leaned over, holding the fish just below the water line. Its strong back muscles jumped and bunched as it pulled the vines from around the fish's body gently. As soon at the fish was free, the mapinguary opened its hands and the fish swam away. It straightened again, standing at its full height and turned back to us.

"My name is Cariget." The mapinguary finally said. "What are you doing in my jungle?" Cariget did not make that question sound accusatory but more confused.

"Before I answer you, I just want to let you know," I told it, "that Ben cannot understand you like I do. I will need to translate."

Cariget nodded, and I continued. "We are here because the Heka needs help. Do you remember what happened during the Flood?"

Cariget nodded again. "Everything was drowned. Even though

the jungle is a very wet place, it was far too wet. When the water went away, I went around the jungle, checking on the animals and plants to make sure they were okay. I discovered that we were isolated here. The Dry Place was all around us. I couldn't leave."

"We call the Dry Place the Wastes," Ben told it. "They separated all the lands of Taikarlu from each other. No mythical animals could leave their home, and gods could not come to the mythical animals."

I picked up talking, explain the same story we had told so many times now. "The Heka was trapped in the Wastes by Malachi. It could not get free. But now, we are walking the Wastes unlocking the oases to free the Heka before Its entrapment kills It."

"Why now?" Cariget asked.

"What?" I replied.

"Why now?" Cariget repeated. "Why did you choose to free me and the Heka now? Why not before, right after it happened?"

No one had asked us this before. I looked down at the ground as I answered. "Because no one knew before. We just found out ourselves. The gods thought that the Heka left of Its own free will. But a lot of things happened recently and it was discovered that the Heka didn't leave, but was trapped by Malachi, a human who had been gifted with immortality by his god, and who had befriended the Heka in the city.

"Bob, Malachi's god, had forgotten that Malachi was old when he gifted him immortality, and failed to heal Malachi's aging body of its aches and pains. Malachi became bitter at this so-called gift and acted out causing all of these problems."

"What happened to Malachi?" Cariget asked.

Ben answered this time. "He was brought before all the gods to be put on trial to answer some other questions, questions about Anna that we thought he knew about. But before that trial could happen, Malachi told everyone what he had done to the Heka and why. Bob got angry with him and killed him, right there in the Joint Commission hall. We don't know what happened to Bob for killing Malachi. We left to save the Heka before anyone did anything about that."

"I have felt It close by. The Heka," Cariget told us. "It is close by. I thought It was hiding from me when I called out to It."

"Not hiding," I told it, "but trapped."

Cariget nodded. "That makes more sense. When the Heka wouldn't come, I waited. I took care of the jungle, protected it just like I always have. I knew there was something wrong, what with the Dry Place all around where it shouldn't have been, but I just kept helping the plants and animals like always and waited. Did I do right?"

I smiled and stepped closer to the mapinguary. "You did exactly right."

The mapinguary looked around the jungle, turning in a circle as it did. "The Heka still feels close by, but now that you tell me, I can sense the wrongness in It. It is hurt, isn't it?"

"Yes," Ben replied. "It is dying. Every oasis we unlock makes the cage the Heka is trapped in smaller. It needs to be free, but the only way to do that is to unlock the oases. So, we have been hurting It more to help It, if that makes sense."

Cariget looked at Ben. "It does. That fish I was helping? It struggles to breath when not in the water. But the only way to free it from the tangle of vines it was trapped in was to remove it from the water. I didn't like hurting it, but sometimes, you must hurt to help."

"Exactly." I told it.

Cariget walked closer to us. It didn't seem to be threatening just curious. It walked by me and sniffed. "You are hurting too."

I nodded. "I am connected to the Heka somehow." I explained. "I am siphoning off some of Its pain, trying to help It last until we can get there."

The mapinguary sniffed me again. Almost thoughtfully, it said, nodding, "Hurt to help." Cariget sniffed me again. "Not connected to the Heka, though."

I looked at Cariget sharply. "What do you mean not connected?"

Cariget kept sniffing around me. My mind wandered back to the discussion with Ben about how I probably smelled bad from sweating and everything, and I felt self-conscious as Cariget walked around me, sniffing. Ben put a finger under his nose as Cariget came closer, attempting to respectfully block the smell that seemed to be emanating from the mapinguary's abdomen mouth.

Cariget finally spoke again. "No, not connected. You smell the same. Like the Heka and you are made the same."

"The Heka wasn't made though," I retorted.

Ben contradicted me, his finger still at his nose. "Actually, The Heka was probably made or born at some point. The humanistic idea that the gods have just always existed is obviously wrong. We cannot, therefore, just automatically transfer that ideology from the gods the humans know to the god of the gods in the Heka. How the Heka was born, created, or made, I have no idea, but logically, if the Heka can have an end, then It must have had a beginning."

"So, what does that say about me?" I asked, my question directed more at Cariget than towards Ben. "I was born from a human and a coordinator. The Heka made humans and coordinators so could not have also been born from them too."

Cariget grunted, indicating it didn't know. I looked at Ben who shrugged. Now, let me see, I thought. I have been called the heart of the Heka, tainted by the Heka, connected to the Heka, linked with the Heka and now am made the same way as the Heka. I wonder if I am related to the Heka somehow, I thought sarcastically.

Cariget was still sniffing around me. I was ignoring its smell as much as possible while it investigated me. Finally, the mapinguary walked a few steps away from Ben and me. Ben exhaled, lowering his finger from blocking his nose.

"Why do I get the sense," Cariget asked, "that your name is different than what you told me? And why do I smell a desperation from you, Anna, that needs me to know that name?"

"Because my name, knowing it fully, is how we fully unlock the oasis." I told it.

"Hmm," Cariget thought. "Is Anna actually part of your name?"

"Yes," I replied. "How do you sense these things? Or smell them? You've used both words almost interchangeably."

"I can smell things incredibly well," Cariget replied. "I can also taste different pheromones and whatnot that animals and plants give off into the air with my umbilical buccal cavity." I raised an eyebrow at that seemingly scientific term and Cariget put his hand on his abdomen, saying, "The mouth on my stomach."

"Ahh," I said.

Cariget continued talking. "These scents and tastes in the air around people, animals and plants help me defend my rainforest home. I can tell if an animal is in trouble and come to protect it."

The mapinguary paused. It looked at me closely. "You smell like you are in trouble, AnnaBella Cain. Had the fish not been taking my focus, I would have smelled you as soon as you entered the jungle and came to your aid." In an offhanded way, Cariget added. "And Ben tastes of concern and attraction. He is not a threat, nor much help to you, but he tries."

I smiled while Ben pretended to be affronted.

"Did I guess your name right?" Cariget asked.

"Yes," I told it, "now, you must do one more thing for us, if you will. I need you to leave the oasis. If you go to…" I thought about my directions for a moment. "If you go to the west, you should be able to stay in the jungle until you reach the city of Taikarlu, where the gods are. They probably have people along the borders by now, watching for mythical animals to show up. Or at least, that is what I would do. If they don't, or you do not want to go to the city, turn north before entering the city and you will come to the land of the unicorns. They will help you as well, I believe."

"I have to leave?" Cariget asked, sounding unsure.

"We believe so," Ben told it gently. "At every other oasis, the Heka's cage did not get smaller, and thus weaker, until one of the residents of the oasis had left the boundary of their lands. While this will hurt the Heka, and Anna, it is necessary to complete the connection back with the rest of the other lands, Taikarlu and the humans. Or at least, we assume it does."

Cariget nodded. "Hurt to help. I understand. Will I be allowed to return to my jungle once the work of connecting it is done? Once the Heka's cage is broken?"

"Yes." I told him. "As soon as you have connected with the other gods, you should be able to return to your jungle. In fact, some of the gods may even want to come back with you, to learn about your jungle and you as we have."

Cariget nodded again. "Then I will do ask you ask immediately. Goodbye Anna and Ben."

Before it turned away, the mapinguary spoke again, but this time from the mouth in its abdomen. "Goodbye, AnnaBella Cain." The voice from the abdomen was a deep, rumbling sound, very different from the higher pitched, more musical sound from the mouth on its face.

"Huh," said Ben, "I did not expect that." We watched the mapinguary as it took off through the dense jungle. When we could no longer see it, Ben turned to me and said, "What I do expect, though, is that very shortly, you are going to be in a whole lotta pain. Want to head back towards the cave?"

I nodded, and we turned back into the trees, following the now obvious path through the overgrowth that we had carved out while looking for the mapinguary. We did not talk much as we walked. I wanted to get back to at least somewhat familiar territory before the pain from the Heka's cage closing in hit me.

Instead, I thought about what Cariget had said about my connection to the Heka. It was becoming more and more obvious that my connection to the Heka was not just a simple friendship, or even that I was just somehow the Heka's chosen messenger. Our connection seemed much deeper, even, then something formed because of the Heka urging my father to have a child for the sole purpose of rescuing It, and me being said child.

Once we reached the pond, we wandered towards the cave without actually going inside it. I put a hand out and gently grabbed

Ben's arm.

'Hey, Ben,' I broached.

Ben turned toward me. "Yeah, Anna?"

"Remember way back when, when Nummi told me that everyone had three parts: a body, a soul, and a spirit?"

"Yeah," Ben replied. "Well, humans have those three parts. Gods are different. Well, most gods." He corrected himself. "You are a human made god, so you are a god with all three parts. Most gods only have an actual spirit, the body is not really real, or needed and so there is no soul."

"Anyway," I broke off Ben's rambling. "I have three parts, Nummi said. My body, which was with the humans, my spirit which had been in Taikarlu, and my soul. Nummi had said that my soul had to be with my body because otherwise my body would have died. My body was sick because the spirit had been away so long. But he told me that, as a human, if my soul left my body for even a second, poof, I would die."

Ben nodded. "Yeah, that's right."

I shook my head. "But Nummi was wrong. I wasn't human."

"You were human then. You aren't now." Ben attempted to correct me, but I kept shaking my head.

"No, I wasn't human then," I pushed. "We just didn't know it yet. I was a god then. The humans had already decided I was one."

Ben sat down next to the pond, crossing his legs and pulling at tufts of grass. "Where are you going with this, Anna?"

I sat down next to him. "Is there anything other than a human that has all three: body, spirit and soul?"

Ben pulled at the grass some more. He picked up a strand and held it to the light., examining it. I think he was buying time to think. Eventually, he shrugged. "No. Animals are body and soul only, no spirit. Gods and coordinators are spirit only, no body or soul. Mythical beasts are body and spirit, no soul."

"What about the Heka?" I asked.

"The Heka," Ben sighed. "I don't know. The Heka had a body at one time. I used to think that Its body was just like a god's body, made up just to make interaction easier. But I'm not sure about that now. I used to think that the Heka was just a spirit, like gods. But again, I am not sure now. Spirits are containable, and the Heka is currently contained but is dying from being contained." Ben dropped the grass and rubbed his face in frustration.

I pushed further. "What really is the difference between a spirit and a soul? A body, I think I get, obviously, but spirit and soul seem so similar."

Ben looked at the ground, his mouth twitching. "Honestly, Anna? I am not sure I really know anymore. I used to think that it didn't matter because that was human stuff, and I didn't need to worry about it. My worshippers had bodies, spirits and souls, I knew. But when they died, the body gets discarded. The spirit would come to the afterlife I had chosen for them, after a brief stop for a meeting with your dad, and I really didn't think about where the soul went. Nummi would be better at answering these questions than I would." Ben started plucking at the grass again, his face in a scowl.

I stopped asking Ben questions. For some reason, he seemed upset by them, so I let him be. He had never had a problem with my questions before, though. Maybe he was frustrated because he didn't know the answers. Most of the time, he had been a really good instructor on the way all this god stuff worked, so he never had to doubt his knowledge.

Sometimes, I forgot that, even though Ben is an ancient, immortal god that has existed for mellenia, he is also just a teenager like me. Sometimes, I had the reverse problem and forgot that Ben was also a god and not just a teenager. I looked down at the grass, copying Ben's movements at picking at it, and wondered if Ben ever had the same problem, forgetting that I was either also a god or not only a god.

I didn't get to wonder for long because a prickling sensation, like pins and needles, started spreading across my skin. Cariget must have left the oasis. I had just enough time to call out to Ben before the walls of the Heka's cage started shrinking.

Ben jumped off the ground and ran around to sit behind me. As the pain of the Heka's cage shrinking started to become overpowering, Ben lifted me into his lap and put his hand on my forehead to pull me back to rest my weight on him. The pressure of the cage pushed so hard my ears popped and my heart felt like it was going to burst. I couldn't draw a full breath and saw spots floating before my eyes. I fought hard not to pass out.

"Anna, just breathe." Ben said gently.

"I can't." I panted. "Too tight."

Ben wrapped his arms around me gently as the pain became overwhelming. The Heka had no more space at all. It was cramped into a space so small that even contortionists would struggle to fit inside. An infinite being inside a tiny box. The pain was unbearable. I thought my ribs would crack. Ben kept one arm around my waist, that hand resting on my hip, and placed his other hand on my forehead, running his fingers through my hair the way a mother would with her child when they had a fever. He kept making soft shushing noises.

The Heka pushed at me in my mind. It was asking if some of Its essence could come inside me, the same way It would bring me inside It when I went to the place where universes were born and died. I agreed, hoping that doing so would give It more space inside the cage and relax some of Its, and therefore my, pain. It helped slightly.

Slowly, the walls of the cages stopped moving. The Heka was able to settle Itself inside the space It had left, what little there was. Once the Heka accepted Its new limited area, I was able to try to accept it too.

I felt Ben put both arms around me again. Somehow, the tighter he held me, the less pain I felt. It was as if Ben's touch grounded me in the reality that I was not, in fact, in the cage with the Heka, but in a jungle styled oasis with plenty of space to stretch and move. As soon as I was able, I turned around to face Ben. I laid my forehead down on his shoulder and wrapped my arms around his back.

As I sat there in Ben's arms, out of the corner of my eye, I saw the spot in the hollow of his neck where I had kissed him to make the talisman brand. I knew, with the Heka growing weaker and the cage getting smaller, the haze in the Wastes was going to be larger and stronger. I should redo the talisman, just for safety's sake.

I lifted my head and told Ben what I was thinking.

"Are you sure you're up to that right now, Anna?" he asked, concerned.

I shifted a little, testing myself. "Yeah," I told Ben, "The Heka and I, we are getting used to the pain of the cage. It's worse every time, but we are also better at dealing with it every time." I did not tell Ben about the Heka moving some of Itself into an unused corner of my mind. I didn't know how he would feel about the Heka basically possessing me.

"Do you, um," Ben stammered. "Do you want me to kiss you first again? To make it less weird like last time?"

"Do you want to kiss me?" I asked in response.

Ben smiled slightly. "I always want to kiss you, Anna."

I nodded in agreement and Ben raised one hand to my face, smoothing my hair. His hand stopped to rest on my cheek. He leaned down and kissed me gently. I leaned in to Ben, wrapping my arms around him tighter, returning the kiss. Ben's hands moved to settle on my hips as he deepened the kiss.

A part of my brain reminded me I was supposed to be preparing to mark Ben to protect him from the haze, not just enjoying kissing him. I wanted to tell that part of my brain to shut up, but it was right.

I pulled my face away from Ben's and, instinctively knowing what I was going to do, he tilted his head to give me better access to his neck.

A different part of my brain wanted to chuckle. The way Ben had moved reminded me of all those vampire movies where the humans are willing to get bitten and bare their necks in preparations. I internally rolled my eyes at this part of my brain and told it to shut up.

Instead of thinking of vampire movies, I closed my eyes and felt for my Heka. It felt different somehow, but I ignored that. I fed the Heka my feelings for Ben, and my ideas of what love is and pushed it out of me as I kissed the base of Ben's neck.

The other times I had done this, Ben had hissed slightly, and there had been a red mark, almost like a small burn, left in that spot. This time, as soon as my lips touched him, Ben jumped back from me, yelping and spilling me onto the ground.

"What the hell was that?" Ben gasped, grabbing his neck.

"I don't know." I said. "It was the same thing I did last time."

Ben pulled his hand away from his neck. I looked at the spot I had kissed and saw the red mark. I watched it, waiting for it to fade like last time. Instead, the red spot blistered and turned pale white against Ben's bronze skin.

Ben felt the edges of the mark with his fingers. "You burned me." He said, accusatorily.

"You said it burned last time too," I tried defending myself. "I didn't do anything different."

Ben stood up and started pacing. "Well, something sure was different. Last time, it burned just a little like a bee sting. This time, if felt like you set me on fire."

"It looks different too," I told him honestly. "Last time, it was just red for a moment or two. Now, it blistered."

Ben stopped pacing and plopped back down on the ground. He sighed deeply. "I'm sorry I yelled. And I'm sorry I dumped you. I was just surprised. That hurt, a lot."

"I'm sorry, too." I told him.

Ben looked at me. "Anna, you have to be honest with me. What was different this time?" I started to say nothing, but Ben shook his head. "Something is, I can tell. What is different?"

I looked at the ground, hiding my face as I spoke. "The Heka put some of Its consciousness in me to escape how tight the cage got."

Ben jumped up again. "What?!" he yelled.

I looked back up at him, and tried to stand. I managed to get to my feet, although shakily. I was still trying to recover my strength from the oasis unlocking. "It was the only way!" I told him. "The Heka would have died from being so cramped down. I think, I think I would have died from the pain of it too. The only choice we had was to make there be less Heka in the cage. And the only place It could go was in me."

Ben rubbed his eyes. "You let an infinite being into your own mind?" He asked, incredulously. The he paused. His body stopped all motion as he stopped speaking. "Wait a minute." Ben continued. "You were capable of letting an infinite being into your mind? And was able to limit it to 'just a little bit'?"

As Ben said this, I realized how impossible what I had said I had done now seemed. I prodded the part of my mind where the Heka seemed to be sitting. It was there, carefully sitting in Its assigned space. It was being careful not to spread out any more than I was willing to let It and not interrupt any major thinking functions, keeping Itself separate from me.

"Yeah." I finally answered Ben, shrugging. I didn't know what else to say.

I had been so used to knowing the things that the Heka was thinking and feeling that, when the Heka piped up from Its spot in my mind, it took me a moment to realize the thought was not mine. I said it out loud to share the thought with Ben.

"The Heka thinks that maybe, when I combined my feelings for you with Heka to make the talisman, I accidentally used the Heka instead of my Heka."

Ben knelt down, resting his weight on the balls of his feet and placing his elbows on his knees, his hands clasped together and his head hanging between them. Ben's hair slung over his shoulder and brushed the ground.

"So," Ben finally said, "not only are you able to connect with the Heka, know what It is thinking and feeling, and able to take some of the Heka's pain to make it more manageable, and able to allow some of the Heka's infinite being to chill out in an unused corner of your mind so that It won't be crushed by Its cage, but now you can *accidentally* use the Heka's power instead of your own without having any idea you doing it?"

"I mean," I tried to explain. "I knew something was off with my Heka, but I ignored it. I assumed it was just wonky because of so much contact with the Heka Itself."

Ben stood up again, with his hands on his hips and stared into the sky. "You ignored it?" I knew he wasn't actually talking to me. "It was wonky, just wonky, so you ignored it." Ben started laughing. His laugh sounded slightly spiteful. He shook his head and walked over towards me.

Internally, I cringed away from Ben. He was angry. I didn't know why he was angry, well besides the fact that I accidentally burned him. But I had no control over that.

"I don't think you understand, Anna." Ben said to me. "This is insane. It's not possible." Ben crossed his arms over his chest, staring at me.

Finally, too frustrated, I yelled at him. "Impossible? It's impossible? You want to talk about impossible? Let's see…" I started pacing, just completely done with everything. "Six months ago, I would have said that one of my parents being anything but a normal human was impossible. I would have said traveling to the world of the gods through a nondescript office building was impossible. The idea that I could be put through the same trials that Hercules did, and completed them better than he did, was impossible. I would have told you that the idea I could do anything magical or supernatural with some power called the Heka was impossible. I am a god? Impossible. I am the only one who can save the god of all the gods? Impossible! That I am standing here, having spoken to eight mythical creatures, freed them from their entrapment, and am on my way to free two more? Impossible!"

I stopped talking, panting. I ran my hands through my hair, tugging at it in frustration. Forcing myself to catch my breath and calm down, I turned to face Ben again. "Everything I have done, everything I have seen has been impossible. And I have dealt with it, rolled with the punches, and took on all the pain, hunger, and exhaustion. And you, Benahahminen, are having a problem dealing with the slight impossibility of me accidentally burning you with the Heka?"

Eilidh's words floated through my mind. *Promise me you will do whatever you can to reach the Heka in time. Even if it means abandoning Benahahminen.* There was no time to argue about this anymore, I knew. I had no time to waste on Ben's frustrations with the impossible things that seemed to just be my life now. I had no more time. The Heka had no more time. "You know what, Ben?" I finally said. "Why don't you stay here, worrying about what is impossible and I'll continue on and just do it alone!"

I turned away from Ben and walked to the edge of the oasis. The haze was right there, right at the edge of the oasis. There was no more space that was only kind of wrong, but only the oases that were the door and the Wastes that were very wrong. I could hear Ben calling my name, begging me to wait and talk to him, but I ignored him. I just didn't have the time. He would either get over himself and catch up with me or he would go back to Taikarlu. Either way, we had wasted too much time. I would continue on to the ninth oasis on my own.

Chapter Nine

AnnaBella stomped through the Wastes, muttering to herself. The pain of the Heka's cage tightening was still affecting her, but she ignored it in favor of her frustration with Ben. "Impossible." She muttered to herself, mocking Ben. "What you are doing is impossible, Anna. What you are doing is insane, Anna." She shook her head as she walked.

"Why is he so worried about what is impossible now?" Bella's shoulders sagged. "When we started it was all 'you can do this, it's all on you' when I had no idea what I was doing. None! But now he is all pissy 'cause I messed up a little. Sure, it hurt him. Whoops, my bad. But that is not even the worst way he has been hurt lately. He lost an entire finger, for cripes sake. He didn't have a problem with me 'accidentally' tapping into the Heka instead of my Heka then, did he?"

Ben had remained in the mapinguary oasis after Bella had left him. He had called after her, hoping to get her to stop and talk to him, but she ignored him and kept walking.

"Oy vey," Ben muttered and rubbed his hands over his face. As he did it, he caught sight of his right hand. He held it up to examine it. The pinky finger was still missing, with just a small nub left. The skin had been pulled over that nub cleanly and seamed together, leaving only a small scar.

Ben laughed sarcastically. "I have a lot of new scars from Anna." He said. That thought made him pause. In his head, he listed all of his new scars and how they had come to be. He had the scar around his leg from the first time he brushed up against the edge of the Heka's cage. The Caladrius had healed that, with Bella's help. The Caladrius had told Bella that the poison in the wound could have tainted her. They could expel that poison, but she couldn't, so she should be careful what she does.

Then there was the pinky finger. Ben had lost that to the Heka's cage as well, and Bella had, once again, healed it with the Heka's power, rather than her own Heka power. The finger had only gone slightly green with the poison that time. Ben looked at the spot where the finger should have been. There was no green tinge. Bella must have cleaned it up and, if the Caladrius were right, tainted herself even more.

Finally, there was the talisman. Bella had caused that injury on accident, again using the Heka's power instead of her own. Ben realized that all three times, Bella had to have used the Heka's power, not her own, on him. This wasn't a one-time mistake she made because she had invited the Heka to bleed a little of Its existence into her mind to make It more comfortable, but something she had done repetitively.

"Anna can use the full Heka's power at will." Ben whispered to himself. "How?" He asked no one in particular. No answer came to him. Bella was right, the number of impossible things that happened around her were staggering. How could Ben possibly blame her for not being able to keep it all straight?

Ben sighed and paced again, his mind full of all the things Bella had done. Her Trials Arena results, her survival as a spirit and physical body separated for so long, every different way she had interacted with the trapped Heka all swirled around in his mind becoming a storm of thoughts and confusion.

A new thought was born from all these other thoughts. Ben stopped pacing to try and pin it down. When he did, he took off at a run after Bella. He needed to tell her before she was caught off guard. He needed to help her, protect her, no matter the cost to him. He ran out of the oasis, scanning the Wastes to see which direction Bella had gone.

She was only a speck on the horizon to the north-east. The haze, Ben noted, was directly outside the oasis. Ben figured if the talisman had been made too strongly, so strong that it burned him, then it was probably powerful enough to withstand this much haze. He took off as fast as he could after Bella.

I reached the eighth oasis before I realized I had. The land had long since changed from pure sand to scraggly bushes and a smattering of trees that were not much taller than I was. I only realized that I was actually inside the oasis when I reached the pond.

Confused, I looked around. Yep, there was the cave, right where it should be. But the usual forest area of the oasis had never fully developed. As I wandered, trying to figure out why the oasis was like this, so different that the others, I realized that the sand had changed from gleaming white to a rusty reddish-brown. By the pond, a beach of sorts had developed, rather than the basically dead run-up lined with rocks that had been in the other oases, and that sand was white.

Because the trees and other plants were so sparse, I could see that to the east the oasis went on for a very long time. There were small mounds out that way. They looked like earthworks that human cultures sometimes built rather than small hills. I walked towards them to inspect them better. The mounds were large, the smallest ones probably three to four feet across and the biggest ones were more than thirty feet across.

I expected, as I got closer, for the pattern of the earthworks to make more sense, but they didn't. The very small ones all seemed to be made close to mid-sized ones but, other than that, they seemed to have been placed very haphazardly.

As I walked closer, I noticed that the earthworks were a mottled brown color, with the small ones being more of a plain tan with less pattern and the larger ones having a pattern of greens and browns and tans that resembles the skin of some lizards. There was also an odd deep humming sound coming from them. I assumed that the sound was probably coming from the mythical animal I would need to talk to. They were probably hiding in the earthworks.

The closer I got, the more earthworks there appeared to be. The mounds seemed to go on forever, over the horizon. Who had built these and why? Was it the mythical beast that built them, or were they built by the humans that interacted with the mythical beasts and the land of Taikarlu had made them part of their habitat?

I had been walking casually, not worried about making noise as I moved. As I passed the last clump of small trees before the earthworks, I stopped. Those were not earthworks at all. They were lizards. Giant lizards. The deep humming sound was their breathing. Or actually, their snoring. All of them were huddled together, sound asleep. The humps that were small and tan were the beasts' young, presumably huddled up against their mothers. The larger humps were probably the oldest, and therefore biggest, lizards.

I moved more quietly now, afraid to wake them. There were hundreds and, from one glance, I could tell they were carnivores. Long snouts with sharp looking teeth protruding through their slightly opened lips, forward facing eyes, and sharp claws all screamed meat eater.

I carefully moved around, trying to identify more about these

171

lizards. They had four legs, each ending in three toes, and a medium sized tail. The front legs were significantly shorter that the hind legs, similar to a t-rex. They probably moved like a t-rex too, balancing on the hind legs and using the tail for stability, while the front legs were used for gripping prey as they killed it.

Great. Well, good news, bad news, I thought. Good news was lizards are usually cold-blooded, and will be sluggish in the cold, and restful in the heat, only active long enough to hunt and mate, which usually they only did once every few days to once a month. Bad news was I had no idea when these particular lizards had last had a good meal and, with so many of them, I would probably be just a snack to the bigger ones. If they woke up hungry, the would fight over me and I had zero chance of escaping. The semi-arid conditions of the oasis combined with the lack of sun movement meant it would always be warm enough for these beasts to hunt well, so I couldn't just try to come at them when it was dark and cold and they would be too slow to really be a threat.

I crouched down, allowing myself to blend into the ground, just in case one of the lizards opened their eyes. Behind me, a noise caught my attention. Something was moving through the brush at my back. I turned very slowly, dreading what it would be.

"Anna." I heard Ben say loudly before I could turn all the around. I rolled my eyes and turned around quickly but silently.

Ben was moving the way I had before I realized that the earthworks were not dirt but animals. I forcefully gestured for him to stop, be silent. Ben nodded and crouched down like I was. He moved slowly and carefully now, making as little sound as possible.

When Ben reached my side, I pointed to the field of sleeping lizards. His face blanched as he realized his mistake. I patted him on the back, trying to show him it was ok. I made the same mistake at first too. Ben's eyes were wide as he looked around at all the rather large, predatory, sleeping lizards.

Ben leaned over and whispered, "Burrunjor."

I raised an eyebrow at him, showing my lack of understanding and Ben whispered again. "Burrunjor. Also called Old Three-Toes by some humans. A nocturnal lizard that eats cattle and kangaroos."

I nodded. "Nocturnal?" I asked.

"Yeah," Ben replied. "Not sure how that works in the land of perpetual day."

"They look like the t-rex." I mentioned.

Ben agreed. "Some humans think they aren't just a mythological animal, but were a type of dinosaur that lasted into the era of people but has since gone extinct, leaving behind just fossilized footprints and legends."

The mention of dinosaurs made me think of a question. I was going to ask it, but didn't. The last time I asked Ben questions about how all this stuff worked, he got angry at me.

Ben must have figured out from my face that I was thinking of something. He asked me what it was.

"Nothing." I told him. "Just more stuff I don't know that gods should."

"Ask me." He replied.

I shook my head. "Nah, you're sick of my questions."

Ben groaned. "Anna. I am not sick of your questions, just tired of all of this. Tired of realizing how little I actually know. Some of the questions you are asking I never thought to ask in my millions of years. And, as you so rightly pointed out, you have only been in this world of gods and coordinators and myths being real for six months give or take, and yet you know to ask the questions I never did. It makes me feel… irresponsible not to have asked them, or cared really, before."

I didn't respond to Ben's quasi-apologetic statement, instead I just asked my question. "How old is the earth really? A lot of people think, because of their faith, it is only six thousand or so, but others and science say it is millions. Dinosaurs went extinct long before humans ever existed and whatever. Which one is right?"

"I don't like to think about it in terms of right and wrong." Ban answered. "Has the physical planet been around for a long time before humans? Yes. Did the dinosaurs exist before humans? Also, yes. But how can you put a value on time before time was created? Humans made up time and if there is anything I know you understand really well it is that time is completely wonky. So, did creation take millions of years or six days? Yes, to both, depending on how you measure time before time was created."

Ben and I sat quietly for a while after that and watched the burrunjor sleep. We had to figure out a way to unlock this oasis without waking the nocturnal lizards that might just decide to eat us rather than listen to us.

"Ben?" I finally said. "Do you think that we could carry one of the small baby burrunjors?"

"I don't think so. They are still pretty big. Why?" he replied.

I shrugged. "I was thinking maybe we could take one of the babies into the cave, where it would be too cold for it to move quickly and

173

wake it up."

"Even if we could do that, without waking up the mother, who would probably be pretty pissed," Ben said, "we can't be sure a baby would have the understanding to help us."

"True." I replied, defeated.

I continued thinking about how to handle the burrunjor without becoming lunch. I even tried poking at the Heka to see if It had any bright ideas. The Heka just pulled away from me, focusing too much on Its ow survival at this point to worry about mine.

"Anna," Ben said, still keeping his voice low, "I have an idea, but you probably won't like it."

"Is it worse than stealing a baby?" I asked him, half joking.

"Maybe," Ben replied. Oh boy. "You are very adept at using your Heka, aren't you?"

I snorted. "Obviously not." I said, glancing at the spot on Ben's neck where the talisman was. It was still raised, blistered and looked painful. A perfect imprint of my lips burned into Ben's skin. Yay, another scar on him that was my fault. What did that make, now? Three?

Ben waved his hand in dismissal. "That was you mistaking the Heka for your Heka, an honest mistake. I mean, no one should ever have been able to tap directly into the Heka's power. How were you to know how to not do that when it was very obvious you could? You only did it like three times on me alone. The only one who could have taught you how to keep them separated was busy not dying."

"Three times?" I asked, glad to hear Ben sounding more like his normal self, sarcastic and a little silly.

"Yeah," Ben answered. He ticked them off on his fingers. "When my leg was hurt. When my finger was hurt. And when you made the talisman the last time." Ben held up his right hand, smiling. He had lowered his thumb out of the way and with the pinky finger missing, he was only holding up three fingers. "Three times."

I shook my head, trying to not smile at what was obviously an attempt by Ben to be lighthearted about his missing finger.

"Anyway," Ben continued. "You are rather adept at using *your* Heka. You silenced the entire Joint Commission, forced a door between the human realms and Taikarlu without a key, made the sand direct us, and did a whole bunch of other stuff without even really trying. Do you think, if you walked up to one of those burrunjor and touched it, you could use your Heka to make it wake up and talk to us without alerting the rest of the herd or it biting our heads off?"

I thought about this idea. "Two problems," I told Ben. "Or actually, three. One, I would have to walk around all of those sleeping mouths without waking any up before I wanted to. And two, what if I messed up and used the Heka instead of my Heka again? I could kill it instead of just wake it."

Ben tilted his head to the side considering this. "Well, one, we would just go for the closest one that looks rather adult-like without being too big and with no baby by it, giving us a better chance to subdue it before it gets mad and wakes everyone. And two, I would say that, before we even move, you pull up your Heka and make sure it really is your Heka and have It at the ready so you don't make a mistake."

Ben waited a beat, then added, "You said three problems but then only said two of them."

I took a deep breath. "You are asking me," I said slowly, "to control a sentient being, with a will of its own, with my Heka. I promised myself I would never do that, Ben."

"It would only be like giving an animal a sedative so you can help it better. Veterinarians do it all the time." Ben countered.

I shook my head. "I made a promise to myself after I saw what I could do with the Heka. After I forced the Avenging Women and the Joint Commission on accident, I promised that I would never use this power that way. That isn't right. Only dictators or evil people use such power to force anything with free will to act against their will. And the path from slightly sedating a wild animal to complete control of hordes of gods without their consent is a very slippery slope. One I won't even step on."

Ben put up his hands in surrender. "I will not ask you to go against your morals, Anna." He lowered his hands and kept talking. "You have the right, as a god, to decide the moral stances that your faith will be built on, what your worshippers or other can or can't ask you to do. I would expect you to respect the decisions I make in those areas, as long as it doesn't violate Commission rules, so I will respect yours in return."

I sat fully down on the reddish sand, my ankles throbbing from crouching for so long. I drew designs in the sand with my finger, contemplating solutions.

"What if," Ben wondered out loud, "you didn't force the burrunjor to be calm and listen to us, but only asked it to?"

"What do you mean?" I replied.

Ben sat all the way down as well, explaining. "I mean, instead of using your Heka to wake the animal, forcing it to be calm and not its normal predatory self or wake the rest of the herd, you just used your Heka to ask it to wake up calmly, we are here to help, would you please talk to us? That wouldn't violate your morals of not controlling sentient beings. It would leave us open to the possibility that its answer would be no, but if we must leave their free will intact, then no matter what we do, we run that risk. At least with this, we give ourselves a few seconds more to react because the burrunjor is still asleep when it answers you."

I nodded. That could work. It would be terrifying, but it would work. I told Ben to scout out a burrunjor he thought would be young enough to not be horrifyingly big but old enough to be at least some form of rational, and childless, for us to talk to. While he scanned the sleeping lizards, I looked inside myself to find, and hold on to, my personal Heka power free of the full Heka. I closed my eyes and searched for that warmth over cold. It was hard to find amongst the noise from the roaring fires and glaciers that was the actual Heka, but I did eventually find It, tame and small by comparison in one corner of my being. I grabbed hold of It and opened my eyes.

Ben pointed to a burrunjor to the left. It was probably fifteen feet long in the body, with another three feet of tail, and was positioned at the edges of the herd. The mothers and babies were all well clear of this lizard, centered more towards the middle of the pack. I nodded that I agreed on that one and Ben and I crept toward it as slowly and silently as we could.

Up close, the burrunjor was beautiful. The one Ben had chosen had a scaly hide that seemed dry and rough. Its coloring was mottled with circles of dark tan ringed with black and fine lines of almost mahogany color zigzagging through it. I tentatively placed my hand on one of its fore legs and pushed my Heka into it with the thought, "We are friendly and don't taste very good. We just want to talk to you, to help you and your herd."

I felt a response from the burrunjor without it even waking up. *Help with what?*

"It's responding in thought, not voice." I told Ben. "Are they telepathic?"

Ben shook his head. "Not that I know of, but I guess they could be."

"I am going to try to talk to it like this." I told him. "Maybe we don't need to wake it up at all. Can you keep watch?"

Ben nodded and stood up fully, his gaze scanning back and forth across the sleeping lizards. "Don't forget, one of them has to leave the oasis. So, it will have to wake up at some point."

"I know." I responded, then turned my attention back to the burrunjor.

You are trapped here, aren't you? I asked.

"Yes." The reply came. *We had been forced into hibernation during the Flood. The water was too cold. Afterwards, we came here. But it is always day now, and too hot. We cannot hunt when it is too hot or too cold. We can only sleep.*

Do you know what caused the Flood and this? You being trapped in perpetual day? I asked.

No, the burrunjor responded.

I told the lizard about the Heka and Malachi. I explained how the oases worked and what Ben and I were doing.

That is a lot of words to say the Heka is dying and I need to wake up and leave to help you save it, the burrunjor replied.

Ok, so it got the gist of the issue. *There is only one part you missed. You have to say my name to help me unlock the oasis so you can leave. Can you speak?* I asked. *Like verbally rather than telepathically?*

I can make noises, the burrunjor replied, *but you would not understand it.*

The Heka will, and whatever is locking the oasis will, I told it, simplifying the issue. *That's all that matters.*

I felt the burrunjor sigh internally. As I watched, the burrunjor opened one eyelid and then another. Its mouth opened wide. Ben and I both took rapid steps back before we realized the lizard was just yawning. The lizard lifted its head and looked around, its gaze falling on me.

"Hello, AnnaBella Cain." The burrunjor said, its voice like nothing I had ever heard before. The burrunjor then stood, stretching and trotted off.

"Woah," Ben said.

I looked at him. "What did you hear when it spoke?"

Ben pointed towards the direction of the pond, indicating that maybe we should move away from the rest of the sleeping burrunjor before talking. Once we got far enough away to feel safe, Ben answered me.

"It was wild." He said, awe in his voice. "It was like two different sounds overlaid on top of each other. The low sound was more constant. It was almost like the sound you hear when two cars are drag racing a few blocks away. The higher sound was more like clicks, almost like aliens do in scary movies. Why? What did it sound like to you?"

"It said 'hello, AnnaBella Cain,' and I know it said it out loud, but its voice was so deep, I felt it rather than heard it. Like its voice was too low for my human ears to hear." I told him.

We made our way back to the pond near the cave and sat down. Ben sat close to me as we waited for the Heka's cage to shrink. I leaned over the water and scooped some up in my hand to drink, then settled back to sitting.

"The next oasis is the last one." Ben reminded me.

"Maybe." I corrected him. "The next oasis is the last mythical beast oasis, if Malachi told the truth about how many oases and beasts there were locking the Heka's cage. After that, we have to actually find the Heka's cage, which could be anywhere."

"We have moved in basically a circle around the city of Taikarlu." Ben replied. "If the next oasis is to the north-west, as I expect it to be, we will have completed a full circle. The Wastes should be basically gone. I would assume that the next step would be to sense out the wrongness that is still left and go there. It would be the only part of the Wastes and the haze that isn't unlocked."

Ben seemed pretty sure of his idea, and I had no different ones. It made logical sense to me, but then again, logic did not seem to be enforced in this part of the world. I didn't know how I would have responded, but it didn't matter anyway because, at that moment, the burrunjor must have left its oasis home boundaries.

The pain from the Heka's cage growing smaller hit me with a force I could have never imagined. Everything compressed on me with pressure like I had dived too deep into the ocean. My bones felt like they were splintering and my heart raced, only able to half-beat under the pressure. Inside my head, the Heka was crying and tearing at Itself. My head throbbed and felt like it was attempting to collapse in on itself.

I put my hands to my head and screamed, falling over into the red sand. I tried to curl up into a ball to lessen my pain, but it didn't help. Neither did stretching out fully either. I ended up writhing on the ground, unable to find any position that eased my shrieking muscles.

Ben was hovering around me, lost as to how to help. Eventually, he just bent down and scooped me up into his arms, cradling me like a baby. He might have been talking to me, but between my screams and the Heka's cries, I could not hear him.

I felt a warm liquid trickling down my lips and at first thought I was crying without knowing it. A small drop got between my lips and I tasted the metallic saltiness of blood. My nose must have started bleeding. My hands, still clenched around my head, also felt damp. Part of me realized that it was not good if both my nose and my ears were bleeding.

How could we survive this? There was still one more oasis to unlock. If this was how bad it was now, how much worse would the next one be? There would be no way we could survive.

A picture started forming in my mind. Between my shouts of pain and the Heka's crying, I realized that, in my mind, I could see a vision. It was the cave in the oasis. I had never gone much further past the opening of the caves in any of the oases. The very first time, with Gavya, I had attempted to go deeper into the cave to see where the rivulet of water that ran through it and out to form the pond came from. But there had been no light source and the cave had gotten very dark very quickly. I had abandoned my explorations, satisfied with just staying in the larger areas just inside the mouth.

We needed to go to the cave in the last oasis. The Heka was telling me the only way It could to go there. But I had no way of walking with this much pressure on every part of my being, both physical and metaphysical.

I tried to open my eyes, blinking rapidly. "The oasis." I managed to squeak out, panting for breath between each syllable.

Ben continued holding me tightly. "What about the oasis, Anna?" The concern in his voice was palpable.

"Go." I whispered. When Ben didn't respond, I took the deepest breath I could and forced my voice as loud as I could make it. "Go!" The word still came out very weakly, but Ben understood.

Ben stood up, shifted my weight in his arms and started running. He ran out of the oasis and into the Wastes, heading north-west. Right at the edge of the oasis, he stumbled as he hit the haze head on. It felt like we had run straight into a brick wall and the pain of that combined with the pain of the cage doubled on me, making me cry out.

Ben caught his balance and shifted me again in his arms to hold me more securely, saying, "Sorry. Sorry," as if he had been the one to hurt me. I had no breath left to tell him it wasn't his fault. Ben wasn't able to run through the sands of the Waste, but he tried. He moved as fast as he could, never stopping.

Even for a god who didn't need to breath or rest, walking through the haze in the Wastes carrying someone else took an intense amount of strength and energy. Strength and energy that Ben's worshippers had never dreamed he would need, and so never gave him. But he never faltered and never stop. Even when he began to sweat and his breath, that he didn't need, came in short pants, Ben trudged on, hell bent on getting me to the final oasis.

Chapter Ten

AnnaBella is coming. Ben is bringing her. I just have to hold on for a little while longer. They are coming.

Ben carried me the entire way to the next and final oasis. By the time we reached the pond, he was drenched in sweat, the muscles in his arms trembling. Ben knelt down next to the pond and set me down gently. Then he sat down next to me, panting as he tried to catch his breath. Neither one of us questioned that he, as a god, suddenly needed to breathe or that he suddenly could sweat. It was obvious that the closer the Heka got to death, the weaker everything, even immortal things like gods, would get.

The haze had not let up when we entered the oasis. If anything, it was thicker here than it had ever been. I knew from my vision that our actual goal was the cave but, between the pain I was feeling and Ben's exhaustion, we had no choice but to take a break and gather our strength.

Ben took off his boots and peeled down his sweat-soaked socks. He shifted himself to sit at the edge of the pond, with his feet dangling in the water. He scooped up handfuls of it, splashing the back of his neck and wetting his face and hair. After resting there for a few moments, he crawled back to me.

"Come on," he said, pulling on my arms to make me move. "Anna, come by the water. You need to drink and cool yourself." Ben coughed from the intensity of the haze, which was so thick it was visible, like fog on a warm morning.

I groaned and tried to help Ben shift my body towards the lake. We sat together, leaning on each other, with our feet in the water. The coolness helped ease my pain some. The Heka was still curled up in the corner of my mind, silently crying, but even It had calmed down some.

As soon as I felt able, I slid into the pond, letting the cool waters do for all of me what it had for my feet. Ben joined me in the water and wrapped his arms around me. I leaned my head against his shoulder and we stood there, quietly, not swimming or roughhousing anymore.

After some time, I pushed myself out of the circle of Ben's arms and dipped completely below the water a few times. I brushed my wet hair back and used scoopfuls of the water to wash the now dried blood from my ears and face. I attempted to scrub at my visible skin, shedding the sand and sweat that had accumulated from me. I didn't have soap or any other bathing things, so it was mostly a hollow action, but it felt better to have at least tried.

Ben watched as I climbed out of the pond and found a nice rock to lean against. The sun was shining through the trees onto the rock, making it comfortably warm against my chilled wet clothing. I sat down and leaned against the rock, closing my eyes. I felt more than saw Ben join me.

We stayed at the rock long enough for my clothes to become mostly dry. I might have even slept but I'm not sure. At one point Ben left the rock then returned. When I sensed him return, I opened my eyes. He was holding an assortment of berries and nuts in his hand.

"Where did you find the nuts?" I asked, my voice hoarse.

Ben shrugged, "Around. Hunter-gatherer society, remember? Now, eat."

I took the handful of gathered food and ate it all. I had not realized that my body was that hungry until I started eating.

As I ate, Ben talked. "We are going to need to figure out where the mythical beast is in this oasis soon, Anna. Based on the state of you, I would guess the Heka is basically out of time. We have to unlock this oasis and find out where It is quickly. The only problem is, while foraging, I didn't see anything indicating the presence of any mythical animals. This seems to be the most stereotypical oasis since the first one."

I shook my head, swallowing the food in my mouth. "Not out in the oasis. We need to go down into the cave. Deep down."

Ben looked at me askance. "Did the Heka tell you that?"

"Showed me, more like." I said. "I think the Heka may be here, in this oasis."

Ben nodded. "Makes sense. It would explain why the haze is so thick here, even inside the oasis." Ben stood back up and I struggled to stand as well.

"No." He told me. "Keep resting. If we are going deep into the cave, we are going to need torches. I'm going to see what I can find."

I watched Ben wander over to a patch of evergreen trees. Searching the ground around them, he found a large stone with a sharp edge and started hitting one of the trees at about shoulder height. He hit the tree over and over as bits of bark and tree wood splintered off and rained around him, sticking to his clothes. After every few hits, Ben would stop and inspect the damage he had caused, then continue hitting the tree again.

After one inspection, Ben must have decided that he had done a sufficient amount of damage. He then turned and started looking around on the ground again. He picked a one stick, examined it then threw it away. Then he picked up another. This one he kept while he continued looking. After a while, Ben had found two sticks he deemed appropriate and walked back to the wounded tree.

Setting the sticks down by his feet Ben proceed to take off his tank top. It used to be a black tank top, but it had become bleached in the sun and had stains on it from his blood. He held the top between his hands and pulled it, twisting it this way and that until the fabric gave way. Ben continued twisting and pulling on the now destroyed tank top until he had several strips of fabric.

Ben put a few of the strips of fabric on the ground, keeping some in his hand, and picked up one of the sticks. He put the stick between his knees, and threw the remaining strips of fabric over one bare shoulder. He chose one of the strips and rubbed it into the wound he made on the tree, allowing the sap that had beaded there to soak the fabric completely. Once the fabric was sticky enough, Ben wrapped it around one end of the stick. He did this over and over until all the fabric strips that had been on his shoulder were now wrapped around the stick. He leaned the stick against the tree, picked up the rock, banged on the tree a few times, and then repeated the whole process of sapping the fabric and wrapping it around the stick with the second set of items.

That completed, Ben walked back over and leaned against the rock. He held up the two sticks for me to inspect. Smiling, he said, "Pine sap torches. Pretty neat, huh?"

I chuckled. "You learn that in the god version of Boy Scouts?"

"Nah" he said, still impressed with himself. "My worshippers taught me that. They're a pretty impressive bunch."

"They are," I agreed. "Pretty resourceful. I would love to meet them someday."

"When all this is said and done," Ben told me, "I promise, I'll take you to them. Maybe we can combine worshippers and become a system of gods together."

"Sounds like a plan," I responded, but some part of me knew that couldn't ever really happen. I wasn't even sure I would still be alive when this was 'all said and done.'

Ben held out one of the torches to me. "You ready?"

I pushed myself up and off the rock, forced myself to stand, and took the proffered torch. "Ready as I'll ever be."

We walked to the cave entrance. Even just over that short distance, the haze thickened. It seemed to be coming directly out of the mouth of the cave. We both took a deep breath as we walked into the cave, steeling ourselves for whatever was inside producing the greasy wrongness that was haze.

The cave looked just like every other one had. A small mouth with a rivulet of water flowing out of it towards the pond. The water had carved a trench directly through the middle of the cave floor. A few steps past the entrance, the cave opened up, making a rather circular area with space on either side of the trench of flowing water. The water was coming from the back of the cave, where the cave walls came closer together and the floor sloped downward into darkness.

Ben stopped just inside the cave. "Give me a light?" He asked holding his torch out to me.

Shakily, I reached for my Heka and convinced It to light the torch. There was barely a spark, but it was enough. The torch smoldered before catching. Ben then used his torch to light mine. Then he set out, heading into the dark of the cave passage.

We walked single file, Ben first then me, down and down and down. The passage curved first this way, then that, getting wider a bit, then skinnier, but there were never any branches off the main passage that we could see. At points the passage got so narrow, Ben's bare shoulders almost grazed either side, and other times it opened up into large chambers too wide for the poor light from our torches to illuminate. In these, Ben and I would circle the whole cavern, making sure there was only one way to go before proceeding on, always following the water. As we walked, the haze would thin and then thicken in puffs, blowing past us as it floated up and back the way we had come from, and presumably, out of the cave. I completely ignored the fact that the water in the rivulet was flowing uphill to run out of the cave. Out of every impossible thing that had happened to me lately, this was probably the easiest impossible thing to disregard and just accept was because it was.

We reached another wide-open cavern and, as we had before, Ben and I followed the wall of the cave to the right first. Ahead of us, shadows played across the cave walls, dancing in a way that made me think there was something large in the center of the cavern. I tapped on Ben's shoulder to get his attention.

He turned to face me, and I told him, "Maybe we should explore the center of the cavern. Based on the shadows, there is something large there. It might be some sort of rocky outcropping or something."

Ben agreed and we walked toward the center, holding our torches high to spread as much light as possible.

What we saw was not a rocky outcropping but a huge dragon. Ben walked a few paces away from me, his mouth hanging open in shock, to spread the light out further and let us see more.

The dragon had blue scales covering a long slender body, limber legs, and a slim tail. It had curled around itself the way a sleeping cat would, its purple wings resting close to its body and its tail sprawled from its body, the very tip waving gently in the air. The wings were not only purple. The phalanges and edges of the wings were a yellowish gold. The two horns growing out of its temples and its claws were also the same yellowish gold. Along the ridge of the dragon's spine were spikes that were purple edged with gold. We could see puffs of haze coming from its nostrils each time it breathed.

"So, this is where the actual, physical haze we can see in this oasis comes from." Ben said quietly.

I nodded. I don't think either of us realized until that moment that there had been a difference between the haze of the Wastes which was just the greasy feeling that was the edge of the Heka's cage and the actual haze of this oasis that was the dragon's smoke and had nothing to do with the Heka's cage.

I looked at the dragon again. Its eyes were closed. It was sleeping, we hoped.

The dragon let out a low grumble and its eyes opened. They were big, one eye was probably the same size as my head, and a vibrant green. Ben and I stopped moving and I held my breath, waiting for what the dragon would do. The dragon raised its head and moved so that it was sitting on its hind quarters. As it shifted, I spied something glittering underneath its body. The dragon moved too quickly for me to see what it was.

The dragon blinked looking from me to Ben and back again. The dragon leaned down its head over me, its mouth slightly open. I panicked but stayed very still. It gently plucked the torch from my hand and stretched up its neck towards the cavern's ceiling. Using the torch, the dragon lit a massive candelabra hanging from the ceiling. The entire cavern became brightly lit. Then it leaned its head down, as if giving me back my torch.

I took the torch gingerly, trying not to show how much my hands were trembling.

"Thank you," the dragon said, its voice almost like music. "I have been in the dark for a very long time."

I looked at Ben and he nodded his head slightly. He could understand the dragon too.

"You're welcome." I said. "I am…"

The dragon interrupted me. "You are AnnaBella Cain and Benahahminen. The Heka told me to be expecting you."

"The Heka told you?" Ben asked.

"Mmm," the dragon hummed. "Yes. A long, long time ago."

"Can I ask your name?" I said.

"Taenna," the dragon told me.

"Thank you, Taenna," I replied. "It's nice to meet you."

"Did the Heka tell you why we would come, Taenna?" Ben asked.

"Yes, Benahahminen." The dragon replied.

"You can call me Ben." He answered. "So, you know you need to leave this cave, then?"

Taenna shook her head. "I cannot."

Ben and I looked at each other. "Why not?" I asked. "Did you come here when you were smaller and now the cave is too small for you to fit back through?"

"No." Taenna said. Her voice almost sounded melancholy. Taenna lifted one leg, shifting it so we could see the glittering thing I had noticed before. They were eggs, bright green like emeralds. Six of them. "Malachi put me here to guard the Heka. He knew that I would stay here because of my eggs, my babies."

"Oh," Ben and I both said.

"Wait, you knew Malachi?" Ben asked.

The dragon nodded and the smoke of the haze billowed thickly from her nostrils. When she spoke, there was hatred in her voice. "Malachi tricked us. Something had been hunting dragonkind, and killing us off one by one. Malachi was so wise and good, everyone said. So, when he came to me and my mate as we guarded our eggs and told us he knew who was killing dragons, we listened.

"He said that we were the last of our kind, and that the killer was on their way. He said he knew of a safe place where we could hide and led us here, to this oasis. Once dragon eggs have been laid, we have no way to move them ourselves, so Malachi helped. We expected him to bring the eggs to the nest we were making near the pond, but instead he brought the eggs into the cave, into this cavern."

Taenna looked up at the ceiling. "The roof off this cavern used to be open. I flew down the opening to get to my eggs. My mate tried to follow, but Malachi was ready. As soon as I was inside, Malachi slid the rock that makes the cavern's ceiling, with its candelabra, in place, sealing it off. Sealing me off. I could do nothing. Malachi killed my mate then, and I could do nothing."

The dragon's voice took on a bitter edge. If she had venom, I thought, it would have been dripping from her. "Malachi came back into the cave, using the entrance, to mock me. He didn't even stop to clean my mate's blood off his clothes. I would have eaten him. I could have, but my eggs. He killed my mate. He killed all other dragonkind. I could not leave them motherless, uncovered, to die before being born. I could not risk it." Taenna looked down at her eggs. Even though she was a dragon, her despair was evident all over her face.

I nodded, tears pricking my eyes. Taenna had made a choice to suffer in the hopes of saving her children.

Taenna continued her story, anger replacing the despair. She breathed deeply, thick haze billowing from her, making Ben and me cough. "The bastard laughed at me. He laughed! Then he cut his hand, making himself bleed. He placed his bleeding hand on my skin and told me 'Guard the Heka with your life. You cannot leave until the Heka does. If the Heka dies, you die.' Then, there was nothing I could do but wait."

I shook my head in confusion. "Excuse me, Taenna. But I don't understand. Why did Malachi do that?"

Ben answered me. "It's a blood oath. If someone gets close enough to a dragon to touch them, they can use their blood to compel a dragon. The person touches the dragon while bleeding and makes a claim on what that dragon must do. If the person lives, the dragon is bonded like an oath to perform whatever that person said. The blood oath is only broken if that dragon, and only that dragon, kills the one who compelled them. If they die some other way, the compulsion still holds."

"That is right, Benahahminen." Taenna said, sadly.

"So, you couldn't leave." I said, understanding now. "It wasn't

---

just your eggs that you couldn't leave, but the compulsion Malachi put on you."

"No," Taenna explained. "It was both. I am doubly trapped. If I tried to leave the cave only, but not the oasis, I could have, as long as I stayed close enough to guard the Heka. But the only way for me to leave the cave is to break open the ceiling. I could not do it without putting my eggs in danger of being crushed. I could not move them out of the way on my own. I was forced to choose. Stay and protect my eggs and guard the Heka from here, or leave the cave, find food and water on the outside, still guarding the Heka but abandoning my eggs to die."

"And Malachi knew exactly what he was doing when he put your eggs here," I finished for her.

"Wow," Ben said. "The more I learn about Malachi's actions, the more I wonder how any of us ever thought he was a good guy."

"It gets worse, Ben." I said, putting the pieces together in my head. "Technically, Taenna's oath ends when we free the Heka, but she still won't be able to leave. If she tries, she destroys her eggs which are the last remaining hope for dragonkind. And I don't know how long you have been down here, Taenna, but you haven't eaten the entire time? Eventually, that has got to be bad for you."

"It already is, AnnaBella Cain." Taenna answered. "I am weak from my hunger, as well as from being cramped in here for so long. I barely have the space to spread my wings. I am not even sure if they would be strong enough to lift me anymore, even if I did manage to break out. This haze coming from my breath is not natural to my kind. It is a side effect of my body failing. The weaker I get, the worse the haze coming from me is."

A thought came to me. "Taenna, when did Malachi trap you here? Before the Flood or after?"

Taenna thought before she answered. "I do not know of any flood, so it must have been before."

"Wow." Ben whistled. "Malachi had this all planned out, didn't he?"

I called out, "Ben!" while walking a few paces away from Taenna. He looked at me, and I gestured at him with my head to come close to talk to me.

Ben trotted over. "What's up, Anna?"

"We have to help her, Ben." I told him, keeping my voice low. "We have to go on and save the Heka, to release It so she is free of her blood oath, but we need to help her too. We can't leave her like this."

Ben nodded. "You're right. We need to figure out where the Heka is and how to release It from Its cage, but then we need to make sure Taenna and her eggs get to safety and freedom too, intact."

"Hey, Taenna." I called out loudly. "Where is the Heka, exactly?"

"At the bottom of this cave, AnnaBella Cain." She replied. "But It is trapped."

"We know." Ben told her. "Anna feels the Heka's pain. Every time Its cage gets smaller, Anna feels it."

Taenna disagreed, "No, Benahahminen. The Heka's cage does not get smaller."

"What do you mean, Taenna?" I asked. "I felt it, each time we unlocked an oasis."

"What you felt," Taenna explained, "was the actual cave getting smaller. I knew the first moment you unlocked the city of Taikarlu. The ground shook and parts of the cave collapsed in on itself. I believe what you felt was not the Heka's cage getting smaller, but rocks falling around the Heka, burying It more and more. The pain could be the debris actually hitting the Heka, landing on It. With each oasis unlocked, the earthquakes got worse. Stones would hit me, striking me, as I huddled over my eggs to protect them. I can imagine the same happened to the Heka, but most likely, much, much worse. An infinite being in a finite space that kept getting smaller and trapped in a place where physical debris hurt their nonphysical body? There is only so many paradoxes one being can suffer under before it is too much, even for the creator of all things."

I crunched up my face, confused. "I never unlocked Taikarlu," I said quietly.

Ben shrugged. "It must have been when you opened my front door in the human realm and walked into Taikarlu. Best as I can guess, anyway."

I paced for a bit. There was a lot of confusing stuff going on, but my sense of what is right said that, even though I desperately needed to get to the Heka, we could not abandon Taenna, even just for a little while. Who knew if we would be able to come back here to help her, no matter how much we may want to.

"Ben," I said low, just for his ears. "You have to stay here."

"What do you mean Anna?" he asked.

"You have to stay here." I repeated. "You stay and help Taenna. Get her food to eat. Water to drink if she needs it. And if she will let you, help her move her eggs to safety so she can bust out of here. I am going to go on to the Heka alone. There is no time for us to stay together and do one then then other, and we can't leave Taenna, hoping that maybe we will come back. We need to split up and do both."

Ben looked like he was about to argue but didn't. Instead, he handed me his torch and took mine. "Your torch looks a little low. Maybe it didn't have enough sap on it. Take mine," he told me. "And Anna?" he whispered, crooking his finger in a gesture for me to come closer.

I stepped closer to Ben. He wrapped his free arm around my waist and pulled me up against him. My free hand rested on his bare chest. Ben dipped his head and kissed me. When he lifted his head, he said, "Be careful."

"You be careful, too." I told him, a little breathlessly. Ben kissed me one more time then let me go.

I walked away towards the back of the cavern. Behind me, I heard Ben tell Taenna, "So, here's the plan…"

Chapter Eleven

She is here. We are here. I am here.

I left Ben and Taenna behind and followed the tunnel deeper and deeper. Just like before the path twisted and turned, but it didn't widen into a cavern again. The walls seemed to close in around me with only the light of one flickering torch. I was in a bubble of light that touched the sides of the cave tunnel, but only spread a few feet in front and behind me.

I could feel the Heka's urgency, but walked slowly anyway. If there was a fissure or a sudden drop, I wouldn't see it in time to stop if I moved quickly. The Heka had stopped crying, but I wasn't convinced that that was a good sign. The only good thing was that the haze was gone. Taenna's breath seemed to travel up and out of the cave. Since I was past her, in effect upwind of her, the haze was moving away from me rather than towards me.

The cave seemed to go on for miles. I didn't plan for the loneliness and claustrophobia that would come from travelling through it alone. I started to sing, badly, to keep my mind from worrying itself into a panic.

I had sung every 1990's song I knew, a smattering of 2000's music, and had moved on to just humming randomly when I saw the first boulder. It wasn't too big so I scampered over it rather easily. A few more minutes, and I found several stones stacked on top of each other. I had to throw the torch over the pile and then climb over it myself. Luckily, the torch didn't go out.

The trench of moving water, somehow flowing uphill, took up most of the cave floor now, leaving only a few inches on either side. What little ground there was left was covered with loose dirt and small pebbles, making it a slippery mess. I moved carefully. If I fell and hurt myself, there was no one to come to my rescue.

The walls of the cave started widening, finally. When they were wide enough that my fingers would only graze either side if I spread my arms out fully, my way down became completely blocked. Large stones and what looked like stalactites were densely piled on top of each other. I could not see through them even enough to see how far back the blockage went.

I sighed. I had no choice but to try to un-dig some of it. I examined the stones, poking them gently with my free hand. Like playing Jenga, I felt for pieces that were already loose. One stone near the right side of the top of the pile rocked a little when I pushed on it. I set the torch down, leaning it against the stone pile on the opposite side than I would be working on, and pried at the loose rock with my fingers.

It was hard to find purchase and my fingers slipped several times. One time, I almost had the rock fully loose and my fingers slipped. The rock shifted and one of my fingers got pinched between it and another rock. I stepped back, trying not to swear.

"One more try," I told myself. I gripped the rock the best way I could and yanked. The rock, and several others below it, rolled off the pile to the cave floor. I jumped out of the way. Once the rocks stopped rolling, I picked them up one by one and walked them up the cave tunnel a little way. I did not want to unbury the way in only to trap my way out.

I looked through the hole I had made to discover... more rocks. "Yay," I said weakly. One by one, I moved rocks from the pile blocking the way down and walked them back up the tunnel. Soon I had a line of rocks marching back up the tunnel like little soldiers. I had created an opening just wide enough for me to side forward while lying flat on my belly. My fingernails were torn and bloody, and my clothes were a mess of dust and tiny tears. Once I was in the hole I had made, I was in complete darkness. I was scared that one of these times, before I opened it up at the other end, I would crawl out of my hole to find my torch had gone out.

I climbed up into my hole one more time, pulled at the loosest rock I could find and shimmied it backwards out of the hole with me. When I climbed in again, I felt around for a loose rock and felt, instead, something soft. At first, I flinched away from the softness. I wasn't expecting anything other than more hard rock.

Once I got over my willies, I felt for the soft thing again, running my bruised and battered fingers over it. It felt like skin. I pushed at the rocks around the soft thing. They shifted slightly. I felt the soft thing again and, in the darkness, recognized the feeling of a person's hand.

"Heka?" I said out loud.

Yes. The Heka replied in my head. *That's me you are touching. Help me.*

"Are you," I asked. "Are you buried in here?"

Yes. It replied.

Oh crap.

I slumped against the stones around me. It had taken forever to dig out this little hole. How could I ever move all these stones to free the Heka? And what if I moved one wrong and crushed It? Oh, to be back in the Trials Arena where everything was easy, I thought.

Use our Heka. The Heka told me.

"Our Heka?" I asked.

Yes. It replied. *Use both, together. You have used mine, and you have used yours. Now use them both.*

"Are you sure?" I asked tentatively. "I don't have the best track record with this stuff."

I trust you. It said, sounding surprisingly bold. *I trust us.*

I took a deep breath and grabbed hold of the Heka's hand. I hoped Ben had gotten Taenna and her eggs clear of the cave, because this was probably going to do a lot of damage. I closed my eyes and searched for all of the Heka power I could find. All of It, mine, the Heka's, I did not discriminate, but just pushed It into a huge ball.

When I had gathered every scrap of Heka power I could find, I clutched the Heka's hand as tight as I could and thrust the Heka ball into the stones. The explosion was deafening. I felt myself flying through the air, but I kept a grip on the Heka's hand. I landed on my back; my eyes still closed tightly as stones rained down around me.

When the stones stopped falling, I risked trying to move. The ground underneath me felt softer than the cave floor. I felt it and realize it was sandy dirt, like the oasis outside had been.

I realized I wasn't holding the Heka's hand anymore. Shoot! My eyes flew open and I jumped up, or well, tried to. I got about halfway to standing when I realized every single muscle in my body was sore and bruised.

"Ow," I moaned, laying back down.

"Bella," I heard the Heka say over the ringing in my ears.

I fluttered my hand a little saying, "Give me a minute. Owww."

"Bella," the Heka said again, sweetly.

I heard that, I realized. Not in my head, but out loud.

I forced myself to sit up. At first, I thought someone had put a mirror in the middle of the oasis. But then I realized I was sitting while the figure in the mirror was standing. She was also much cleaner than I felt.

I stood up quickly, ignoring my protesting body. "Heka?" I asked the being that looked like my reflection.

It nodded Its head. "Yes, Bella." It spoke with my voice.

My brain felt like it was shorting out. The Heka looks like me? Sounds like me?

"Do you look like this just because I happen to be the one looking at you?" I asked It. "If Ben was looking at you, would you look and sound like him?"

The Heka shook her head. "You know what this is, Bella."

It was right. I knew. I had a connection with the Heka from that moment in the Trials Arena. I always had. I knew what It was thinking, what It was feeling. I heard what the Heka heard. I knew what the Heka knew, even if I didn't let myself know I knew it.

"You're not really out here, are you Heka?" I said more than asked.

"You know where I am, Bella." It replied. "You know who I am, and who you are."

I looked away and closed my eyes. I had to admit that I did know. I probably had always known. "I am the Heka." I whispered. I felt the Heka smile.

No.

I smiled.

The Heka was my soul. Nummi had been wrong when he said that only my spirit was gone from my body. But then again, Nummi had thought I was only human, the child of a coordinator and a human. But I wasn't.

I was a god. I was human. I was a coordinator. I had created myself to free myself. I led Dad to want a child, pushed him into it, to create a new body for myself. A real one, a human one, this time. One someone could not strip away from me so easily. Human bodies come with both a spirit and a soul. But this body, I created with only a spirit. Human body. Coordinator spirit. God soul. The trifecta within the trifecta. Unbreakable.

I am AnnaBella Cain, the Heka.

Epilogue

Ben had found me next to the pond and knew instantly what had happened. Of course, he did. Gods obviously knew the Heka when they saw It. Me. He had gotten Taenna and her eggs free before I blew up the cave. He showed me where they had settled. Apparently, exposed to the light, Taenna's eggs finally decided to hatch. Six beautiful blue dragons were crawling around on their mother. A few of the dragonets had green tinges to their wings, but Taenna had stopped breathing haze after a good meal of pine needles. Pine needles, of all things. Who would have guessed that dragons were herbivores?

I could have just Heka'ed us back to Taikarlu, but Ben and I decided to walk. It gave us time to discuss things. It would be rather difficult for Ben to be dating the Heka, we decided. So, for now at least, we would cool things off. Maybe in the future, when all the craziness that was definitely about to happen calmed down, we could reconsider. I was okay with that because I knew that in a few years, Ben's worshippers would not stop talking about the myth of how Benahahminen had helped save the Heka and how the Heka used love to save Benahahminen. With a story like that, how could we possibly deny that we were destined for each other?

But we had some time until that happened. For now, I needed to focus on bringing the gods back together. I needed to learn from my past mistakes. I would keep the law of gods and coordinators not having children with humans, that much I knew. But everything else? The system the gods had put in place in my absence seemed to be working well. It was fairly democratic. A few tweaks here and there, with me as a sort of president rather than dictator, and the Joint Commission as a senate or parliament, would be a good way to go. The rest, the gods and I would solve together.

One of the things I would need to solve though was Bob. I was not sure what to do about Bob. There were so many things he did wrong, but he never did them out of spite. One thing I learned from Ben during our trek through the oases was how very little I had taught the gods about the world they occupied and what their place in it was. A lot of Bob's mistakes were really my mistakes. Could I truly punish him for things he didn't know? And the way he killed Malachi? He did that in my defense, even if it was in anger. In the end, I decided that I was not the right one to judge Bob's actions. There was a Joint Commissions trial for him and he served a prison sentence for killing Malachi, but I think they went easy on him, commuting it to mostly time served.

When we reached Taikarlu, it had changed significantly with the return of all the mythical animals. Ben and I found Nummi first, and had him get a message to Dad. I wanted to see him and Mom because, no matter who I was, they were still my parents. Explaining to Mom what had happened was no mean feat. She finally just decided that the whole thing was a paradox and stopped trying to understand that they had given birth to the Heka so that It could save Itself that already existed. After a brief tour around the new and improved Taikarlu, Mom chose to go back to her home in the human realms and her job there. She said she would visit from time to time. Interestingly, Albert went with her. Based on the way Mom and Albert were smiling at each other, I think I may have a new step-dad/god-dad in the future. Even I didn't see that one coming.

The Speaker of the Joint Commission immediately abdicated her position upon my return, or at least tried to. I asked her to stay on, as a favor to me, until we could get things sorted and calmed down enough to hold a fair election to replace her. I told her it would only take a hundred and fifty years. I knew she would be glad to go back to her little tribe of worshippers after that. And if we never saw her in the Joint Commission meeting again, I would understand. She had served in her position well during some truly trying times and deserved a rest.

As far as my religion, my worshippers, and how I set up all of that? I don't know. Why don't you tell me?

About the Author

Kefira Zink is an author from a little town in Michigan. She has a bachelor's degree in Sociology from Arizona State University and a master's degree in Sociology, with a specialty in Religion and Deviance from American Public University. She loves buying books, especially rescuing old books and giving them a loving home as well as reading books (which any reader will tell you, buying books and reading them are two very different hobbies). She is married to her wonderful husband/muse and together they have six grown children, two cats, a dog that thinks it is a cat, and a lizard that thinks it is a dinosaur.

Connect With The Author

Website: https://sites.google.com/view/kefira-zink-author
Email: kefirazinkauthor@gmail.com
Facebook: Kefira Zink Fantasy Author
TikTok: kefira_zink_author